A
COUNTRY
DIVORCE

A
COUNTRY
DIVORCE
BY ANN T. JONES

DELPHINIUM BOOKS

harrison, new york   encino, california

Copyright © 1992 by Ann T. Jones

Library of Congress Cataloging-in-Publication Data
Jones, Ann T., 1930–
A country divorce / by Ann T. Jones.
p.   cm.
ISBN 0-671-76056-4 : $20.00
I. Title.
PS3560.04574C6   1991
813'.54—dc20   91-31200
CIP

First Edition   All rights reserved
10 9 8 7 6 5 4 3 2 1

Published by Delphinium Books, Inc.
P.O. Box 703
Harrison, N.Y. 10528

Distributed by Simon & Schuster
Printed in the United States of America

Jacket art by Milton Charles
Text design by Milton Charles
Production services by Blaze International Productions, Inc.

To my husband, Jim,
who makes my writing possible.

ACKNOWLEDGMENTS

Grateful acknowledgment is made to Michael Cunnane for his wonderful recall of life in County Mayo, Ireland; and to my agent, Harvey Klinger, for his support and encouragement.

CHAPTER
1

Morgan Riley announced he'd take a wife, a woman to help dear Annie. She'd milk the cows, feed the hens and the pigs, keep a kettle on the hook before noon. She'd wash and mend, knit and bake, and keep a pipe for his smoke by the fire. There'd be a stool for his feet and a lamp lit. She'd see him soothed on a wet November day.

Morgan Riley measured his days in fields plowed and bushels of rye. He was calm with the turf dug and piled. His zeal for the farm bordered on veneration. "Isn't it for this the Almighty made us?"

His sister Annie, too, reckoned her worth by the farm, by cattle bought in the great spring fairs. Annie loved the quiet rewards: a full hayrick, turnips in the haggard, a slab of bacon hung from the rafters.

Annie was a tall woman, big-boned. When Morgan plowed, Annie spread the seed. When he cut the turf, dripping wet out of the black bog, she was there to catch it. She raked and stacked and bound the hay.

For all of that she was a gentle woman, patient and quiet, a household sort.

The farm itself lay well off the road out of Westport, sixteen acres at the edge of the bay. It was a lonely piece of crop-land. At the end of a boreen, it bordered steep cliffs, where, far below, the ocean washed the vacant shore. But there were green, fertile fields.

Away from the water the fields rose, until the arc of green

was suddenly cut by stark ridges of grey, the remains of an ancient glacier. The house and haggard occupied a brief, level plain, but the fields dropped off sharply. Except for the high rocky ridges they seemed to flow in swells toward the sea.

Between the house and sea stood four wind-shorn oaks, gnarled, grey bare branches bent toward the cottage. The wind off the sea had frozen the trees into fixed curves. A clothesline stretched between two of them and, when the rain held off, there was a flutter of drawers and shirts.

The two-story cottage lay nestled in a cluster of outbuildings. There was a cabin for cattle, a shed for the tools and carts, two separate sheds for crops and seed, and in the middle of the haggard a great straw-covered pit for turnips and mangels.

Each summer Morgan and Annie built a great hay rick with the winter's supply of fodder.

They had lived alone since the death of their father Edward two years before. But now Morgan was about to take a wife. The match came about in an odd way; at first Morgan thought the idea was preposterous.

The evening of the suggestion had begun with the men from the neighborhood gathered as usual. (It was to the Rileys' cottage they'd always come. With Edward Riley's death the custom had continued. But when the old fellow was alive Morgan occupied a stool at the far end of the kitchen, well beyond the heat. Now he had his rightful place, close to the fire.)

This particular evening Pat O'Donnell had brought along his cousin Denny. Denny O'Donnell came once or twice a year the long ten miles from his own village of Ballyrea. When he'd finished his business he stopped with his cousin in Kilmaragh. So just as naturally Pat brought him along to Morgan Riley's.

The evening began on a cordial note. It was a clear, cold winter night, no moon, sharp bright stars overhead. Denny's presence at first had a leavening effect, but before long the usual trouble began. Michael Barrett, just turned sixty at Christmas, launched into a tirade. "A digger should stand facing the turf bank," he shrilled. "Thrust your spade horizontal. No good standing on the bank, tiring yourselves."

Colman Ronan, fifty-two, with a young wife, turned immediately scrappy. "Sure, what would we want to be goin' down into the muck for?"

"I'm only just wanting to look at all sides," said Barrett.

"All sides of what? There's only one way we've ever cut turf in Kilmaragh."

"And why do you want to be bringin' dissension?" asked O'Dowd, who inevitably sided with Colman Ronan. (O'Dowd worked a farm with a wife and six sons.)

Duffy, a bachelor, kept quiet. (Though since he'd a brother in America, he was surely entitled to speak.) He removed his cap, ran his fingers swiftly through his hair, ruffling the grey wisps. He looked from Ronan to Barrett, then back to O'Dowd.

O'Dowd bristled at the intrusion, despite Duffy's Yank brother.

Duffy lowered his eyes to the floor.

Ronan looked squarely at Barrett. "Any man's held a slane knows underfooting's the way. Would you argue with success?"

"Have you seen a breast-slane?" Barrett's eyes circled the room. "Any of yez?"

"Any boob?"

"Ronan's the expert!" cried Barrett.

"Now, hold it," said Morgan, from his chair in the front. "Remember our guest. Keep your heads cool."

"But there isn't a man can't profit by a better way," argued Barrett.

"Now, there you go again," snapped Ronan, ignoring Morgan's frown.

There was a sudden stirring near the hob. Old John Mulrenin was pulling his bones upright. His ancient sharp eyes gleamed. "There's methods and there's methods," he said, voice rolling solemnly across the hearth. It seemed, for an instant, he had nothing more to say.

But his eyes bored into the flustered Barrett. "There's men dug these bogs for sixty years." He paused. The words hung threateningly. The younger men shifted uneasily. *"Are there them that thinks they know better?"*

"Why doesn't Annie make the tea?" said Morgan.

The remainder of the evening passed quickly. Barrett had lost his bravado. So that, passing Mulrenin at the door, he inclined, then nodded—Morgan thought he might even be going to genuflect. But the moment passed.

Ronan, behind Barrett, touched his cap.

Both men stood back while Mulrenin sailed out the door.

It was while Annie was piling the cups and her back was turned that Denny O'Donnell whispered his news. Morgan wasn't sure, at first, what he'd heard.

Denny repeated it. "This Minnie Maughan's like nothin' in this world . . . Didn't the father come to me? 'Is there a good fellow over near Westport?' he asks—I without a thought in the world. 'Someone of substance,' he sez, 'wantin' a match.' . . . The Maughans are fine people. But Ballyrea's the end of the world . . . I'd leave it myself." Denny dropped into a chair, calling out to his cousin, "Go along, Pat. I'll be home in a bit."

"Sure there isn't a moon at all," said Pat, hesitating. "You'll go over the cliff."

"Oh, I'll find my way by the stars."

"The devil himself'll snatch you."

Morgan closed the door behind Pat, stunned by his own eagerness. He beckoned to Annie to leave them alone. But wasn't it nothing but curiosity? What could the girl've to do with himself?

Denny sized up Morgan. "By God, it's yourself's the man for Minnie Maughan!"

Morgan stared. "Me? What would I care about marrying? There's Annie. And I give her the help she needs. Not a cross word. The house in great style. What put a thought like that in your head?" Morgan laughed. "Kilmaragh's no place if you'd marry."

"But Martin's married."

"The brother? Martin's the marrying one." Morgan felt a stab of envy over his brother's lovely wife. He ached for the pleasures. "And Martin was thirty-five. I'm an old man."

"Forty-three?"

"I know. I know." Morgan's tone was light, but he felt a heaviness near his heart. Who could give him hope? Not a marriageable woman for miles around? And the few that there were'd rather a young buck, surely. Not one past his prime like himself.

Denny beat time while whistling a tune, the same three bars over and over. The primitive melody trailed to an end in a thin wisp of sound. He took a deep breath, plucked a scrap of paper from his breast pocket, dug hurriedly in his pants pocket for a pencil. He placed the paper on the table with all the careful formality of a legal document. "I'm writing down the girl's name," he declared, "and I'm puttin' beside it her ma and her da. There's a nephew, too . . . His name doesn't matter . . . Oh, what the hell, I'll write it too." Laboriously he wrote out the four names. When he finished he sat back in his chair, a smile revealing his long front teeth. He snapped his suspenders, settled his elbows on the table. "You'll never see her like. Didn't the da come to me himself to ask about a match?"

"I never knew you to be in the matchmaking up to now, Denny?" Morgan had an uneasy feeling that he'd be wise to simply give Denny a lantern to keep him off the cliffs, then bid him good night. A voice in his head warned, "Ignore the subject of this young lady and her father's aspirations."

"Now you're right on that score, Morgan. Right as rain. I'm new to the matchmakin'." His eager eyes took in the comfortable kitchen. What a fine sight to impress the Maughans. "But don't let that discourage you," he said hurriedly. "John Maughan is the best farmer you'd want to meet, no tellin'. They've a fine fortune to give."

Morgan looked long and hard across the table at his visitor.

"Now, I know Ballyrea isn't much," Denny offered quickly. "But nevertheless, here and there's a good farm. A grand large piece, the Maughans.' "

"Have they now?" Morgan felt his resolve slipping, though he'd determined to say nothing more.

"Thirty acres." Denny waved a hand through the smoky air, as if the kitchen were a spread of pasture. "The best cows and pigs. Nobody gets the price John Maughan does . . . One would keep you in bacon for the winter. And the milch cows. Butter enough the coins'd jump in your pocket."

"I've a fine lot of animals myself," said Morgan.

Denny sensed a lack of firmness. Wasn't he still using the same old plow horse, near dead the day his father died? "There's nothing like Ballyrea's high ground," he pushed, "if you want the most from your cows." Easy. Easy, he cautioned himself. "There'd be hopes of a little one," he said, switching abruptly, ashamed almost of his slyness.

Morgan tensed. His guard was up.

"I don't know should we be talking like this, Denny. I'm forty-three. Not a thought of a wife in years. You put it aside, the long years, while you're hoping they'll give up the farm. *You* know."

"I do. By the time I get mine I'll be so old I won't know the first thing . . ."

"You'll get the hang of it." Morgan's sudden burst of playfulness caught Denny off his guard. But he recovered quickly. He joined in Morgan's hearty laughter. "Sure, who would have me?" he said, wiping tears of merriment from his eyes.

"Or me, either?"

"Now, don't trouble yourself, Morgan. Listen to me. These Maughans are itchin' to raise themselves . . . Not that you'd be gettin' a bad bargain yourself. This Minnie Maughan is a darlin' girl, only twenty. She'd set the heart of any man to poundin' . . . She'd be grabbed up before this, don't you be thinkin' otherwise, but for the father."

"What's wrong with the old man?" This had gone far enough. He wished to God Denny'd leave.

"Not a thing. Nothin' at all. Don't be puttin' out ideas that have no substance. Old Maughan's a fine man. One of the best. He has firm ideas for his daughter's marriage. As I said at the outset, he wants a connection. Over this way. An 'alliance,' you might say. Something to move the family up in the world."

"And you've come to *me*?" Morgan snorted derisively. He looked at his worn work shoes, brushed a streak of dried mud from his trousers. He'd often suspected there was a bit of a crazy bird flying around between Denny's ears, but this was the first proof. "Come on now, Denny."

"This girl is a beauty." Denny ignored Morgan's innuendos. He gathered his courage. "Will you come talk with the father?" He paused, gave Morgan time to recognize sound ground. "I'll put the two of yez together. And there'll be no hard feelings if it doesn't catch on. We'll say no more about it . . . But if you like old Maughan's proposition we'll give you a look at the girl. See how it goes from there. Fair enough?"

Morgan stood up and stretched. His back was to Denny.

The room was cold now. He stared into the dying turf fire. He took up a poker to stir the ashes. When a lick of flame showed he threw on a sod.

What harm, indeed, to talk? There'd be nothing to say he couldn't come home, forget that he'd even the thought. But in the middle of winter, a ten-mile walk? Five miles you walked, from the Westport road, and even then you weren't in the uplands. And after that?

Desolate bog. An uphill climb. And what did you have when you got there? Three or four decent farms out of the lot, perched smack on the sides of the hills. Not sense enough to put the houses on the flat plain. Graze the cattle on the hills. And this Maughan himself? What thinking man would build a house like that?

Still, the girl might be worth a look.

What craziness. He was as wild, himself, as Denny. This woman? Who'd look at the likes of him?

"Well, Morgan?" Cap in hand, Denny waited by the door. His face was tranquil. He peered the length of the room into Morgan's soul. "Shall I be telling them to look for you?"

"I suppose it wouldn't hurt. The horse is hardly fit, so I'll have to walk. You'd have to put me up. I couldn't be home again, if myself and the father are to have any time at all."

"I thought you'd say yes." Denny spoke quietly, soothing Morgan. The way you'd talk to the animals when they'd had a bad scare. "Don't put another thought into it until you've a look for yourself. The father'll be delighted you're coming."

"Sure, it's only for a lark I'm going up there. Don't raise any false hopes. Don't give these Maughans the idea I'm a marrying man."

Now that he'd agreed Morgan grew tense. A buried sense of resentment swept over him, something from deep in the past. Vague, unstoppable, it was the savage indignation of the long lonely years. When he'd waited without hope. Waited. Cap in hand. Eyes on the floor while old Eddie Riley gave out the do's and the don'ts.

What made them so resistant, the old men?

But he knew the answer. Why would they give up the land? When every important thing in life was accorded them? Didn't ownership render the best seat by the fire, the first voice, the charge of all the money? It was to the father they'd all to submit, no matter that age was upon him, as long as he held to the land.

He glared at Denny. "Don't you be telling them people the lies," he cried fiercely. "I'm only a poor farmer. Nothing grand."

"I'll not tell them a thing. Just that you're coming. And not to get their hopes up."

Morgan stood by the open door, watching the yellow light

from Denny's lantern. It bobbed across the slope. Off in the darkness, to the west, waves hit against the rocks. Spray boiled up the side of the cliff. Salty foam peppered the winter grass, splashing off the steep rocks in great, drenching blasts of spume.

He took a deep, angry breath, filling his lungs with salt air. Calmed, he shut the door against the blackness.

Alone in the moonless dark Denny picked his way along the boreen, with only the lamp and stars to show the cart track. A good day's job, the work well started, he exhilarated. And with the help o'God, he'd finish it.

In half an hour he'd reached O'Donnell's.

Morgan, meanwhile, sat alone by the hearth. His anger had died. The old despair was back. It crept from the corners of his mind. The faint surge of hope had evaporated, leaving the old sense of futility, present whenever he thought of anything but the farm itself. If he kept to the crops and the furrows he was fine. He gloried in clean ditches, drains taking the rain from the roof, fresh to the barrels below. The farm was his whole heart's desire. One year followed the next. He knew he'd the Almighty's blessing.

But let him lie in his solitary loft bed, awake under the rafters. Then emptiness would take hold, terrible and black. Over him would wash a bitterness, a melancholy awareness that scythes and spades, cows and cabbages were not the whole of life. Where was the woman to share it?

Where were the soft curves, the fragrance of her hair? Oh, the delights of a lovely woman's hair.

Morgan sought comfort in his pipe. He puffed harder. Blue clouds spiraled.

"Morgan?"

He pretended not to hear. He felt the solace of the clay stem against his lips.

"Dear brother?"

Morgan half turned. Annie crept out of the darkness, her stockinged feet noiseless on the concrete floor. She had wrapped a great shawl over her bed gown. Pulling a chair close to the hearth, she waited for her brother to speak. But when he only smoked in silence she took up the poker, began stirring the grey ashes.

"Leave it."

Annie dropped the poker, shivering. "Ye mustn't . . ."

"Don't meddle where you've no business."

"Oh, dear brother . . ."

"There's not a word to be said of it." But his tone had softened. He stared into the hearth.

"You'll go? At least have a look?" Mother o' God and all the saints, turn down the chance of a match? For this lonely life at the end of the boreen?

"Who'd be wanting the likes of me?" The growl was back. "Twould be grand to have another woman," Annie began timidly.

But Morgan jumped to his feet. He strode across the room, stopping at the stairs to the loft. He turned, face pale. "I don't want to hear of it in the morning," he said.

Sharp hay stalks scraped Minnie Maughan's back. She squirmed and twisted. The stiff dry stems cut harder. "Ah, let up. Mattie, come on. I'm gettin' the worst of it."

His hands slid under her petticoat, rough fingers on her flesh.

"Na, Mattie . . .tis sinnin' . . . Ye have to stop . . . Ahhhhh."

He slid sideways, lay over on the brown stubble, breathed deeply. He was quiet.

Relieved yet disappointed she settled her skirts around her ankles. "For the love of Jesus," she began, rolling over to look at him. "I'll be confessin' 'til doomsday, don't you know? And the penance I'll get." She laughed quickly, throwing herself down again on the new-cut hay. "The ma would skin me alive . . . Mattie? Are ye listening? Mattie."

The great giant of a man was snoring heavily. He lay flat on his back, work shoes pointing at the blue sky. His arms were motionless by his sides. She watched the huge chest moving up and down with a kind of grace. "Is it dead ye are?' she asked playfully, bending to kiss him. Immediately he was awake. "Dead, is it?" He jerked himself upright to grab her, arms around her knees. He spilled her over on top of him. "Ah, no. Ah, no," she cried. Her voice was a high note of gay adventure, peeling out across the cut field.

CHAPTER
2

Annie raked the ashes, put on fresh turf and the fire caught at once. From outside in the frosty haggard she heard the cows mooing. Hens clucked. It was the week following Denny's visit, and when she'd come out to the kitchen she heard only the animals. Not a bit of a noise from Morgan upstairs.

But as she threw another sod the kitchen door burst in. Morgan, face alight, stood framed in the early-morning greyness. His shoes were wet, his trousers damp.

"You're soaked," she said.

"Ah, no. I cut across a field or two."

"And I thinking you were asleep upstairs." Annie grabbed the milk bucket from in front of the dresser, but full of curiosity she set it down.

"I sent off a letter to Denny. I'll speak to the father Monday next."

"But the mailman isn't . . ."

"Ah, no. I wanted it early. Pat's going in to Westport."

"You've been all the way to O'Donnell's and it isn't even breakfast yet?"

Morgan took a light for his pipe from the fire. He puffed vigorously, avoiding Annie's eye. But when he finally turned he let her see the broad smile he couldn't contain. "So they'll know I'll be there Monday."

"Glory be to God," said Annie. "Isn't this the grand day, that finally saw it happen."

"Nothing's happened yet. There isn't a thing known to the girl."

"Surely to God she'll not turn you down?"

"That's not for me to say. I've done my part."

"Well, it's a lucky girl to get a man like yourself." Annie wiped her eyes with her apron. "Wouldn't dear ma be proud, God rest her soul?"

"Now, don't be leaping ahead. I'm only walking over. We'll need a lot of talking. Denny's the message, that's all."

"The long walk. Ballyrea, God help us. Couldn't you wait 'til the spring?"

"Not on your life. You have to get the negotiating."

"But you'll dress warm? What bride wants a man with consumption?"

"Oh, for the love of God, Annie. A chance for a bride and you talk of consumption?"

"Don't be putting me off. Ma, herself, would warn of a chill. Going all that way in the winter."

"Ma's dead. And when did I last have a chill? We've a new life."

Annie sat down to give it her full attention. "Ma thought the world of you," she said. "Even on her deathbed, breathing her last. 'Find yourself a wife, Morgan. The minute he gives the farm.' "

"And did he give it?"

Annie flinched. Morgan's bitterness stirred her own forsaken hopes. Her own bitterness. The grief at the hopes undone.

What chance had there been, Morgan having to wait? The father not giving the farm? In the early days, with Martin home, the mother alive . . . she'd thought long and often . . . a little cottage . . . a bit of land . . . a few animals. The husband they'd find for her. There were still young men. Not everyone had gotten the idea of America.

Her anger surged. But, "Aren't they all that way?" was all she said.

"All of us grey-headed with waiting."

"We'll put it behind us. Think of the future. Forget the past, the way you're always scolding me."

"That we will. We'll start out new."

Annie jumped up. "I'll boil us an egg." She hung the kettle, set a blackened saucepan into the red coals. "She'll not be able to help being taken with you."

"I don't know if I'll see the girl. It's mainly to talk with the father."

Annie stopped in her tracks. "I think I've gone daft, don't you know?" She grabbed up the milk pail. "The mind has gone out of me, thinking the cows could wait. I'll be quick. Watch the eggs 'til they come to a boil."

On the Monday next, just after seven, Morgan set out for Ballyrea. He was dressed for the weather. His best corduroy pants. Heavy overcoat. A tweed cap on his head. And every warm sweater Annie could find. "I'll never get there with the weight of me," he argued. "And would you come home with your death of cold, from all that wild, wet bog land?"

Annie had her way.

The morning was cold but the day was clear, which meant only that no rain was falling. There was a sharp, raw wind off the sea. But he knew it'd be easier on the bogland road, where he'd not be fighting the Atlantic gale. He covered the three miles north in good time, pausing occasionally to watch a car pass.

Yet as the turn-off approached his misgivings returned. Was he a lad? The bright bloom of youth still on him? What in the name of God sent him on such a venture?

Annie was right. He should have waited. Spring was the only fit time. April. The dry earth beneath his feet to give him courage.

Apprehension drenched him like a rainsquall. And matching his mood, the weather failed. Vast grey masses of clouds blotted out the pale January sun. Until his last bit of luck collapsed and a cold mist fell.

His feet slowed. He was well past the Westport road on nothing but a turf pad. The narrow strip between cuttings was a track for carting the turf home. On each side of the high ground were great stretches of peat, a waterlogged, dreary scene. His spirits plummeted lower. Should he abandon the trip, before he'd a chance for more foolishness?

Overhead a pale disc of sun emerged. The mist slacked off,and a cold bog-breeze picked up, blowing off the flatland. He pushed ahead, face down against the breeze. His heart was heavy.

Again the mist fell, icy droplets off the tip of his nose. And he'd two more miles before the uplands.

Despair screamed off the turf bogs: Lie down, old man. Surrender yourself to the black muck.

The blood pounded in his head. He raised angry eyes to the sky, to the unfeeling Deity who'd ordained this. "Does it give you pleasure?" he cried. "Did you count the years that I've waited? Two decades. The old fellow hanging on. And look at poor Annie!" What was there for her? Hair gone grey, bright eyes faded. Dreams crushed.

The bog was marked here and there by patches of scraggly meadow, where effort had been made to reclaim the land for crops. The road crept upward. Coarse grass and moss changed abruptly into rocky pastureland. Morgan made his way around two massive boulders, smack in the middle of the road. Wouldn't you think they'd clear a way? Damned poor job to get a cart over *this* road.

Occasionally, when he stumbled, oaths rang out. Would to God that no one heard him.

At last—it must be close to noon—came a flat upland plain. (Denny said it was a skip and a jump from here to the village.)

The sky had cleared somewhat, a pasty sun against the clouds. He rested his pack on the ground. Off in the distance thin sunlight played over stark, wintry hills. Here and there small farms dotted the slopes, tiny against the fields. Stone walls crisscrossed in every direction.

The road ahead was level. Somewhere close lay the village, nothing more than a crossroads. Ballyrea had a public house, according to Denny, and a store, everything from tea and sugar, thread and needles, to orders for clothing from Westport.

Morgan sat eating his lunch by the roadside. He heard voices ahead, where the road snaked to the left. After a small rise a wide swath of bog cut through the flat fields, and the sounds came from there.

Two men approached, one carrying a loy, the younger man behind him wheeling a barrow loaded with stones. "Good day to you," said Morgan, scrambling to his feet. He stuffed a hard-boiled egg in his pack.

The two men seemed extraordinarily surprised. "And good day to yeerself," said the older one.

"Would you be good enough to say how far to Ballyrea?"
Morgan smiled. He touched the brim of his cap.

"Oh, ye've just a field or two, and then there's a small
hill . . . What business might ye have?" The farmer leaned on
his spade. His face was long and bony, and his sharp, inquisitive
eyes remained fastened on Morgan's face. "Not that ye need
say, unless ye've a mind to." He nodded to the younger man,
who rested the wheelbarrow and came forward.

"The Maughans," said Morgan. "Well, it's not the house
I'm after. We're to meet at the public house. John Maughan."

The sharpness went out of the old man's eyes. He turned.
"It's John Maughan he's after. He wants the way to the public
house."

The younger man pulled a grey rag from his trousers to wipe
his hands. "It's a long day's walk ye've had." He smiled, inching
close to shake Morgan's hand. There was a great gap where one
of his front teeth was missing.

"Perhaps ye'd like a rest?" he said. "We're only over the
fields. What do ye say, da?"

The elder man cleared his throat with a great racket, before
spitting a brown mouthful onto the ground. "Ye think he'd like
that?" he asked. (Father and son seemed to be enjoying a private
speculation.)

"When do we ever have a visitor?" The son looked eagerly
at Morgan, waiting for the old man to make up his mind.

By the time the three were crossing the swath of bog to the
O'Neil cottage both father and son—John and Mick O'Neil,
they'd introduced themselves—were talking animatedly of Morgan's journey. What had he to say of the condition of the road?
Was there a soul at all on the way? How in the name of God did
he leave the likes of Westport for a godforsaken spot like this?

"Oh, it's not in Westport that I live. I'm only a country boy
myself," said Morgan. The three men laughed together. "Westport's the nearest town. I'm from Kilmaragh."

He followed his hosts to a thatch-roofed cottage, into a dim
room that at first looked empty, but as his eyes grew used to the
darkness he saw a huddled figure in the corner. The woman
began to move. She pulled her shawl around her shoulders but
kept her back to the door.

"Ma," called out the son. "Look who we've brought. Get
the tea, he's long on the road."

"Get up, now," shouted the farmer. "He's not all day. He's on his way to the Maughans."

Morgan smiled bashfully at the old woman, who turned frightened eyes. She bent quickly to the fire, stirring the dull ashes.

"He's from Westport." John O'Neil beamed at Morgan. He indicated one of the two chairs. There was a small wooden table.

"Oh, I'm three miles out, and then over a bit, towards the sea," Morgan corrected him. "There's nothing at all of Westport. We're poor farmers like the rest . . . Oh, I've a bit of good ground, and the place is nice and tidy. We've a good roof." He stopped, embarrassed, fearing he might have offended. He looked at the blackened ceiling. There were breaks in the boards, and the roof thatch hung down into the room. But no one seemed to notice.

The old woman, relaxed now, was busily making the tea. She set out cups and soon she was ready with the pot. She filled Morgan's cup.

"It's grand to have a good roof," she said amiably. "And what is your business, Mister . . . ?"

"His name's Riley," said John O'Neil.

"And ye've business in the village? Whatever-in-the-name-of-God kind of dealing's a man like yourself in Ballyrea, God help ye?"

"It's not exactly 'business.' " Morgan squirmed. The old woman quickly refilled his cup.

"Sure, what're the Maughans but farmers?" The old woman let the question hang. Her silence demanded an answer.

"They've a fine place," offered the husband.

The son leaned next to the fireplace, smiling at Morgan expectantly.

When Morgan merely sipped his tea John O'Neil said, more firmly this time, "A fine place."

But still Morgan said nothing.

The son stared across the smoky room. "It's not often we've company," he said, smiling. The gap in his teeth showed.

"Ye've a wife at home?" The old woman tried a new tack, ignoring her husband's scowl.

"Ah, no." Morgan blushed. "I've no wife."

"Well, it's a long walk for a man with no wife."

"We've no business," growled the farmer, but his wife turned her back. She snatched up the poker and stirred the fire. "Ye wouldn't be the one I've heard of, would ye? For the daughter?" Her voice had become sweet as sugar.

Morgan's face burned but he looked her in the eye. "There's nothing settled," he said carefully.

"Aha!" she cried, her grey, withered face breaking into a gleeful smile. "Isn't it a wonder? No sooner ye'd stepped in the door I said to myself, 'Here's a man soon to be wed.' "

"There's not a thing at all arranged," Morgan protested.

"That's the very thought crossed my mind," continued the old woman, as if he hadn't spoken. She turned to her husband. "Isn't he a fine specimen of a bridegroom?"

"Now, ma," said the son, mortified.

"Leave the man to his peace," growled the elder O'Neil. "Finish yeer tea," he ordered Morgan. "Ye'll be late for the Maughans."

Morgan stood. "I'll say 'good day' to you," he said. "And thank you for the tea." He put on his cap and overcoat and edged toward the door.

"Now, come again to the O'Neils'," said the old man.

"It'd be the death o' me if I didn't hear how your business went." The wife smiled invitingly. "Ye'll never leave us wondrin'?"

The son only smiled.

Morgan nodded. The smoke in the room made his eyes smart and he lingered at the door rubbing the itch. But in the cold winter air he breathed deeply, and his eyes cleared. He saw the long walk back to the road.

"It's a warm welcome ye'll have," called out the old woman.

Morgan set off towards the black bog.

CHAPTER
3

Morgan approached the public house. Unaccountably, he felt both apprehension and elation, sorry and eager. At one moment he wanted to flee, the next he could barely wait.

He crossed the barren square.

The public house stood waiting, half-doors shut, window shade fully raised, so that boxes of fresh eggs and a row of sweets' jars were in full view in the window. A bicycle leaned on the front wall, and at the other side of the door were two flat breast-spades for cutting turf.

Morgan came closer. A hand reached into the front window, snatching up a box of eggs, replacing it with another jar of sweets. He pushed open the half-door. "Is there a John Maughan?" he asked of the woman behind the counter. "Oh, this is the grocery," she said eagerly, pointing to a doorway out to the back. "Himself's in the pub."

"Thank you kindly." Morgan's face went crimson when several women left off buying groceries to stare at him.

"When yeer through the door go past the partition," burbled the shopkeeper, as flustered as Morgan. "It's *the fellow,*" she whispered loudly as Morgan crossed the short hallway to the large room at the back.

The pub was nearly empty, only three old men drinking at the bar. One table was occupied by the publican in his white apron, sitting with a weathered old farmer in his Sunday suit. Denny O'Donnell sat with them, his back to the door. But at almost the instant Morgan appeared in the doorway Denny whirled, leaped to his feet to rush across the room, scattering sawdust in his haste. "How grand!" he cried, shaking Morgan's outstretched hand. He propelled him swiftly to the two men.

"This is Michael McNulty, and I want you to meet John Maughan."

"Have a glass on the house," said the publican. "Sit and enjoy yeerselves, while I handle the refreshments. Ye've the whole afternoon, with no one here to bother ye."

Negotiations proceeded briskly.

Morgan bought the second round of drinks, John Maughan the third. The publican rushed back and forth filling the glasses, maintaining a respectful silence.

Denny, in his capacity as "speaker," polished off drinks while encouraging the preliminary questions. Eventually he settled back to let old Maughan take over. "Ye've already the farm?" said Maughan.

"Oh, yes. The farm's mine."

"Two years the father's gone," chirped Denny.

"Nineteen twenty-eight he made it over. When he felt himself going."

"A great hand with the soil," said Denny. "Morgan learned it at his knee."

"And ye've a slate roof?"

"To be sure. A fine house. Annie's the downstairs, but if there's a wedding we'll have it. She'll move to the loft."

The farmer shifted position, uncomfortable in his Sunday clothes. His old sun-beat face had the look of a man well into a hard bargain. "How many cows?" he said.

"Two milk and two dry, and three fat pigs. There'll be more in the spring."

"Only four?"

Morgan bristled. Hadn't he surplus to sell, always calves for the market in spring? "Four's plenty for Annie and me."

Denny grew nervous. "They've a fine house. And you'd never see the like of the pasture, a sweep of green right down to the sea."

"Ye mean there'd be great work for a young girl? Takin' her strength from the chief duty?"

"Not at all," Denny insisted, "that's not the case at all. Morgan's a great one for the heavy work."

"Sure, my sister Annie does the work of a man." Morgan

blushed. What man'd keep a bride from her duty? Then a
fearsome thought struck. "The girl's not weak?"

"Minnie Maughan's as strong as a horse!" Denny's voice
rose. He began snapping his suspenders.

"If there's illness I've got to know," said Morgan.

"God, no," said Denny. "There's no bad blood in the
Maughans."

"She's not a day of sickness in years," said the father,
bristling now himself.

Morgan felt relieved. "And the rest? Are they well?"

"Oh, she's his only one," said Denny. "The one fair jewel
he has."

"And are ye far from the road?" asked Maughan.

"You've got me there," Morgan admitted. "We've a damn
good hike over the boreen."

"But he's grand fresh air from the sea," cried Denny.

"We was hopin' for a house on the Westport road," said
Maughan thoughtfully. "Not that we won't take a nice slate
roof. If it's not too far in."

"Not too far for this grand fellow to walk the long ten miles
to Ballyrea!" Denny nearly shouted.

Old Maughan rubbed his chin. "Do ye get in often to
Westport? Ye say it's three miles?"

"Whenever I've the notion. Me and Annie's been pretty
content at home."

The bargaining continued. Cows and pigs. Slate and thatch.
Turnips, oats and rye. John Maughan bought another round,
Morgan the next. Morgan, not much of a drinker, felt light-
headed. His hopes soared and fell.

Maughan set his glass on the table. He glanced over at the
bar at the three old men who'd never turned around, then
fastened calculating eyes on Morgan. "Here's my proposition,"
he said quietly. "I'm a man with a bit of ambition, ye know
that, I'm sure."

"To be sure," put in Denny, his words slurred.

"If a man's only daughter were to see a bit of Westport, get
used to the wider world, so to speak, no time at all before the
family'd have a kind of broadening themselves. Do ye know
what I mean?"

"Don't be givin' it a thought. Morgan knows exactly."
Denny formed his words carefully. Victory was in sight.

"For that kind of connection I'd gladly go two hundred fifty pounds."

More than a little dizzy himself, Morgan pondered the offer. "It was three hundred I had in mind. But it's true about Westport. I don't go often."

"Two hundred fifty's a grand fortune," Denny said.

The publican rushed to the shop for his wife. They leaned on the bar, breathless. "Twould be a shame," he whispered, "for it to bog down. Just for hardly goin' to Westport. Damn fool to mention it."

In the end it was settled. Two hundred and seventy-five. They'd go straight to have a look at the girl. If she suited, the offer was fixed. And if the daughter agreed, he'd send Denny around to arrange the day.

"Minnie Maughan, where've you been? The word's come over from the public house. He'll be here. And not a sight of ye to be found." Katie Maughan was mixing bread. "Ye think he'd like raisins?" she said. She spilled a handful into the sticky batter.

Minnie watched guardedly. Her thoughts were across the hills. A web of pleasure held her.

"No tongue in yeer head?" Katie spooned batter into a pan. She glared at her daughter, who stared at the floor, relishing her silence. Her deep soft place awaited the return of her man. She felt his tight strong body fitting into her soft flesh. Her breasts were taut.

"Minnie."

Startled out of her dreaminess Minnie's anger flared. She glared sullenly. Have ye a match for the wonders, old one? What do ye know? Had ye the Great High Heaven, known only to Mattie and me?

In summer they spent their passion in the upland meadows, danced their delight in the new-raked hay. But in the cold of winter they fled to the O'Malleys', to the old decrepit cow house. The ramshackle shed was their great wild Eden, where they flung themselves in a wordless reel. After which, spent and giddy, they lay for hours on their bed of hay.

This morning, after they'd exhausted themselves, they lay grieving. "Am I cattle to be bargained off?" Minnie'd cried, knowing this was the day the farmer'd come. Mattie gazed up at her. He fashioned a pad for his head from the hay, struggling for words. But the pain was too great. This was the day.

"Ah, Mattie. It's yeer own kisses I'm wantin', not this farmer from God knows where."

"Then don't let them do this," he cried. "Run away with me. To America!"

"Ah, if it was only that easy. I'd be packed and off."

"I've a cousin that went. There's boats all the time."

"Had we the fare I'd go. Ye know I would. But I've not a cent to my name. Isn't it the fortune they'll give for the farmer?"

"I'll *steal* the fare. There isn't a locked door in the village."

"Yeer crazy. Hardly a one's the price o' the oil. Aren't they forever turnin' the lamps down? That's why my da's so keen on Westport, for people with a bit more like himself."

"I'm sure I could find a few shillings."

"That's not enough. Besides, stealin's wrong. Don't ye listen to the priest? Nothin's worth burnin' in Hell for. I'm ashamed ye'd even think of it."

"Hell? I'd murder if I could have ye."

"Murder? God help us! The Civic Guard'd be takin' ye."

"Only if they caught me."

"Yeer sayin' wild things. Crazy things. And who is it ye'd murder?"

"The farmer. Who else?"

"The farmer? That'd surprise them . . . But ye've no gun?"

"There's ways."

"And even if ye shot him, God forbid, they'd be sure to find another. Ye couldn't go on murderin'."

"Then it's yeer da I've to take a gun to."

"Yeer not serious? The da who raised me? Glory be to the saints. Put away yeer wild talk. Give me a kiss. I've to go meet the da, and the farmer."

Katie Maughan spooned batter into a second pan. She slipped a metal oven down into the coals, covering it with red fire. "Ye'll find yeer tongue quick enough," she said.

Minnie gazed on the hot coals. "I'll not. Isn't it only to have a look he's come?"

"It won't hurt to be pleasant."

"They've not even the writings."

"The writings, is it? Aren't ye ready with the answers, when ye feel like it? Yeerself without a cent but what we give ye? . . .

Besides, there's not much to work out. Only the sister's to be provided for."

"I may not want to live with this Annie Riley. I may not even like the look of himself."

"Whisht! No more of that. Ye'd turn the sister out?"

"I never said that."

"What is it has ye so cross?" Katie measured flour and milk for another loaf. She added soda to the flour, stirring vigorously. "I've been worrying the heart out o' me. Ye'll wreck the whole endeavor. Tell me where ye were."

"Walkin'."

"In the middle of winter?"

"And wouldn't ye know that nothin' but a rest would put me up to the long walk home. So I stopped in."

"Mary Maughan, ye've been over there! No matter that I forbid it. That Mattie O'Malley! . . .Wait'll himself gets in. He'll put a stick hoppin' on yeer backside. See if that young buck'll look so good."

"Ye'd have me screamin' with welts on my back when your grand fellow comes to call?" Minnie planted her feet rebelliously. She put up a hand to ward off the slap.

Crack! A sharp blow on the cheek. She backed against the dresser. "I won't do it!" she cried. "It's Mattie I'll wed. There's not a thing that I'll do with this stranger. I'll have Mattie O'Malley or none."

"Ye've been hangin' 'round the O'Malleys. I can hear it in yeer voice. On the very day. Mary Maughan."

"I'm not Mary Maughan. I'm Minnie! And I'll be Minnie O'Malley or it's dying I'll be. So help me."

"You're swearing oaths? We'd right to put ye in harness with the likes of that crowd?"

"They're fine people, the O'Malleys. They're warm. Always smilin' and laffin', and havin' a bit of a joke with themselves."

"A tinker bunch. Tinkers, the lot of them."

"They're not tinkers! They've a house! There isn't a drop of gypsy blood in his body. Why, his da is . . ."

"I know exactly what his da is, and his ma, too. If ye really want to know."

"I won't hear another word."

"Well, want to or not. Sit down. Right by the hearth. Don't make a move from that chair. Ye'll hear what I've to tell ye."

Minnie's face was ashen. She put her hands to her ears.

"Do ye think ye can shut out the truth?"

Minnie sat frozen, unable to meet her ma's eyes. She made a great effort to keep her knees from shaking. Morgan Riley? Was she really to marry this stranger? An old man, past forty? Was life to be lost, so the Maughans could better themselves?

"The O'Malleys don't cut the hay 'til the fall," said Katie Maughan. "What's left of it." She fixed a cold stare on Minnie. "What kind of shiftless crowd is that?"

"They haven't starved," said Minnie. Her voice trembled. The O'Malleys' decrepit cabin rose in her mind, the miserable tin-roofed sheds. The sagging farmyard gate. The near-empty hayrick.

"Have ye ever seen the like, meadow land goin' to waste the long summer? The rest of us mowin' and rakin', dryin' and stackin'. What rest is there 'til ye save the hay? Ballyrea out from mornin' 'til night, the whole month of July.

"But what o' the O'Malleys? What are they doing? Nothing. Nothin' at all. Sittin' by the old dung heap in front o' the door. Eight strappin' children—oh, I know there's some o' them babes. But not one'd do a day's work any more than the father. The wonder of it is they're healthy as hogs. Not a day but they're out for all to see, instead of hidin' their heads in shame."

Minnie bowed her head, her face twisted in pain. The ma's voice droned on, cutting the heart out of hope. Her someday dream of a little cottage, herself and Mattie in charge. A few acres, a cow or two. A little garden, enough for a man and his wife.

But a match with the O'Malleys was not to be. Her father'd lie dead in his grave. The money he'd saved in the hands of Con O'Malley?

But why not give herself the money? Place it into her own hands? She'd buy a piece of land, a little cabin. Make a life for herself and Mattie, doing what they'd always wanted—making love by night, working together by day. Wasn't Mattie strong as an ox? Hadn't he the makings of a farmer, a good one, all he needed was a push?

"And if ye ruin yeer character with the likes o' them, at the very moment yeer da is makin' the match . . . Well, you'll be lucky to ever get a man at all, once it gets around. There isn't one'll have ye."

Minnie looked up. Tears welled in her eyes, but her voice held steady. "They're happy there. I never hear them cross. Even the da laughs."

"Oh, indeed they're happy. Isn't a bird happy, flyin' around in the tree tops, not a thought in his head from morn until night but a branch to rest his wings on? . . . Well they might be happy, the O'Malleys."

"The ma's always a child in her lap. Even the da holds the babe when he cries."

"What else does he have to do? Not rakin' in the hay, I'm sure."

"I hear the wee ones singing," said Minnie, gathering courage. "I've been walkin' by the door, and sure as I'm born isn't there one or the other hummin' a tune. And never the ma's voice screamin' to be quiet. Doesn't she be joinin' in herself?"

"Singing for their supper? No more than a song to feed them."

"Yeer makin' it wrong. Yeer tellin' them like they're not at all. I know. I've been with them." Minnie's voice grew soft. Nothing could destroy what she'd learned from the O'Malleys. Not even this Morgan Riley, this farmer from Westport. "I've been with them," she repeated firmly.

CHAPTER
4

The last round of drinks was done. Now for a look at the girl.

Morgan's head spun. Caught up in dizzying happiness he was unable to stop smiling. An imaginary fiddle played in his head, and he longed to leap to his feet for a four-hand reel.

Denny had troubles of his own, trying to keep his feet on the floor. His heart danced. Old John Maughan wore a grin from ear to ear, and between the three of them there were enough smiles to cause the old men at the bar to leave off drinking. They got up to shake their hands.

When the three had sailed out the door the publican motioned to his wife. "Is it settled?" she whispered.

"Old Maughan's to pay two hundred seventy-five . . . The girl's gettin' a fine house with four cows . . . There's a horse that's lost his legs, but the buildings are in great shape. Two big sheds, with a cabin and the cows. And doesn't he be cutting the turf when spring's barely begun? A grand farmer indeed. They've hens, too. The sister's a great hand with the hens . . . and pigs, three fat ones. Did ye ever hear the like?"

"Isn't it a fine fellow ye've been servin' this day?" Her eyes grew big with wonder.

"They're goin' now for the girl. He's not had a look at her."

"Minnie's a beauty. He'll rave at the sight."

"Denny's a great hand with his first match," said Michael McNulty. "It'll go to his head." He swept the floor, putting down fresh sawdust. "But it'll be a long day before he'll find another pair in this poor place. It's not many makes a living, or like yeerself out there sellin' the groceries."

"Sure, everybody drinks," said Mary McNulty. "And they've need of the tea and sugar. But a decent man for the few young girls? Who can save the fortune, scratchin' a bare livin' to keep from starvin'?"

The publican poured himself a glass of stout. His wife stirred the fire, and when it blazed cozily she came to sit at one of the tables with him. "Ye think she'll have him?" she said softly.

"She'd be crazy. Sixteen acres, Mrs. McNulty? O'Donnell says it's great pasture land. The cousin gives him all the particulars."

The wife looked around carefully, satisfying herself. She made a quick Sign of the Cross. "Well," she whispered. "There's more than one's seen the girl in the hay. She's lucky . . . Many's the one weds in a hurry, no fortune at all. The clothes on her back and what the parents'll give them, so mad they are."

"Whisht. Not a word. If it gets about we ruined a girl's character not one'll be stoppin' for a drink."

"Well, aren't I only whisperin' it between the two of us? I'm not tellin' it at the crossroads."

"Whisht. Whisht."

"That O'Malley's a strappin' lad. Isn't it a shame there's not a shilling to their name? A girl wants to look up, you know."

"Well, there isn't a thing stoppin' her. Morgan Riley's a good solid man. Isn't his face as upright as they come?"

"I know. But it's the O'Malley she wants. No good can come of it."

"Will ye be quiet."

"Sure, the girl's only twenty." Mary McNulty was not to be stopped. "Did you ever see the like o' the rich brown hair? Curlin' and sweepin' over the shoulders, 'til the ma's half crazy keepin' an eye?"

"All the more reason to settle it. Then old Maughan can bring in the nephew. Isn't he waitin' to sign over the land?" Michael McNulty got up to pour another drink.

"It's a sad thing when a farmer's no son."

"The nephew'll give it the name. Isn't he waitin' to marry?"

"Wouldn't it kill old Maughan if all they had was girls? Him goin' to all this trouble, sendin' to Kilmaragh for a match for his own?"

The two talked on, examining John Maughan's situation from every angle, dissecting the peculiar plight of a farm with no heir. "Is there a family alive," said McNulty, "wouldn't bring in a relative when there's no son for the name on the land?"

Morgan breathed the steep upland air, trying to clear away the giddy delirium. Occasionally he stumbled, only great concentration preventing a fall. How foolhardy, consuming so much drink, with the girl yet to be seen.

"Don't give it a thought," whispered Denny.

The two floundered clumsily along after John Maughan, who appeared to have no trouble at all on the hills.

The Maughan farm lay at the far end of a glen, on the side of a hill, the glen itself stretching oddly back from the flat plain. Beyond the hills loomed a mountain, brooding over the short, steep hills.

The farm seemed a haven when it became visible. The low, whitewashed walls stood bright against the brown, the house in fine repair.

"Are ye ready for the girl?" whispered Denny. John Maughan looked over his shoulder. "Is the walk too much?"

"Ah, no. We're fine." Morgan tried to sound confident.

"Don't be giving it a thought," Denny comforted him. "There isn't a reason in the world we can't complete the deal."

Morgan's mood, since leaving the pub, had swung from optimism to terror. One sweep of the pendulum filled him with confidence. Of course the girl would have him! A fine farmer, with the place of four cows, a great hand with a scythe or a plow? Then abruptly, like lowering clouds on a spring day, his assurance would vanish, leaving him soaked in a shower of gloom. Despair tumbled out of the past. She would think him too old.

He soared repeatedly, only to crash again into desolation.

The house came into close view. The crazy seesaw halted. The pendulum hung motionless. He was a man of substance, come honorably to the girl. He'd the respect of Kilmaragh, his neighbors' good will. So why not be hopeful? Light-hearted? Himself and the father'd a good bargain struck, now he'd show himself to the girl.

The Maughans' kitchen was large and cheerful, with a brisk fire crackling in the hearth. From the fireplace crane hung an enormous kettle, steam gushing. A lamp burned brightly on the dresser, and on the wall a second lamp was lit.

The large table was laid out for tea, with a white cloth, china plates, and two steaming loaves of soda bread, the golden crusts painted with butter. Plump raisins fairly burst from the loaves. Morgan drew a deep, contented breath.

"They've cooked a goose," whispered Denny, pointing out the platter of sliced meat on the dresser.

"Are ye here?" cried Mrs. Maughan. She set a butter dish on the dresser to rush to Morgan. "Ye must be Mr. Riley?" Her plain country face broke into a smile. She grabbed Morgan's hand and shook it. "We've waited long for this honor."

"Aren't I honored myself?" Comforted, Morgan took a chair by the fire.

"Take off yeer heavy coat."

"Oh, isn't it the way?" said Morgan, getting to his feet, embarrassed.

John Maughan settled Denny by the fire, before taking a place by the dresser. He rested his feet on a sack of oats. "Where's the young one?" he asked his wife.

"Feedin' the hens. She'll be along in a minute . . . Don't be actin' the stranger," she said to Morgan. "A bit of somethin' to warm ye?" John Maughan rose quickly, but just as swiftly Morgan stopped him, hoping to God they'd take his word. "I've had more than plenty already."

"Oh, but a drop?"

"No. No." What he needed was a cool head, not more drink spinnin' him around. The girl'd think him a drunk.

"I'll take a drop," said Denny.

"Oh, here's the girl," said John Maughan. "Come in, daughter."

Morgan gazed. The girl was like none he'd ever seen. Not very tall, but full in the breasts. A tiny waist. Hair that spilled over the shoulders until it seemed he saw heaven itself. Rich, brown swirls.

"Look up, Minnie," ordered the father. At first she ignored him, but when she raised her face to Morgan he felt the whole room whirl. She had the loveliest imaginable eyes, green they were, like a summer meadow, tiny flecks of gold like summer sun.

(In the distance, Denny babbled to old John Maughan. Was he readying for spring? What a great thing he'd the nephew. And from Maughan, No, indeed, he'd no need for a month.)

"Step forward, Minnie. Shake the man's hand."

Morgan pulled himself up. The girl made a tentative approach, her eyes taking him in. She relaxed slightly. But when she offered her hand it was icy. There was no confirmation in her neutral glance. Morgan held her hand as long as he decently could. Afterwards he put his hands in his pockets to cover his embarrassment. The girl was clearly shy.

Minnie struggled to assess the man, took in the light brown hair, bunching up in little tufts over the ears. The eyebrows, too, were bushy. And he had farmer's hands, large, work-worn. A strong man, tall and broad, arms all muscle. But what of it?

"I'm pleased to meet ye, sir," she said.

The farmer nodded. Minnie saw at once he was shy. The face was of a man you could trust, the eyes kind. But I'm given! she wanted to cry out. The deepest, true part of me's owned.

"Sit up to the table, Minnie. I'll be pourin' the tea."

Minnie did as she was told, though Denny was sure he saw signs of rebellion. So that when they were comfortably settled, drinking tea and eating, he threw out a few points in Morgan's favor. "Have ye ever considered what a blessing it's been, me goin' down to Westport? Bringin' all the news. Many's a one'd never know nothing at all." He put the question to John Maughan, across the table, but with a corner of his eye on the girl.

"We'll be goin' that way ourselves, now we've a reason." Maughan lit up his pipe.

The wife agreed. "I'll be buyin' a new shawl, don't ye know?" She flashed a great, broad smile, beaming across at Morgan, until she saw his plate was empty. She rushed to fill it.

"Oh, I'm stuffed," said Morgan, savoring the tender goose meat. He poured hot tea into his saucer. "Some of that wonderful bread," he said. "And a bite of the meat."

The Westport talk spun on, banter on the wonderful world outside. "It's a long road out," said Maughan. "But grand things ye find at the end of it," said Denny. "Oh, glory!" cried Katie. "We'll see somethin' besides Ballyrea."

The girl took no part, barely lifting her head. Not a bite of her food had been touched. Morgan, glowing from the warm reception, nevertheless felt unease. Once when the girl'd looked up for an instant he saw her green eyes spark with resentment. Later, the ma urging a bit of friendliness, he felt sure he saw hopelessness.

Was it the duty? Not knowing a thing of the flesh?

But how could that be? With all the animals. A country girl. Feeding and tending, and birthing. Surely they were better at it, in a backwards place?

Or was it lonesome for the ma she was, just thinking about the leaving? Sick for the family, many's a bride. If that was the case she needn't suffer. Who was to say they'd not have a visit? And there'd be christenings and Christmas, no matter the dead of winter. More than that he'd do, to be husband to Minnie Maughan. Husband. He savored the word, rolled it on his tongue like a mouthful of sweets. It called up visions of paradise, this darling woman every day by his side. And in the evenings they'd sit by the fire, her hand in his, talking over the day's affairs. Oh, it'd be grand.

And then there'd be the nights. His face reddened and he put up his hand. Mrs. Maughan, thinking he wanted more tea, reached for the teapot. Glory be, if the mother only knew!

Across the table Minnie abandoned even the pretense of eating. The haze of despair that had hung like a cloud for five days swelled into a thunderhead, pulling her up, up.

"Mattie!" her heart screamed. "My darlin' Mattie, come save me!"

Around her the talk went on. When to plant the potatoes? Should the rows be down by St. Patrick's? Was there a better way for the root crops? Oh, and did he think the garden was best turned in November? Gab!

"Ye've sat long enough, Minnie." The ma's voice broke her reverie. Minnie lifted her head to see her future husband looking at her. His eyes under the bushed brows were both awed and eloquent, and she saw hunger. But there was no greed in the look, no craving. Only hopeful, reverent worship.

Dear God in heaven. Was she to break two men's hearts?

Morgan continued to gaze, and Denny—cursed matchmaker—wore the smug look of a man with a good day's work. A pox on his efforts.

"Isn't she strange?" said Katie. "Food on her plate when she ought to eat hearty?" She laughed, but threw a severe look at her daughter. Minnie seized bread from her plate, but it stuck on her tongue. Only with great effort was she able to swallow. She sipped tea to calm herself.

"Go out to the cows, Minnie," her father said. Minnie took her hand from her eyes. Only the farmer sat with her. Denny and her da smoked their pipes by the fire.

From the cow house came sounds of mooing and bellowing.

"They're heavy," said the farmer, and Minnie heard the kindness in his voice. "We'll be off." The farmer nodded to Denny, who got slowly to his feet. "Sure, isn't it late?" he said comfortably.

"Ye'll take a lantern?" said Katie Maughan.

Minnie crept off to the cow house, with Denny's farewell in her ears.

The farmer said nothing, only smiled shyly.

The only sounds were mooing, the slap-slap of tails in the darkness, Minnie's feet brushing the straw. The cows, heavy with milk, lowed steadily, and in the back stalls the dry stock bellowed. She hung her lantern on a hook. Around her, great dark eyes gazed trustingly.

"They've not even fed ye, so busy they were." Minnie glared in scorn at the empty troughs, but quickly her anger fled. She crooned, "Ye poor darlins." The warm sweet cow-smell filled her. She breathed the aroma of dung and hay.

Adding fistfuls of hay to her bucket of parsnips and turnips, she stirred the mixture, then brought in a pail of water. Darting from side to side she spread the feed. The animals comfortably settled, she dragged the milking stool to the first of the milk cows. She jumped to her feet again, threw herself on the animal's neck, touched ridges of bone and flesh, felt the hump that slid downwards. The cow mooed. Minnie clung. She wept soundlessly, tasting her own tears. Hot thick cow-smells surrounded her. She pressed nearer, stroking the wet, soft nose, close against her cheek. Sweetness flooded her. She settled on the stool, wiping her face with her apron. Her fingers worked surely.

Softly at first, then louder, she crooned a lullaby. Her hands flew.

When the milking was done Minnie shoveled the trenches, piling the dung on the manure pile back of the shed. She swept the floor, spread fresh straw. "There, me darlins," she said. "A nice, warm bed for the night."

She plucked the lantern from the wall-hook and carried the milk pail to the kitchen.

CHAPTER
5

In the morning, before anyone was about, Minnie slipped out to the cow house. The cows milked, she wrapped herself in a shawl. Before the mist had cleared the mountain she was down the barren hills. She raced through the sleeping village, across the flat plain, over the swath of bog.

"It's done!" she cried, when the O'Malleys opened to her pounding. Con O'Malley rubbed sleep from his eyes. "God be praised," he mumbled. He clutched grey, ragged underwear to hide his hairy chest.

Mother O'Malley, yawning, lumbered from the tiny room off the kitchen, enormous in her shapeless gown. She stared, uncomprehending. But seeing Minnie she smiled. "I'll wake Mattie." She shuffled to the ladder and stiffly, yanking her nightgown above her fat knees, began the steep climb to the loft. "Go to bed," she ordered Con over her shoulder. And to Minnie, "Don't have a care. I'll get him for ye. Sit yeerself b'the fire."

"The ashes, ye mean," said the husband mournfully. He moved obediently toward the bedroom. "They'll freeze." Con shivered in his worn underwear.

"They can blow on it," Mrs. O'Malley called down briskly. "I'm sure they'll find a bit of heat."

"I've a few sticks I been savin'," said Con. "If I'd my pants on."

"Oh, no," Minnie protested. "Ye'll need the warmth for the little ones."

"Here's Mattie," Mrs. O'Malley called down. "His head is after liftin' and one eye is open . . . Blow on the ashes, Minnie."

By the time Mattie had dressed the elder O'Malleys were snoring. Their door was shut. Minnie sat in the kitchen's lone chair. Mattie battled the ashes. "No matter," she said, hugging her shawl. "The news I bring is all the fire we'll need."

"Then don't tell it," he said, throwing his arms around her. Minnie pried herself loose. "Sit on the hob," she said gently. "You'll have to hear. And today's as good as any."

Mattie scrambled up the ladder for a blanket. The raggedy covering was dirty and frayed. Bundling together, they sat on the hob.

"So you see, they shook on it," concluded Minnie, after telling the story. "All that's left is to walk the land, and the writings. So it won't take much. My da'll give over, and we'll be set for the wedding." Her voice broke at the terrible word.

"And did ye see the man?"

"A kindly look he has—he's well thought of. He has the place of four cows, so he's a catch . . . Hasn't Denny been makin' himself sick runnin' back and forth to Kilmaragh?"

"But what's in it for Denny? That he should set himself up? I'd like to kill him."

"Ye mustn't talk of murderin'. Denny wants a contact. Someone he can know in Kilmaragh."

"Doesn't he be braggin' o' cousins? Ye'd think he owned the town, with all the travelin' he does to Westport. And doesn't he be visitin' Pat O'Donnell? What more does he need?"

"Denny's ambitious from waitin' so long for the farm. He needs to be occupied."

"Then let him make the match for us. Can't he arrange for ye to wed me?"

Minnie's resolve evaporated. She broke into heartbroken weeping. "I'll die," she shrieked. "It's not a weddin' they're sellin' me to but a funeral." A circle of O'Malley faces lined the opening to the loft. Several of the smaller children burst into tears.

Below, the bedroom door flew open. Mother O'Malley, immense in her voluminous gown, rushed to Minnie. "Oh, darlin'. Darlin'," she said. Waving her arms like a ship in full sail she embraced the two young people.

"Is it trouble?" Con's mournful face appeared at the door.

He was struggling into his trousers. "Murder. Nothin' short of a wee killin'll stop these scoundrels."

"No," said Minnie, emerging from the tangle in the blanket. She stared in horror at her lover's da. "They're only doin' what they must," she pleaded. Terror gripped her. Had they a weapon hidden? Her mind flew around the ragbag farm. The tangle of outbuildings. *What if Con O'Malley shot her da?*

"They don't want me left," she said reasonably, but her voice shook, and she wiped her eyes.

"Left?" shouted Con O'Malley, beside himself with rage. "Our own Mattie eatin' his heart out? Isn't it married ye'd be in a minute, my own son havin' his way?"

"It's no use," said Minnie, agonizing over how to put it. "Yeer a backward people, they say. They say backward places die out. They've no big fortunes." Her heart beat strangely at sound of the terrible words.

"Little they know the happy times I've had." She looked from Con to his wife, and then at Mattie, who appeared tortured. "Who's yeer like?" she said. She looked to the loft, at the wonderful sisters and brothers, their stricken faces peering down.

"Isn't it a wonder ye are?" she continued sorrowfully. "Never complainin', yet not a shilling to yeer name. There's not many does well with their fate."

"Come live with us," cried Mattie. "Forget a weddin'. It's *here* is yeer place." He leapt to his feet. Excitement had thrown him into a frenzy. Grief, rage, hope blazed from his eyes. "Yeer to come to us, I tell ye. We've room. Yeer to come."

"To be sure," cried Con. "Not a stick or a stone isn't yeers if ye want." He waved an arm, sweeping the room. "It's all yeers."

"Indeed," crowed the wife, shivering in her nightdress. "Con, darlin'. While Minnie's decidin', run out for yeer few bits of sticks. I'll get us a bowl of porridge."

Minnie regarded her beloved friends. Their sparse odds and ends of furniture. One lone chair, Mother O'Malley's. She looked at the soot-stained walls, cracked, blotched where leaks ran down from the sagging roof. There were two tiny windows, curtained with melancholy rags, one tattered cloth on a peg for the few cracked dishes. "Ah, no,' she said softly, contemplating the room she'd call home if she chose. She stood motionless, suddenly firm and sure.

She faced the O'Malleys, the grief of all the world in her eyes. Sadness streamed from her. But at the same time she exuded an aura of grandeur. An ancient queen, she appeared to her friends. They were dazzled. "It's settled," she said, just above a whisper, but with no hesitation. She looked at all of them steadily. "My da wants it. We're to move up in the world. I canna go against him."

She settled her shawl, smoothed her skirts at her ankles.

Never would she forget Mattie's face when she left him. His bleak eyes. The hard jaw. A smoldering rage emanated. He appeared ominous, a revengeful young bull. He'd not yield peacefully. He hadn't her own practicality.

Life had to be lived, Minnie knew. Ye had to put up with it. Things were what they were.

But not to Mattie, God help him. He'd never accept. He'd continue to do battle, hopeless though it was. God only knew the grief might come of it, when a man was set on revenge.

So that she made a concession. She would meet him once more.

But the meeting must be secret. *Very secret.* If her character was ruined, there'd be no tellin' the consequences. "Oh, darlin' Mattie," she cried, "how could I stand it? They'd drive ye off to America . . . Who knows what they'd do to me? My da would never get over it, the family name destroyed . . . There'd not be a husband at all, no one would want me."

"And is it done?" cried Annie, the instant Morgan walked through the door. She'd a place set, and she snatched up his plate from the hearth, where it sat warming.

She turned up the wall lamp. Bright yellow light bathed the room, so that the fine wood of the table shone rich brown. "Was it a cold walk?" she said.

Morgan ignored her, and, without a word, began wolfing down potatoes and bacon. All the ten miles he'd brooded, the whole way home, his mind on last evening's farewell, if you could call it that. What ailed the girl, the angry look she threw?

"Is it done?" said Annie. She heaped Morgan's plate for the second time, scrutinizing his face for a sign.

Still the stubborn silence.

She filled his teacup, growing ever more apprehensive. (These backwards people do be tricky sometimes, the girl not all they said.) She plucked a bit of mending from the dresser, settled herself in a chair by the hearth. Abruptly Morgan pulled a clay pipe from his pocket. When it was drawing nicely, he turned to Annie. "It's settled."

"Praise be the saints. Isn't it my prayers answered?"

"We've struck the bargain. They've still to walk the land. And we've met, the girl and myself."

"Great Jesus. And when is the walking?" Annie's mending had dropped to the floor, and she left it. "But they're coming?" she gasped.

"The father'll send word. If the match is agreeable."

"She didn't *say?*" Annie gave a whoop of indignation.

"They never do. Doesn't the young girls always be thinking it over?"

"She'll surely agree? We need time to paint the house."

"The house is fine," said Morgan.

"A little whitewash, surely to God. We'll have to kill a goose. And there's whiskey and porter . . . Should we borrow a few cows?"

"Not at all. The father knows what I have. You wouldn't believe all the praise Denny gave us . . ."

"Pat would lend us three cows. A few extra, standing around, if only for the mooing? Cows make a good impression."

"And where would we put them? Out in the cold?"

"It wouldn't hurt," said Annie, miffed at being mocked. Wasn't it only for his happiness?

"The fellow knows, and he's very well pleased. Doesn't he want a connection? And would you believe it, we're it."

"Sure it's the lass that's fortunate."

"Ah, I don't know. I'm only an old fellow at that. Our luck's this Maughan wants a tie with Westport."

"Kilmaragh isn't Westport," said Annie, suddenly gloomy.

"But you've never seen the likes of Ballyrea. A backward place. It's the end of the world. But for the few grand farms on the hills . . . Maughan's place is a wonder."

"What about when they see how isolated we are ourselves? The whole thing might come apart."

"Oh, I told him we're three miles out. I said it enough times. But we're close enough, I could see. We're a grand connection. They're moving up in the world." Morgan's laugh pealed out. It seemed to bounce from the small cabin walls. But still Annie frowned.

Morgan grew sober. "Maybe we'd better put on a coat of whitewash," he said. "And be sure the goose is a fat one."

The men came in the first evening after Morgan's return. It was cold, clear, moonless, the same sort of night as that of Denny's proposition. Except this night something was uppermost on everyone's mind. Had Morgan made the match?

Morgan was apprehensive as the neighbors filed in. Surely to God they'd not ask. Shyness overwhelmed him, the fear of looking ridiculous. It was one thing to be off in Ballyrea, but another entirely to break the news in Kilmaragh.

There was Colman Ronan, for instance. "Have you given it enough thought?" he'd ask. But what he'd really mean was, "Whatever did she see in him?" Morgan had been asking the question of himself since yesterday, almost from the moment he left Ballyrea. Doubts kept him awake near half the night.

With the evening in progress, it seemed he needn't have worried. Brendan Duffy, as usual, said nothing. Barrett was on his best behavior, Ronan hadn't a single caustic thing to say. O'Dowd, who'd have been sure to have sided with Ronan, pronounced the evening a grand success. Morgan concluded the same. Either the word hadn't gotten out, or else they were respecting his privacy. At any rate, nothing was mentioned. His secret was safe, at least until they'd walked the land.

But unaccountably the whole thing came out, almost by accident. Pat O'Gavagan, so old he seldom spoke at all, offered a friendly remark, the kind no one could take offense at. "February, and we'll be plowing again," he said.

"Well, *some* of us," snapped Colman Ronan. A gasp swept the room. Even Ronan wasn't generally so impertinent. "Begging your pardon, but I meant no offense," he corrected quickly, throwing one of his exaggerated smiles at O'Gavagan. "I've done my share of plowing," he retorted, voice echoing the remembered strength of his youth. He carefully refrained from looking at Ronan.

"Don't we know it? You've plowed more than any man your age."

Mother of God, worried Morgan. Whatever was wrong with Ronan?

The old man turned his back on Ronan. He sat smoldering into the fire, shoulders hunched, and began to rock back and forth. For one horrified instant Morgan feared he'd tumble into the fire. But the moment passed. O'Gavagan grew still. Yellow light from the fire played across his sunken cheeks.

"When your father was alive . . ." (He addressed his words to Morgan, ignoring Ronan entirely. His voice commanded total attention.) "When Edward Riley was alive there wasn't a spring we didn't hitch our two horses to the same plow . . . Rows and rows of potatoes we had, into the ground by St. Patrick's. A partnership, my old crony and me . . . And now all the world is gone." He paused. The room was silent except for his labored breathing.

"Or if we were bringing in the hay." He brightened. Some of the tension in the room eased. "Many's the load of hay we brought in together. And other neighbors with us. But always the two of us, however many were with us . . . And a nine-gallon barrel of stout, never a haying without that barrel. And all the hay came in on the same day."

"Sure, aren't we still doing it the same?" interrupted Ronan. From across the hearth old John Mulrenin's ancient sharp eyes glared him into silence. "You were great pals," he said, voice cracking. Every head in the room nodded. A tense silence set in. Ronan held his breath. What in the name of God was wrong with old Pat? Taking offense at nothing at all? Of course his plowing days were done. Wasn't it but for the nephew the farm'd not be worked at all?

He wished to God Annie Riley'd serve the tea, so they could all be off home. "How're things up in Ballyrea?" he said quickly, turning to Morgan to relieve the awkwardness.

Morgan's face flamed. He looked around desperately. Where was Annie with the tea?

The tension in the room deepened. Pat O'Donnell, picking up Ronan's lead, laughed knowingly. Ronan laughed too. Morgan sat with his lips clamped, so Ronan added, "Come on now, Morgan. Give us a bit. We're parched for news."

"Nothing's settled," said Morgan at last.

"But you had Denny draw it down?" Pat laughed again. Weren't they all dying to know? "He's not been travelin' back and forth for nothing, I hope."

"We've only started," said Morgan uneasily.

"Started, is it?" Pat's loudness covered his own nervousness. This was a tricky business. "Are ye saying Denny's not great at the match?"

"Sure, this is his first attempt," joked Ronan. "Wait 'til he's been at it a while." Everyone laughed, even Mulrenin and Pat O'Gavagan. Except for Morgan.

"Come on now," said Ronan, with a sideways look at O'Dowd, who cooperated with an exaggerated wink. Emboldened, Ronan walked over to Morgan. "Give us a hand," he said. "Let me shake the hand of a man who's to wed . . . Come on now, boys. Let's hear it for holy wedlock!"

There was a loud cheer. Followed by foot stamping.

Morgan was mortified. He refused to leave his seat. The laughter grew, until soon everyone except old Pat and Mulrenin had gathered around him, grinning, laughing, giving little pokes. Pat O'Donnell and Duffy the bachelor, linking arms, danced a jig while Barrett whistled the tune. The room resounded with good-natured joking, so that finally Morgan stood up to shake hands with each of them.

After a few rounds of whiskey the evening was over. Everyone left in high humor, with even Morgan caught up in the general enthusiasm.

"Let's hope they're right," he said to Annie, closing the door behind them. "It'd be a terrible thing if I lost it now."

"God save us, don't even think it." Hastily Annie made the Sign of the Cross. "Sure, wasn't it the good Lord put the thought in Denny's mind?"

"Ah, no, Annie. Nothing like that. There aren't many to choose from, that's all."

"Well, I say the good Lord is rewarding you. For the long years you've waited."

"But there's many a one's waited as long." Suddenly Morgan was swept away with sympathy. Annie's lonely life leapt out at him. "There was a lot o' years," he said, shaking his head. He thought of Annie's lost prospects, the two fine men she hadn't married. How could she, without a fortune?

"Ah, don't say it." Annie sat down at the table, grey, faded eyes wistful. Her fingers toyed with a glass. "They were good men, those two. Either would have suited."

The words came from an Annie he scarcely remembered, an Annie grown dim with the passing years. "You have to wonder," he said. Annie nodded, wiping away a rush of tears. "Why do you think he didn't?" she said quietly.

"None of them wants to give over. The land is all they have."

"But we're all *we* have." Annie's eyes suddenly blazed. Morgan stared, wordless. This was the Annie of old, whose heartbeats had thrilled with hopes and dreams.

"Oh, Annie. What can I say? If there was a thing I could do?"

"It's not your doing. You'd have married. Who wouldn't?"

"They just can't give it up, not a one of them. Isn't Denny sick to the death of waiting for the land?"

"Poor Denny."

"They think they're done when they give it. And do ye know, they are. The land's all."

"But are we to be done without ever having had it?" The angry words hung in the air. Annie's rage was palpable. "At least heaven is putting right your lonely life," she said.

"I can hope."

"Do more than hope, Morgan. Believe it."

"Ah, Annie, no one in the lonely world but yourself knows how badly I want to believe it."

"Then do. Don't give a look behind you. Get the writings signed and the wedding date set." She got up. "Enough of this talk." She turned down the lamp on the wall. "We'll put it into the hands of the merciful Lord and His Blessed Mother. There isn't a thing in the world not helped by prayer."

CHAPTER
6

The Maughans came to walk the land on a Monday like none all winter. For by the end of February (unlike the month preceding) the weather had turned unexpectedly mild.

Morgan was out of bed at dawn, earlier even than on a normal day, before Annie'd raked the coals and laid the new sods. After inspecting the cows and the horse he fed them their water and hay, caught the goose and, after breakfast, Annie plucked and dressed it. When the bird was safely roasting Annie joined Morgan outside. Together they scanned the boreen for sight of the Maughans' trap.

"Do you think there'll be sunshine?" Annie worried. Gusts of wind had carried a soft spring rain in off the ocean.

"Ah, now, the house looks grand," said Morgan. Annie silently agreed. Whitewashed inside and out, clean curtains on every window, and even the haggard buildings painted, the place looked as good as any, even with the grey day. "Don't be giving it a thought," he said.

But still Annie fretted. Didn't Morgan have a worry at all, these backward people thinking something grander than they'd get? So that when they saw the loneliness of the place they might think themselves little improved?

Or was the strange mild weather an indicator? New life peeking up in every patch of spiny pasture shrub?

The day cooperated. After an hour or two of gentle rain the low clouds parted. There was a peep of real sunshine. The sky turned almost blue in the sudden light. Across the slope to the ocean, the fields showed every sign of greening. Where the fields rose, the stark ridges of grey rock sported the faint beginnings of flowers.

Annie told her brother this was the happiest day of her life. "The long years," she said, in a voice grown soft.

"If only we'd a match for yourself," said Morgan wistfully, "now there's a fortune coming in."

"Well, the day is past," said Annie, with forced cheerfulness, not to spoil his mood. "Aren't they all for America? Only the bachelor Duffy, in his ramshackle excuse for a house? Seeing yourself settled's enough."

"But it's not fair." Morgan set his jaw stubbornly.

"Sure, what did they know of fairness, the old people?" said Annie in a mollifying tone. What in the name of God would the in-laws think, Morgan before the door like an angry guard? "It wasn't an idea they had time for, so busy they were staying alive," she said to calm him.

"That's not all they didn't know," cried Morgan. His breath came fast. "Justice! Did they know the word?"

"Ye mustn't, Morgan." Annie grew desperate. The Maughans' trap was now in sight. "The grave will hear you," she said, crossing herself.

"Don't be daft," snapped Morgan. "There's no ears in the grave."

As they were speaking the sun came full out. A luminous glow, golden and beautiful, bathed the fields. The house and outbuildings gleamed. Beyond, the sea sparkled. Morgan caught sight of the trap, moving smartly from the direction of O'Donnell's. His anger evaporated.

When the trap was almost within hearing, a cry burst forth. "Here they are," Morgan shouted. There was joy and eagerness in his voice, a wonderful, resonant vibrancy.

"Glory be," whispered Annie.

The Maughans were tired, the ride had been a strain, long and wet. Their patience was taxed. Denny, crammed into the back, worried they'd turn down the match after all. Especially after seeing the here-and-there look of the land, once they'd turned onto the boreen. But all that changed when the Riley house came into view. Abruptly the situation became more promising. The cottage was a delight, the fields grand.

The farmer and the sister stood smiling outside. "These

fields are mine as far as you can see," Morgan told them, waving his arm. Even beyond the ridge of rock, and all the rolling swells. All of it his, he told them proudly.

Denny hopped down from the trap, stretched his legs, smiled.

Annie brought Katie inside. "Sure, keep your nice shoes dry."

Katie was flustered. She smiled nervously, flushed beet red, then alternately turned from pale to pink, while her hands played agitatedly with the ends of her damp, bedraggled shawl.

"Now, your wet shawl, I'll take it," said Annie, draping the visitor in one of her own. "It's kind ye are," said Katie, dropping tiredly into a chair by the fire. Her gaze fell with joy on the room. The place was a wonder, the walls fresh—whitewashed, with even a fresh coat of paint on the floor. Bits of sunshine, orange-yellow and golden, filtering through the small front windows, danced white diamonds off a cut glass bowl on the table. There were china plates and a wind-up clock on the dresser, and besides the four well-made chairs and the table—fine-grained and smooth—there were three painted stools near the door.

Annie, though, had been thrown into confusion. Old concerns rushed from the corners of her mind. Hard on the heels of her initial friendliness, a sudden panic had swept her, even as she shot a smile at the visitor's eager face. There was the all-of-a-color drab brown woolly dress, the kind the country women kept for Sundays. That is, God help us, when they weren't still wearing black.

For a moment she tried to be hopeful. The dress could have been black, or worse still, down to the ankles. But the shoes were black, near the kind of ugly thing the gypsies wore. Laced high. Boots almost. The shoes were a bad, bad sign.

She felt her knees go wobbly. She studied the woman's chunky figure, the braided hair, tied at the back of her head. Were they all to be laughed at, no matter the woman owned a grand farm? The last shreds of her enthusiasm vanished. A black cloud seemed to whoosh from the chimney, obscure the fireplace, turn the bright white floor into stark, bleak black. She found herself staring at a foreigner, mother to the stranger coming in.

They were sliding into an abyss, herself and Morgan, tying

for life with a backward group. How could it be otherwise, the woman knowing no better than woolly tweeds and sturdy shoes?

And as for the daughter, how could they allow it, herself and Morgan? Not even the grand money could justify. One fact stared her in the face, indisputably. The match, whatever else, meant an outsider.

Annie's panic worsened.

Would the bride think her an "old woman"? Someone to be defied? That it was the sister was the intruder? What then? Where would Morgan's loyalties lie? Of course with his bride.

Cleave unto the wife, the Gospel said. So that if worse came to worst they'd turn her out, alone on the side of the road! No money but what Morgan'd feel bound to give. Glory be to God, there'd be no living at all without a roof over her head!

Heaven save us, she prayed. The match was a dreadful mistake.

But there was no way out of it. It was drawn down. The bargain'd been struck. At this very moment they were outside, busily walking the land. She turned to Katie Maughan. "Now, did you have a nice ride for yourselves, all the way from the country?" she said, with great cordiality. The brown dress looked better, her own bright shawl giving a bit of color.

"Sure, we hardly noticed, so eager we were," said Katie Maughan. "Ye've a grand house." She smiled broadly. Annie saw her fine, strong teeth, white and even, not at all what you'd call "country" teeth. "Isn't it kind of you to say?" said Annie, ever so slightly cheered.

"And isn't he the fine sight of a man, yeer brother, the luck o' the world come on us the day that we met?"

Annie's spirits rose. She smiled back. The thing might work out after all. The daughter a regular jewel like Morgan said . . . Though it was hard to know.

Yet, wasn't it a hopeful day and a hard one, all in the same?

Outside, John Maughan and Denny walked the land, Morgan making sure that every bit was seen. He showed them the cows, the horse, the hayrick, still partly filled with last year's hay. They saw the sheds, the tools, the fields, the chickens, geese and pigs. And last of all he handed John Maughan a spade to check the soil.

"Oh, ye've a grand place," said Old Maughan, testing the depth. Satisfied, he returned the shovel to Morgan.

"But yeer not quite so handy to Westport, the way Denny presented it," he complained, on returning to the cottage. Katie Maughan, hearing him, threw a withering look. "Sure, who's to be runnin' in and out to Westport?" she said tartly. It would be nothing short o' crazy, lettin' a few miles of boreen throw them off.

Morgan remained silent. He warmed his hands by the fire.

He supposed they were out of the way, though he'd be hard put if it bothered them. Wasn't Annie on her bike, whenever she felt the need? And every Sunday in Kilmaragh for Mass, half the day gone, with Annie so hot for the news? If the girl wanted Westport, he'd buy her a bike and they'd go.

"Will you have the whiskey now?" he asked. "There's wine for the ladies."

Katie Maughan sipped her wine, a sharp eye on her husband but her expression bland. Don't be ruinin' it, she fumed. *This was it.* A fine man. A grand house. And if the meal was half as good, it'd be many's a trip she'd be makin' herself.

Besides, Minnie was a handful. Glory be to God, with the sneakin' off, who was to say her character wasn't ruined? So that what chance would there be? They'd to get her away from him soon. That Mattie.

The meal was a wonder. China plates. A roast goose. A grand bowl of potatoes, and the sister had added turnips. There was a plate of bacon, and fresh hot bread. More whiskey for the men. And last of all, in a cut glass dish, thick cream for spooning over the cake.

Afterwards, the men smoking their pipes, the ladies enjoying a second glass of wine, Katie Maughan pronounced it a happy day her Minnie'd be joined with a household fine as this. "It'll be grand to have her," said Annie, flushed and happy. Her worries had faded. There wasn't a thing in the world but the Maughans. The wonderful daughter promising to be almost as good as their own dear ma come back to life. Or brother Martin at home, not off on the far side of the world in America . . . She poured a third glass of wine for Katie, impulsively refilling her own glass. She raised the sweet liquid to her lips, caught up in grandeur. This was like the old days. When not a day passed but the dear ma said only in the family was happiness to be found.

The men were on their second pipe-fill before the arrangements hit a snag. "There's no need for an attorney," insisted Morgan. Didn't he already own the farm? So why the trip to Westport?

John Maughan was adamant.

"All that way for a formality?" Morgan could be stubborn too. The negotiations could be completed right here.

"Humor him," whispered Denny, pulling Morgan aside. "Ballyrea'll be laffin' if he doesn't get in to the town . . . No good'll come of it."

So that next morning—the Maughans spent the night at Denny's cousins, the O'Donnells'—they all squeezed into the trap for the three tight miles into Westport. John Maughan was enthralled. He'd seen the celestial city! Broad smiles from ear to ear, pride, satisfaction, contentment streamed from his happy face. "It was a grand day ye put me in touch with Morgan Riley," he told Denny.

Morgan, too, felt elation, once the attorney had put his hand to the writings. Morgan Riley was a man to be wed.

But it was only after the Maughans had departed, the wedding to go forward after Easter, that he felt the full extent of his joy. At last, years of loneliness at an end. His own woman in less than two months' time.

His mind's eye swept her body, sucked from her great breasts' plenty, kissing, licking, at last slipping inevitably downward. Down to the hidden, mysterious place. The secret region of enchantment. Ahhhhh! He gave a loud cry. Minnie Mary Maughan. Minnie Maughan Riley. Minnie Riley.

God help him, he knew happiness.

As soon as the trap carrying Denny and the Maughans was out of sight Minnie hitched up her skirts, threw a heavy shawl over her hair, and bolted across the wet fields. This was her last chance. Once they had the writings it was lock and key.

She skirted the cluster of farms, scampering down the slope to where the valley shot off at an angle, pushing on toward the flat plain. Behind, in the distance, the bare rock face of the mountain hung like a giant, omnipotent presence.

Past the decrepit village she struck out across the swath of bog, by the house of the O'Neils, until finally, spent and breathless, she stopped.

The O'Malley farm was a jumble of sheds, with a great heap of old dung in the yard. A thin stream of smoke snaked upward from the low chimney.

Minnie stumbled across the yard to the half-door.

Mrs. O'Malley broke into tears. Minnie hurled herself at her breast. The countrywoman clasped her.

"The end," she cried. "There isn't a way in the world I can help."

Minnie wept, pressing deep against the other woman. "How am I to leave ye all? Oh, Mother O'Malley, my heart is broke."

Around the dim room the O'Malleys were like solemn, grieving statues, the younger children close on either side of the hob, several of the older ones on low stools next to the fire. The tiny baby lay mournful in his cradle, while the father occupied the only chair.

Mattie leaned against the far wall, by the dresser, hands in his pockets, his broad shoulders slumped. His face was pale. "Minnie," he croaked, before his voice broke. "Mattie, Mattie," was all Minnie could answer, and she clung to him, while behind her a chorus of wails broke out.

"It's a damned shame," growled Con. He jammed his cap on his head and pushed open the half-door.

"Now, don't be late," said his wife, knowing he'd come reeling home at midnight. The room fell silent. Minnie's grief held everyone. Tears poured down her cheeks, and Mattie hid his face in his hands. "God help the lot o' us," said the ma. Then rallying, "Get out the fiddle," she ordered Clare, the second girl. And to Mattie, "Bring down the penny whistle."

Obediently Clare fetched a battered fiddle from the dresser. Mattie scrambled up the ladder to the loft. When he returned his sister was already tuning her fiddle, and Mrs. O'Malley had settled her bulk on the chair by the fire. "Now, let ye play us a tune," she commanded, making the best of the heartbreak. "We'll give a grand send-off to our darlin' Minnie . . . Sit here on the hob, Minnie. Let me enjoy the sight of yeer face."

Minnie dried her tears, struggling unsuccessfully to smile. Her courage wrenched Mattie's heart and he nearly broke down. But he resolved to try valiantly, and his reward was seeing Minnie brighten. She sat close to Mother O'Malley, her head against the older woman's knee.

"And when we've all had our fill of singin' I'll boil us a grand kettle of potatoes. And a bit of soda bread."

"But ye mustn't go hungry yeerselves," cried Minnie, her anguish returning. Weren't the few bits of vegetables she occasionally brought all they had at times? Whatever she could snatch, with the ma keeping her sharp eye? Now the O'Malleys'd have to fend for themselves.

Clare struck up a lively reel. The cottage rang with music, and there were shrill cries as one after another, all but the mother and the infant, crowded the tiny dirt floor, Minnie at first only watching, finally joining in. Cheeks flushed, she spun back and forth between the half-door and the hearth. Mattie's eyes followed her, and when everyone stopped for a rest he grabbed her in his arms, kissing her noisily before the entire family.

Later the music settled into quieter tunes. Everyone gathered at the feet of the two musicians, crowded together on the floor. Delicate strains of love and sadness poured forth from the fiddle and whistle, falling on the upturned faces. The room was silent except for the music. Occasionally the mother, infant now at her breast, hummed along with the ancient melodies.

It was well into the afternoon before they tired. "Someone to peel the potatoes," said Mrs. O'Malley. There was a general chorus demanding that the meal be a festive one. The few pieces of chipped china were taken from the dresser, and Mrs. O'Malley brought out her one treasure, a well-mended linen tablecloth. The older girls arranged the dishes. Clare insisted on making the soda bread. "But ye must be tired," said Minnie. "Ye've given us hours of pleasure . . . and yeerself, dear Mattie?"

"I'm not tired a bit." Clare fastened on a ragged apron. "Music's fun."

By the time the meal was finished darkness had fallen. Mrs. O'Malley said there was nothing to be gained from destroying the happiness of this last day. "Ye'll remember us all yeer life. Whenever yeer feelin' down ye'll think o' the singin' and dancin', and all the love ye've here. Not one o' the O'Malleys without a heart full o' caring . . . Even himself over at the public house, gettin' sick for the morrow. Not a time ye stepped through the door but didn't his cares seem lighter. He'll miss ye, God help him.

"Let Mattie see ye home in the dark," she said. "Aren't there devils out o' the mountain? Wouldn't it be the saddest thing, one o' them carryin' ye away?"

"Oh, but I've my beads," said Minnie. Better to put everything behind her, the sweet sounds of the music echoing in her heart, Mattie's dear face surrounded by all the brothers and sisters? "Besides, there's no devil on the mountain, me da says. An old tale, that's all. Haven't I always found my way in the dark?"

"But isn't it the work of the devil to interrupt people's plans? Mattie'll see ye safe . . . Go on now." She pushed her son toward the door. "And never forget yeer friends the O'Malleys," she called out.

The moonless night was black. Coming up the hill, it seemed the mountain had indeed turned evil, swallowing up the cottage and barns. There was only the black sloping hillside. Even the hayrick had vanished into the night air.

The house stood empty and dark. Minnie unlatched the door. "I knew there'd be no real harm afoot," she said, stepping into the kitchen. She felt immediately cheered by the small fire, still glowing in the hearth. "Wouldn't they have after me, if I'd let the fire go out!"

She pulled Mattie inside, and in no time she had the fire blazing. The room turned rosy in the firelight. "Now what devil would dare show his face?" she said lightly. A look of pain flooded Mattie's countenance. Minnie turned away, feeling her own composure slipping. Mattie came close, took her hands in his. His hands were icy cold.

"Oh, Mattie, I'm a grief to ye."

"There isn't a word for it."

"But we mustn't spoil what yeer ma's give us. We want to remember it. It's the penny whistle and the fiddle we're to think of. Not part with our hearts breakin'."

"Minnie!"

The agonized cry swept away her good intentions. She'd only thought she could bring it off, the entire long walk through the dark wet bog, the hard long climb up the hill. But here alone, without the ma and the da, her resolve could only be flung into the hearth, up the chimney, out into the night, to drift with smoke from the crackling fire. There was only Mattie now. His blazing eyes, the reflection of her own desire. She threw herself into his arms, crying out. He clasped her, so that she scarcely breathed. Stumbling over one another, they grappled their way into Minnie's room, tearing off each other's clothes as they went. When they stood naked, they gazed on each other's bodies, rosy in the faint light from the fire. They filled themselves with the sight.

"Yeer all the man I'll ever want," cried Minnie.

Gently, not wildly like all the times in the hay, Mattie laid her on the bed. She opened her arms and they lay together. There was only their passion. The room disappeared.

Afterwards they made love a second time, and when they finished Mattie lay back with his eyes closed. "Yeer to wed," he said.

"I wanted ye." Minnie cradled his head against her breasts. "But that's not all." She spoke softly, confidently. "Ye'll be with me now when I go to him . . . I'll have ye after all. That's what I want. To have ye with me forever."

"God help us!" he cried. "What have they done to us?"

CHAPTER
7

During the weeks until Easter Morgan gave himself to the tasks of springtime. He plowed and harrowed the rough ground. He birthed the calves, bringing them in to Kilmaragh for the fairs. There was seed to be spread, potatoes put down, extra market trips with the spring butter, and with all of that the day-to-day checking of the cows and the horse, giving them their hay and water. He was out to the fields on the good days, inside the sheds during the rains, his energy unslacking. With no amount of work too hard for a man about to be wed.

Throughout, Annie did every bit of work a woman could handle.

Life had also erupted in Ballyrea. New lambs. New calves. Fields plowed, furrows planted. And when the sow was ready there was straw in the kitchen for piglets, Katie Maughan standing watch. "Isn't it a hard thing," she said to her husband, "a mother crushing her litter?" "Not with yeerself doin' the watchin'." John was proud of her, and when the new dozen were safely birthed he carried them off to the yard.

Oats for the hens, corn for the geese, the entire haggard seemed to have exploded into life. Freshened cows meant extra churning, and when the firkins were filled, the added job of market day. John Maughan brought in the firkins, believing only he could get the price. But the young nephew Brian had a stronger hand now at the plow.

Minnie's spring work was clearcut—to her were entrusted the cows. Milking. Feeding. Driving them up to the newly greened hill pastures so that, safely staked, they could have their fill. Occasionally she led them down to the hill pond where, noisy and greedy, they jostled in the shallow water.

On the first day she busied herself staking, woodenly determined. A wet March wind blew off the mountain. She settled her shawl for warmth. But soon the first shower of the morning ended and there was a peep of sunshine. The clouds parted. Bright spring light penetrated the thin mountain air. Minnie let the sun pour down on her upturned face. "Warm me," she pleaded. Obligingly, the brief tender beams licked the icicles from her heart. Opening her shawl she lifted her arms, felt the healing warmth against her breasts. "Musha," she began to weep. Tears ran unchecked and she thought back to recent days. Days of grief and turmoil.

"Leave me to my heartbreak!" she'd cried out at the ma, back from Kilmaragh with news of the writings. The Westport man's farm was a wonder, the sister full of charm. The fields were grand, and there was a whitewashed house—couldn't she be pleased?

But Minnie'd wept inconsolably, and she'd wept every day since. No amount of scolding made her cheerful. "Can't ye have sense?" the ma'd demanded. But the da looked worried, with it signed and settled. Only with the ma telling him loud and often of the wonders of Westport was he able to do more than slouch by the fire, so lost in gloom was he. He felt crushed with the weight of it. And only now, with the lambs and the calves, the planting and furrowing, was the lift back in his step. Once again he was eager. And Minnie was alone in her heartbreak.

By the time she finished staking, a thick mist fell again. She gave a loving pat to each cow, extra endearments for the calves, and struck out across the green meadow for a crumbling ruin of a cottage she often used for shelter. Long abandoned, the cabin was set crazily where the meadow backed up to the mountain. The rise on which the old cabin perched was dotted with boulders, rocks off the mountain, and here and there clumps of last year's bushes. The house was built directly into the hillside, only the room with the hearth remaining. The bedroom, and the shed to hold the cows, had long since fallen to ruin, except for one wall of rocks. There was a tiny rectangular window in the wall, near where the roof had been.

Inside the hearth room, surprisingly, were several bits of furnishings. A wooden bench, unpainted and splintery, stood next to the fireplace, and resting on the bench, as long as Minnie could remember, were two ancient, rusty teakettles. There was a wooden chair with a broken seat, and from the rust-corroded crane in front of the fireplace hung a rusted pail, its entire bottom a jagged hole. Otherwise the room was empty, the dirt floor littered with straw. The tin roof, almost miraculously, had survived.

Occasionally when Minnie used the house she scoured the meadow for sticks and weeds, proud that her skilled hands could make do from the bare hillside. Then, with the hearth glowing, she'd eat her simple lunch by the fire.

On this day, the quick fire blazing, she spread bread and a potato on the bench beside her. The fire and the food brought calm. Her heart warmed. She broke open the potato and sank her teeth into the mealy delicacy. The potato comforted her. But then abruptly she thought of Mattie. If only he were here. They'd have a feast.

She closed her eyes. The rough kitchen walls disappeared. Sweet sunlight suffused the hearth, poured over the wooden bench, smoothing away the splinters. Brightness colored the battered kettles, ground away the rust, so that fresh water boiled in a gleaming pot. Steam rose, billowing downward again from the ceiling, to float in clouds over the wooden bench.

Where there'd been only dirt and straw, now stood a table, painted blue. Blue as the summer sky when she'd first run laughing over the flower-strewn hillsides, her hand in Mattie's. "Life's ours," he shouted, catching her in his arms. They fell laughing into the deep, sweet grass, where hidden among the tall flowers, no one but the cows hearing their love sounds, they blended their hearts. The mountain danced in ecstasy.

"Minnie. Minnie, darlin'."

The beloved voice cut through Minnie's daydream. She opened amazed eyes, stared at the great bulk of a man in the doorway. "How did ye find me?" she whispered. "Have ye come for me?"

The earth stood on its head, did cartwheels. A cosmic wind swooped into the cottage, sent her hurtling into space, out into the heavens. She was saved.

Just as suddenly the earth became still. The firmament

steadied, the sun resumed its place. The wind ceased. Only Mattie remained, watching her from the doorway. His arms were extended, expecting her touch. He shuddered. She hurled herself at him.

Later they went outside. Over the green meadow, and beyond into the cleft between the hills, the sky shimmered in wondrous shades of violet and blue. Even the bare mountain was transformed. The grey, harsh rocks gleamed wondrously in smoky shades of purple and brown. Everywhere the thin mountain air smelled clean and wonderful. There was the fresh smell of spring grass. Mattie sat on a rock beside the door to lace his heavy boots. "Is it heaven we've been to?" he asked.

It was the uncles gave him shelter, he said, so that he'd only to pass her house once. Keeping a wary eye for the Maughans. He'd been spending his nights on the far, grassy side of the mountain. Every day he came to watch for her. Sometimes by the pond, waiting sometimes where the little rise jutted out, before the rocks began. "But I slept with the uncles," he said, "so there wasn't a chance in the world of yeer ma and da seein' me."

"Weren't they grand to let ye stay?" said Minnie.

The two sat quiet, savoring their joy, peaceful just being together. Occasionally Minnie's eyes strayed to the mountain. She thought of the two old bachelors, sad pair that they were— but wasn't it the best of good fortune? Them providing shelter, so Mattie could sneak past her house only once? The ma and da without another opportunity to catch him. Musha, good things happened.

"But isn't it sad they never gave over?" she said wistfully. "Two old men holding a farm they barely work? While yeerself hasn't a stick or a stone? There might have been a house for us."

"Sure, where would they go themselves?"

"We could've kept them. Ah, I know. It's only one room. But we might've added on. People do sometimes . . . But why didn't one of them marry?"

"It was the ma's fault. She lived too long. And she couldn't decide between them. Not able to give it up either. So there ye are," said Mattie, hopeless with the injustice of it. But then anger swept him. "The future might've been different." He glared at the mountain, seething. "I'll tell ye what," he said harshly. "Those two old celibates'll give me one thing."

"What is it yeer saying?" Minnie touched his arm, but he shook her off, red-faced. "There's one thing I'll take when I leave. And use it, too."

"Good Jesus! Do ye want the Civic Guard?"

"Because I steal a gun?"

"Is it out of yeer mind ye've gone? I told ye, there mustn't be talk of guns."

"I'm not talkin'. I'm for doin' it. So help me God, I'll take a shot at someone. There's someone has to pay."

"Mattie O'Malley! there's a bee in yeer brain! Buzzin' the sense clear out o' ye. Switchin' a fine young man into a first-class murderer. No more talk of shootin'. *I won't have it.*"

Mattie quieted down. But when they led the cows to the pond for a drink, she raced off as many prayers as could be squeezed into their constant conversation.

The afternoon wore on. When milking time arrived they clasped for a final kiss. Minnie led the cows down the hillside, head high, her heart beating happily. Tomorrow they'd meet again. And the day after that, and the next day, too. Not a word needed to be said of it.

So each night Mattie returned to the mountain, to the two old men. And every morning, when Minnie appeared with the cows, he raced across the hillside, capless, breathless, shirttails flying in the breeze. Straight out of the mountain, it seemed. He'd throw himself upon her, and only after they'd hugged and kissed were they able to stake the cows. After that, struck dumb with happiness, they'd hurl themselves onto the dirt floor of the cabin. Their frenzy grew wilder each day. "Ye've become me," gasped Mattie one morning. He lay amidst their scattered clothing, gazing at his beloved. "There's only 'us.' We're one. Ye've entered the heart and soul o' me. I'll not be wanderin' the fields by my lonesome. Ye'll be with me, a part o' me. It's magic!"

With the arrival of April the hills erupted with color. Daffodils, daisies, buttercups. Masses of flowers dotted the meadows. The sun shone, days grew warmer, and the lovers roamed the hills, delirious. Sometimes they lay in the fields. As the mood struck, they gathered armfuls of tall grass, daisies, shrubs. With consummate skill Mattie would fashion a soft bed by the hearth. Queen Minnie, perched on the splintery bench, would await her courtly lover's invitation. "To yeer bower now," he'd announce, when the festive mat was ready. Regal and lovely, she'd discard her royal robes, one by one onto the dirt floor, stepping forward at last to satisfy her courtier's admiration.

Occasionally, when the April sun was high, they'd lie outside in the shelter of the half-ruined wall. Safe from cool breezes, they'd hold one another, stupefied with passion. Again and again they pledged their love. If heaven could arrange it, they vowed, they'd find a way to come together, despite the farmer.

As long as Minnie kept up appearances at home, the cows fed and fit, no one took notice of her preoccupation. There wasn't a word said each day when she crept out of bed at dawn, rushed to the cow house, and with the milking done drove the cows to the hills. "Mind yeerself, now yeer to wed," the ma would call after her. "I will," Minnie would throw over her shoulder, eager eyes on the hills.

Katie and John Maughan, if they knew, said nothing. Their earlier, stern, almost harsh attitude was absent. As if, with the writings signed, nothing at all could go wrong. So that if Minnie chose to amuse herself, why, it'd be a cruel ma'd deny the girl. Sometimes though the da grew testy. "Where's Minnie?" he'd demand, coming in late from the fields. But Katie would shake her head, throw her hands in the air. "Soon enough she'll be gone entirely," she'd say.

But John Maughan was not to be mollified. Minnie thought he watched her oddly. Not as if he suspected but as if, in the evenings, with the hard work of the day over, he took time to reflect. He'd sit toward the fire but then slowly, at first so you'd hardly notice, he'd turn. Once when he'd been watching her closely his eyes filled, Minnie was certain. Surely those were tears? Was it possible he regretted? Was remorse what made him quiet? Once he stuffed his pipe viciously, clamped it between his teeth and stamped off out to the yard. "Isn't it a hard life when ye've to check on the cows yeerself?" he muttered, banging the door after him.

The ma, it seemed to Minnie, regarded her with a new tenderness, reminiscent of the old days. The days of childhood carding and spinning, when they'd cleaned the wool and spun the yarn. Whether they were feeding the calves or hanging the kettle there wasn't a minute the ma'd not Minnie by her side, givin' her treats and pleasures. There wasn't even a trip to the weavers didn't mean a stop at the sweet shop. Oh, glory. A mother's love.

"Isn't Brian the fortunate fellow?" said Katie, several evenings before the wedding. The three were sitting by the fire; Minnie had been very late coming home. John Maughan had waited in the haggard and, after the milking, demanded to know what kept her. "It's trouble yeer up to," he said menacingly. But at the sight of her stricken face he'd immediately softened. Later, after the meal, he settled into a profound and doleful gloom, hunched near the fire. His usually shrewd eyes stared unseeing, and if his cap was off or on he hardly knew.

There was only the occasional snap of burning peat to break the silence.

"But for yeerself givin' the farm, he'd no chance for a place at all," persisted Katie cheerfully. She was determined to put a good face on these last days.

When the husband's silence only deepened she turned to Minnie, who sat huddled with her knitting. "There's not many with the luck o' the nephew?" said Katie.

The ma's gone daft, worried Minnie through her fear. I should cheer for Brian's luck while my own heart breaks? The blood in my throat near chokin' me? . . . It's the greed that's got to her. She's too hard after Westport, not a thought of me . . . Three more days, if I'm lucky. God help me.

"Don't they all be envyin' the lot o' us?" went on Katie, as if the other two were hard into the conversation with her. "It isn't a day I walk in the village but I don't see the sideways glances."

"How do ye know it's envy?"

Katie stared at her husband. But he only hunched his shoulders, leaning so drastically towards the fire she feared he'd fall in. "Now what is that yeer sayin'?" She made as if to grab at him. "Won't we be the talk o' them all, everyone wishin' they had what we'll have?"

"And what is that?"

Minnie's head came up. It would be a long year before she'd hear that sad voice again.

"And what is it we'll have, that they're all scramblin' to have for themselves?" Old Maughan turned suddenly harsh, a scowl on his face.

"What's come over ye, John? That yeer lookin' and talkin' so queer?"

"Is it queer ye think, that I'm feelin' bad?"

"I don't know what else."

John Maughan spat into the fire. After a long silence he turned to gaze somberly at Minnie. Minnie felt her face redden. She rose to her feet. "The cows will need me early."

"They will indeed," said her da. "And it's early the sun is up." He turned his back to his wife. There wasn't another word to be gotten from him. It was hard for Katie to know if he was in the world or out of it. Only the long plume of pipe smoke, rising blue toward the ceiling, gave a sign he was still with the living at all.

The last day on the hillside was the most singular in Minnie's memory. Easter was one day past and the wedding two days more. There were peaks and there were valleys, and in its last moments it held a level of pain almost too great to be endured.

Mattie was late to the hill, so late that Minnie had all but lost hope of his arrival. She had staked the cows, laid the fire, eaten her potato, and only when she was outside the door, finishing the last of her bread, did Mattie appear, feet buckling from exhaustion as he reached her. He lay against the doorway, gasping and out of breath. Only after several minutes was he able to talk. "I'd to wait," he said at last. "Didn't I fear they'd never leave?"

Only then Minnie noticed the gun, lying where he'd dropped it. She stared at the long grey barrel, partly hidden in the grass, and her head reeled in panic.

The gun.

Somewhere above her head a scream seemed to be breaking loose, but when she clapped a hand against her lips the scream sounds poured through her own clenched fingers. "Ye've stolen!" The words pushed the screams aside. "Ye've stolen the uncles' gun!"

"Ahhh. Didn't I only borrow it?" Mattie sat up. He swept his unkempt hair from his sweat-streaked face, wiped dripping hands on his shirt. "They've no need," he said offhandedly. "Sure, can't they get rabbits with a trap?"

"Give it back, Mattie. Ye've done a terrible deed. Those old men live by their hunting."

"After lyin' for hours in the nettles, waitin' for the fools to leave? Christ, look at my arms?" He pulled up his shirtsleeves, revealing an angry rash. "Ye think I've all that for nothin'?"

"I can't believe what ye've done, them takin' ye in. They've been kind, and there's not a rock that'll grow in those fields. If they haven't the rabbits they'll die. I won't have this on my conscience. Or anything ye might do with the gun. Take it back, before ye add an evil deed. Sure, didn't the priest just yesterday tell us the Risen Christ is all around us?"

"Hah! I wasn't there to hear."

"Don't scoff. The Lord God Himself'll get the message soon enough. Too bad Lent's over. I'm thinkin' ye need a long time for penance."

"Aren't ye the little saint now?" He pulled Minnie to him, his hungry mouth covering her face with kisses. "How's that for a bit o' penance?"

Minnie pushed away from him. He left her free. But she'd seen the blaze in his eyes and she felt her own resolve weakening. "D'ye think I can go to the farmer with that gun on my mind?" she pleaded desperately. The hot sweet warmth was beginning near her knees, spreading rapidly upwards. She pulled her skirts tight to her ankles, moved away from him. But he grabbed her. In a flash his hands were under her skirts, so that the warmth in her thighs became a great flood through her body. "Ye've taken what doesn't belong," she cried, but she was breathing fast now. She tried to push his hands away, at the same time relishing his touch. "I won't have it. I won't."

The mooing of the cows awakened them. The hour was late. Softly luminous shades of evening sun bathed the bare rock face of the mountain. Golden rays glimmered where the rough rock mass jutted from the green slope. A stream of mellow light turned the low clouds to purple, rose, and azure. "It's like we've gone to heaven," whispered Minnie, sitting up. She was covered only by her long, silky hair. Mattie reached up to gently touch her softness. "Ah, no," she pleaded gently. "No more. It's over."

"Never."

"Yes, it is, Mattie. There's nothin' now but good-bye." She began pulling on her clothing, her face masking the dull agony near her heart.

"Good-bye, Mattie. That's the work o' this hillside today. Our last task, to say our good-byes." Minnie feared she'd fall to the ground, so hard and sharp and fierce was the pain. She put her hand to her breast, but it was no use. The burning was in her soul, not with the body at all. It festered in the great deep place where only the spirit could reach. So that there was no soothing.

"Now, I've a final word," she said when they'd finished dressing. She led Mattie into the cottage and they sat together on the wooden bench. He laid the gun by the hearth. "It's about the uncles. The sunlight could have them yet in the fields."

"Plantin' rocks?"

"Don't joke me, Mattie. Go right up there now. They'll never even know the gun was missing. It's worth tryin'."

"I'll not," said Mattie. She tried to force him to look in her eyes but he stared at the smoldering ashes. "I took that gun and I'm for usin' it."

"And are ye for the prison?" she asked angrily. "That yeer ma'll be visitin' ye in her old age?"

"Ye have it all wrong. Those two will never miss their gun. Sure, they hardly knew they had it, so seldom they hunted. I wish ye could see the place, they barely leave the fire. There isn't a thing they do but smoke their bit of tobacco. That rag of field they dig wouldn't no more than keep a bird alive."

"And what do ye plan to shoot? God save me, I can't believe I'm askin'. Can we shoot our way out of the match?"

"Ah, don't worry yeer head, I'll not do harm. I'll not be killin'. But a bit of fear in some wouldn't hurt."

"The Civic Guard'll have ye. There's no doubt in my mind."

"Save me then!" Mattie blazed into life again. He faced her eagerly. "Save yeerself, too. We'll go to America! They'll never catch us."

"Livin' takes money, ye know that." Could she stand a life like his ma's? Hardly. Minnie tried to imagine life by that ghost of a fire, thin smoke wispin'? Shiverin' in the breeze from the holes in the roof? Havin' to keep a happy face, no matter the day's crop or the lack of it?

"We've not starved yet," cried Mattie, flushed, with renewed hope in his eyes. "Only a bare shillin' once in a while keeps us goin' . . . If ye won't take the boat, come to us. Share what we have."

"Ye've me wrong. I'm not the same as yeer ma. She's a great, bottomless heart, that darlin' woman. She's a well that never runs dry. That's how she stands it."

"And so's yeerself. Ye've love without limit." His eyes were fiercely black. "Come join us, darlin'. Don't go to the farmer. And if they come after ye . . ." He patted the gun.

"Ye'd shoot me da?"

"I never said it. Yeer makin' the wrong conclusion."

"It's no use. I canna come to ye."

In the end Mattie agreed to give up the gun. Though whether he'd return it to the uncles or throw it into one of the mountain's rushing streams he'd not say. "Ye've no fear," he said. But even while he reassured her the gun lay on his lap. He stroked the long, scuffed barrel with a lover's touch, over and over.

By the time they were pulling the stakes, readying the cows for the long trip home, Mattie had grown distant. He had the look of a low, smoldering fire, banked for the night yet waiting for morning. A sad way to part, but not a word that could change it.

Again and again, as Minnie unfastened each cow from the stake, she wished it could be different. But to no use. The grief of the ages swept over her. I'll go to the farmer, she wept silently. Marryin' was the only solution—there was more than Mattie knew. There was a child, their child. She put a hand to her belly. Mattie must never know. He'd surely shoot the farmer. He might even shoot her da.

The last she saw of Mattie he stood firm on the hillside, one arm raised in farewell, the other clutching the gun. The sun was low now, mists beginning to form between the hills. Pale light shone in streaks around his head. The grass, rocks, the great masses of daisies and daffodils gave off a strange, luminous glow. But where the rock face joined the grassy slope a thick patch of lemony buttercups had faded to dusty yellow.

When the mountain blocked the last of the sun's rays the entire field turned to charcoal.

CHAPTER
8

———

The wedding took place on Wednesday. Morgan and Annie, in a cart hired from Westport, set off along the boreen under a clear sky with the sun full up. A rare gift near the ocean, the day was clear. A perfect day. Morgan's joy swelled and soared.

Life was wonderful. Today gave proof. The pilgrimage, after all, was a good one. For hard work, firm faith, a back bent to the plow a man would reap his reward, no matter how unaccountable. Hadn't his own prize appeared at last?

Who would have believed, that cold winter night of Denny's proposition, there'd come a day he'd be off to his wedding? The long years ended, yearning done, bliss approaching. The bride-to-be was a treasure. The wonder of it defied comparison.

Behind him on the cart Annie purred with contentment, her own joy near equaling his. She gloried in this alliance of equals, Morgan himself owning the farm, the Maughans with no other to be provided for. That was the best way, having the girl's family prosperous too, no pack of sons and daughters needing settling, fighting over who'd get the dowry, who'd have the farm.

She turned sideways for a look at Morgan, handsome in his Sunday suit, with a new tweed cap and the boots he'd only since Shrovetide. She drew a long, contented breath, made the Sign of the Cross three times. God help us, the only thing grander would be having a match made for herself.

Annie gave a quick laugh at her own foolishness, fiddling with her dress and straightening her hat. Morgan turned to look at her. "Won't we be passing O'Donnell's?" she said hurriedly. Saints. If he could read her mind.

Morgan flicked the whip on the horse's back and the cart bumped and jolted along. "Just wait 'til the Westport road," he said. "We'll have a grand ride for ourselves."

At O'Donnell's Pat was out behind the house, with his wife Anna waving gaily from the door. Pat ran up to gesture with his pitchfork, making as if to fling a load of dung. "Godspeed," he shouted. Morgan tipped his cap, and Annie waved exuberantly.

The three miles north on the Westport road were a wonder after the boreen. Morgan pushed the horse hard, with Annie hardly knowing which side to look. Occasionally, when a car passed, he pulled the cart over. On the ocean side were the white breakers, with the shore gleaming rocks and white sand; while inland every field was a jewel of a meadow, the green grass striking in the sunshine. "A vision," Annie murmured. "A dream."

But the dream evaporated. The narrow cart track, once they left the Westport road, had the little horse dodging rocks and boulders. The animal reared and stumbled. On both sides lay nothing but stretches of wet, mucky bog land. At times Morgan was forced to climb down and lead the horse, until the road would unaccountably improve. "How in the name o' God does this crowd be standing it!" he said, squelching the oaths he'd be swearing but for Annie.

"Sure, aren't they used to it?" she said reasonably. But it'd be a long day before she'd come again, God help her. After the five long miles to the uplands she was sure of it.

Ever since the Westport road fluffs of clouds had dotted the sky, growing heavier. Until by now there was a sudden lowering. Annie pulled an enormous shawl from under the seat but by the time she was covered the big drops were falling. "I'll be ruined," she said. Morgan opened an umbrella when the quick shower turned into a downpour. He swore audibly, shaking his fist. The horse shivered, slipping on the wet rocks. "Cripes, Almighty!" Morgan yelled. "Damned fookin' bog track!"

"Now, don't be getting anxious," Annie said. "Them people'll be glad indeed to have you, wet or dry. Isn't themselves taking a few drops on the way to the church, too?"

"Ah, it's not so much the rain, Annie," said Morgan. "Or

even the rocks. Though I hate both of them. I could even put up with the damned wet bog land."

"What is it then, brother?"

"Are we doing the right thing?" Morgan groaned, long, low, mournful. The sound began at his boots, slithering all the way to the top of his head, it seemed. Annie shivered. "They do be a backward crowd up here," Morgan said hopelessly. "The Maughans themselves is grand people, but it's a long way we're going. Not as if I went in on market day and heard of a family that's looking. Someone we know."

"And how many are there? With them all running off to America? It's not many has the chance Martin did. Besides, wasn't it their own fine trap they came in, not having to rent like ourselves? Think about *that,* brother. Oh, we're getting a bargain."

But even Annie's tune hit a sour note when Ballyrea finally appeared. Two bare streets. Only the church occupying the square's far side. Three small buildings clustered on the road to the north, with here and there a few villagers lingering. A flat plain cowered before the stark rock face of the mountain.

She sent up a prayer.

The cart moved into the square.

From McNulty's pub came a shout. Three drunken farmers, long bony faces protesting, emerged by the door of the pub. "And let ye be off," shouted Michael McNulty, the publican, arms folded over his white apron.

"The Lorda mercy," said Annie, rushing off a quick Hail Mary. "Do they be always like that?"

Morgan shrugged. "Sure, what else?"

A chill raced up Annie's back. What of the Maughans? "The land's no good?"

But Morgan reassured her. "It's theirs is grand, and a few others. The rest is sad, indeed. So why wouldn't they drink?"

"Without the land to keep them sharp?" Annie said, suddenly longing for home. For her own green fields. The fine town with its busy square, Kilmaragh jostling with life. Lively crowds in and out of the shops at every hour.

What end of the world had they come to?

From across the road a mother, black shawl down to her ankles, led a string of raggedy children in the direction of the jaunting cart. "An offering?" she cried out.

Annie grimaced. She fixed her look on the backs of the retreating farmers, while Morgan tossed a coin. "Isn't it brazen some of them does be?" she whispered. "Herself surely seeing we've business?"

The country woman moved off.

"And will you look at the skirt? Don't they be knowing the styles?"

"Ah, there probably doesn't be a paper getting this far." Morgan tied the horse near the church. He smiled nervously at the crowd gathering in front of McNulty's.

Annie scrutinized the pub and the church. "Is this the lot of it?"

"Oh, it's hardly more than a crossroads. And that's as far as most of them goes," said Morgan, pointing. There was a burial ground, off behind the crumbling wall of the church. Two rusty bicycles lay just outside the stone walls, wheels off, one bicycle lacking handlebars.

"Don't they be taking care?" Annie said, forcing a smile at a group of women who had moved, mysteriously, to just in front of the chapel door. Some had their faces half covered; others wore their shawls draped carelessly, now that the rain had stopped. All had eyes on the strangers. Eager eyes.

Several women moved as if to come forward, smiling shyly. But overcome, they waited in embarrassed silence for the men and boys. The throng seemed to have simply materialized, and it was only then Morgan realized they'd been waiting all along, out of the rain at the grocery. McNulty himself still stood in the doorway, the wife's face plainly in the window over the jars of sweets and the eggs.

"Good day to you," said Morgan. The crowd parted, allowing them to enter. Morgan moved briskly forward, with Annie nodding and smiling in response to the greetings. "You'd think they knew me," she whispered.

Inside, except for the altar, the chapel was dark. But when Morgan's eyes grew accustomed he recognized the Maughans and Minnie. Behind them, near the altar, Denny O'Donnell stood with a stranger, a red-haired woman. She must be Chrissie O'Bannon, the nephew's bride-to-be. But where was the nephew?

Denny would serve as witness, the O'Bannon woman apologized. The nephew'd to see to the farm.

Denny flashed long teeth, smiled reassuringly.

Morgan struggled with an escalating sense of unease. The long wet ride had left him hard put to compose himself. He pulled his face into a nervous smile, stiffened his shoulders, hoped for an appearance of confidence. Carefully he peered across at the young woman next to the ma. The bride? He scarce knew this young one. This somber, ashen-faced stranger.

Where was the wild, bright beauty of his springtime imaginings? Even the eyes, green as he remembered them, had faded. She'd only a dull, listless stare. He peered closely at the girl, at her sullen, back-country gloom. Bad vapors surrounded her, spreading insidiously through the dank, bare, decrepit chapel. Anger swept him, sent sparks. Who was this imposter? This deceiver in the bunching skirt, with her hair bound and hidden, making him look the fool?

Abruptly the anger faded. Grief flooded in. He recalled what he'd chosen to forget. The evening of the match flashed before him. It blotted out the altar. The sputtering, flickering candles. The waiting priest with his book. It obliterated the servers. The foolish, innocent boys with freckles staining their faces.

Nothing remained but that evening. It rose up, accusing. He saw the girl's angry, fierce stare when the ma said, "Go to the cow house." That told him. He'd known the truth then. Known it all the ten miles to home. He'd known it when Annie set the potatoes and bacon before him. When she poured his steaming tea. He'd known when he pulled the clay pipe from his pocket. Lit the match. But by the time the air was blue with smoke he'd forgotten. It was easier that way.

The girl hated the sight of him. She hated his worn face, his bushed brows, the straight hair that bunched on his ears. She hated his great, country body, could almost pull the plow, not even a horse, God help him. He repelled her. He was detestable. Even now, with the priest's prayers rising like incense to the rafters, she was cursing the day they'd ever sent over the bog to Kilmaragh. Musha, God help him. That the day should come when he'd be found odious.

"Will the couple to be joined stand front. The witnesses beside them." The girl stepped forward. The priest cleared his throat to begin the vows. "Father, hear our prayers for Morgan Riley and Mary Maughan, who today are united in marriage before your altar . . ." Denny felt for the ring. The altar boys jiggled and jumped, but when the priest glared they became as two statues. The priest nodded and one freckled statue proffered holy water. "Morgan and Mary, have you come here freely and without reservation . . . ?"

Morgan's mouth went dry. A dull pain took hold of the pit of his stomach, quickly working upwards, until in a flash he became one great ache, a shriek of silent resentment flung heavenwards. His rage swept to the rafters like candle smoke. "What *pleases* you?" he hurled up at the Almighty.

Sickened, almost dizzy, Morgan mumbled the words the priest put to him. Yes, he'd take her for his wife. That he would. In sickness and in health. Unto death. Afterwards came the girl's faint reply. Low, but with none of his own stumbling. Promising love and honor, to obey him. 'Til death parted them. Now they were man and wife, the priest saying it grand and big. Bouncing the claim to the rafters. Flinging it sideways, one moss-stained wall to the other. So that by the time the words settled again on Morgan's own head he was almost ready to believe them. And why not? What else was there but a hand to the plow? Force the turnips to grow. Stand firm through the rain and the shine. Let it never be said that Morgan Riley of Kilmaragh'd have an empty pit in the haggard!

"Father, by your power ye have made everything out of nothing." The priest sang out his final invocation. Man and woman, two in one flesh, the one blessing not forfeited by original sin. The wife to follow the holy women, the husband to give trust. And after a happy old age, blessed with children and their children's children, the kingdom of heaven.

"Amen!" cried out the two freckled statues in unison.

Morgan scrutinized his bride's face for a sign. It sounded grand, but would she give it a try? She looked more settled now, lovely even, though hardly serene. But there was a quiet dignity. A wifely peace. The wife of a man with a good slate roof and four cows. And why wouldn't she be at peace? Wasn't it cherishing her he'd be doing? Not a day go by but he'd work the farm, 'til they'd a grand fine life?

Surely the girl knew all this, the ma'd have told her? So that with the deed done there wasn't God's own power could come between them. And when she'd sight of the grand house, with the little room off the kitchen just for the two of them, she'd have a long day's regret but for the match.

He offered her his arm, the others falling behind. Denny followed, grinning, and the O'Bannon woman took a tall, proud stand for the family about to receive her. "Aren't they the pair?" she whispered.

The crowd outside was ecstatic—half the town, it seemed, had assembled.

The bridal couple, timid on the chapel doorstep, blushed and waved. John Maughan, somewhat subdued, made great sweeps with his waving arms, and when his name was called out gave a bow. The wife, chunky in her red shawl, flashed strong white teeth on each one stepping forward. Shaking hands, she seemed transformed. Her plain country face had a brightness approaching beauty. "Isn't it a wonder?" she asked repeatedly, and to one old woman's "Will ye be movin' to Westport?" her laugh rang across the square.

Old Maughan himself didn't seem quite so struck with the festivities. His face had a solemn cast. And whenever he wasn't waving or bowing he grew serious. Too serious for the occasion. So that there were a few who shook their heads privately after the entire party rode off.

Mary McNulty, for one, watched the whole ceremony from the grocery shop window. "Poor Minnie. 'Tis a sad day," she lamented to her husband. "That's a rented cart," she said. (The sister and the bride were assisted up onto the seats.) "From Westport, I'm sure. It's a grand connection. But I still say, 'Poor Minnie.' Crazy about that other fella. So how is she to manage?"

CHAPTER
9

The feasting got under way promptly. Roast goose, shop bread and jam, Katie's own soda bread, gravy smothering the potatoes, and whenever the porter appeared running low John Maughan saying, "Don't worry, there's more in the barrel." As for the whiskey, the cork was barely out of one bottle when he was pouring a good glass from a new one.

Most of the feasting went on in the yard under the warm sunlight, where a long table had been set up out of boards. Morgan and the new Mrs. Riley, however, sat in the kitchen, where, Minnie said, she could watch the jigs and reels. She wanted the violins close by.

Her earlier hopefulness, brief as it was, had evaporated. It was a strain now to give more the look of a wedding than a funeral. Reflection had exposed the inescapable. She'd pledged herself to a life sentence.

There was also the matter of guilt. Carrying another's child to her wedding had seem right enough. Keeping Mattie with her. Bringing a part of him for comfort with the stranger. But in the chapel, seeing the farmer, a good man, and watching the tall, proud sister, that was different. That was a scene. The prayers and the vows ringing down the Almighty's grace on an imposter.

God help her, had the priest known the sin that he'd blessed. There'd been a mighty procession fast out o' the church. Ah, she'd done a bad deed.

Minnie stared at her plate, at the cold thick gravy clumped

sickeningly on the goose meat. Her stomach lurched, and for several terrible moments she feared she'd vomit. She wiped her face, felt the cold, anxious sweat. Dizziness made the room whirl briefly. But when her head had cleared a new mood struck. A fierce, resolute anger, deadly in its clarity, had displaced the guilt. What of *their* deed? *Their* guilt? Draggin' her off in the bloom of her youth to marry one twice her age? Callin' her "wife" when she'd no feel at all for the truth of it? What deed was that? Wasn't it a cold face had the Almighty when He wrote out the rules in that book!

Had she no say?

She lifted her eyes to her husband opposite, saw her ma heap his plate for the second time.

"Don't I love your ma's cooking?" said Morgan, catching her gaze.

Quickly she lowered her head, flustered by the first words since the vows. The man had a quiet voice, and his eyes rested fondly—but wasn't it the food he loved? Shovelin' in the roast goose the likes she'd hardly seen? Was he stokin' the fires? Readyin' for the long night of takin' the thing she'd not now to give? I've given it, her heart shrieked. Not a prayer in the world can reclaim it, no matter the ones may condemn me.

"And don't you be liking the food?"

Her husband had addressed her. At first she wasn't sure, so gentle was his voice. But he spoke again, asking, "Is it worn out with the strain of it all? It does be hard, this getting married." He laughed gently, as if only the two of them knew the joke.

Minnie turned crimson. She clamped her lips shut, jabbing her fork at a slab of cold meat. "Oh, have a fresh piece." He quickly transferred a small slice onto her plate. "Isn't it a great hulking traveler your ma thinks she's feeding?" Again he laughed, and there was goodness to the sound. Despite her misery she softened. "Ma's great with the meals," she said shyly, cutting a tiny piece of goose meat. She chewed slowly, discovered herself famished. And why wouldn't she be? The last bit of food to pass her lips the night before last?

"Have more," said Morgan when she'd finished. "Put a little gravy. With a bit of spuds."

The warmth in Morgan's eyes embarrassed Minnie but she ate ravenously. Each time he shifted food to her plate she devoured it, gobbling so fast she felt breathless. "I'm like the pigs," she apologized, surprised to find herself smiling.

"You were starved," he comforted. When she was silent he merely sat patiently, keeping a watchful, hopeful eye. At last, when she had put down her fork, he caught Katie Maughan's eye across the noisy kitchen. Katie beamed on her new son-in-law. "You've wine for the ladies?" Morgan said.

Minnie sipped the strange, rich liquid, letting the sweetness slide across her tongue. The wine was comforting and delicious. After a second taste she drank freely until the glass was empty. Morgan poured another, while a relaxed flush spread across Minnie's face. "Now you'll feel better," he said.

Minnie relished the soothing warmth. It spread through her body, easing the paralyzing rigidity of the past two days. A deep, forgiving sensation of lightness encompassed her, gave a sense of floating, of drifting among the dancers who whirled in an eight-hands-around. She smiled at the merrymakers. At the spinning feet. At the hearth fire next to the fiddlers. She smiled at the dresser. At the spinning wheel in the far corner, heaps of fleecy wool, dirty grey, loose and soft on the floor.

Her dreamy gaze played across the room, paused at the little bedroom, abruptly focusing. "And do you be fearful?" said Morgan. His quick glance took in the room off the kitchen, where he could see her small bed, standing low to the floor.

Minnie looked away at the dancers, at their rowdy whirlings and turning. She turned again to her husband. "Ah, no," she almost whispered, so that Morgan leaned forward. "It's not fear has me troubled." And what is it? Morgan wanted to ask, but he turned towards the dancers himself. The violins were faster now, bows darting, strings singing, so that the room rocked in a frenzy of dancing feet. A glass smashed to the floor. An exclamation. A voice apologized. Katie Maughan, hearty, insisted, " 'Tis only a bit of glass."

Suddenly Minnie was ill. Morgan's hand reached out quickly. "We'll get the air." He led her, skirting the dancers, supporting her giddy legs with his arm around her waist.

Outside, behind the house, the air smelled clean. Morgan fetched an old bucket, upturned it, sat down on a rock nearby. "It was hot inside," Minnie said, seating herself. She fastened her eyes on the hills, and on the fenced-in lambs standing quiet in the sunshine. An old ram nudged against the fence, beyond the enclosure. She studied his futile efforts. Up on the hillside sheep ate the new grass. "When I've not the cows handy, I've the sheep," she said.

"I've no sheep," Morgan said, hoping a bit of gab might help, not that he'd a thing in the world worth saying. But if he gave it a nudge, she might hoe the row.

"But ye've cows."

"Will four be enough?" Morgan laughed quickly, then let his face grow serious, hoping she'd know he was only being friendly. Not a thought at all of taking her lightly.

"We've eight, ye know. But four will do me . . . And I'm used to milkin' three. The rest is the dry stock."

"Oh, we've two dry ourselves. And two for milking . . . I bring the butter to Kilmaragh."

"Do ye now?"

"Annie's great with the milking."

"And will she be doin' it?" Disappointment spread over Minnie's face. The quick, faint flicker of optimism fled from her eyes.

"Ah, no. You've only to say," he said. He jumped to his feet, fighting the urge to grab her into his arms, so lovely and mournful she was, hands in her lap, bountiful hair streaming over her shoulders. Hadn't she the look of an angel while she grieved over cows? Musha, wasn't it strange the things that gave happiness?

"Ye'll have the milking all you like," he said tenderly. "Sure, Annie's so much work there isn't a thing you can't have if you want." He laughed softly, hoping she'd enjoy the joke along with him. But she merely stared pensively at the fenced-in lambs, brightening after a moment. "It's a comfort there'll be cows," she said.

Morgan hesitated. And after a long pause, "Will I suit, little lass? Do I suit you?"

With the words out in the clear air, Morgan was horror-stricken. He threw himself down by her feet, overwhelmed by remorse. But he was unable to take his eyes off her, unable to stop feasting on her dear face, her sweet mouth, the wonderful eyes. Passion fired his hopes again. His heart cried out to hers. Ah, love me!

When Minnie finally spoke her voice was low and strained. "It's not suitin' I'm after."

"What is it then?" Morgan shifted on the grass. He moved closer to the bucket, careful not to touch her. He mustn't frighten her, if that was it. Was there a bride alive didn't be having fear of the bedding? "Tell me, darlin', what's troubling?"

By now Minnie's cheeks were aflame. "Suiting's long past," she said, so low he barely heard. She swayed from the effort of the words, so that he feared she'd fall from the bucket. "Ah, don't speak," he urged, wishing he'd said nothing at all. There wasn't a thing didn't improve with time, and if the girl got used to him, why, there was a long life ahead. "Have a care not to upset yourself," he said.

"There isn't a thought in my head at all," said Minnie. She looked at him solemnly, spoke softly. The green eyes, clear and lovely, spread the heart of her womanhood before him, until he thought he'd swoon himself, so great was her spell on him.

Glory to God he'd to control himself. Quickly he moved away from her. He lay on his back on the grass, eyes closed to shut out her magnificence.

"Minnie?" God Almighty, it was the ma. She stuck her head out the back door. Morgan, breathing hard, sat upright.

"Annie's wondrin' will ye be goin'?" Katie Maughan called out. "Annie's the cows on her mind."

Morgan forced himself to look at his mother-in-law. "If we're late there's a neighbor," he said, wishing to God that Annie'd more sense.

But maybe it was Katie herself put her up to it, thinking the quicker gone the sooner settled? Did she think the girl'd take a spell? Not that the guests would notice. There wasn't one not gay with the drink, them all dancing themselves to a fit.

Yet they were right. The time had come to go. Mightn't the girl be cheered, once she'd the leaving behind her? That was it, surely. It was parting from the ma and da that troubled. Himself and Annie'd have to make it up to her.

Inside, keeping an eye on the back door, Katie Maughan sliced raisin cake and prayed. Since the truth had come to her she had prayed each morning and night. Not that Minnie'd said, but was there a ma alive couldn't guess? The daughter with an illness for days? First thing in the morning, Minnie just out of bed, a foot to the floor? Wasn't she runnin' for the outhouse? Not another thing it could be.

God keep the farmer from guessin'.

How'd that O'Malley done it? With herself and the da keepin' the eye o' the hawk these many weeks, Minnie nowhere but up with the cows? Was that it? Those long days on the mountain?

A chill went up her spine. That's when he'd done it. And *done it he had.*

She grabbed a raisiny morsel, gobbling quickly.

Wasn't her own guilt near great as the girl's? Turnin' her head, lettin' her up there, not pennin' her up in the cow house? Ah, there was God's good price for indulgin' yeer child! For hadn't that been her intention? A last free romp, not a thought of that fella at all? Only Minnie runnin' free, a bit of the joy of her youth, before the yoke o' the plow was upon her?

Musha, wasn't it a hard thing when yeer plans go awry?

Not a thing for it now but to seal up her lips. The bargain'd been struck, and hadn't the farmer the look of a man well taken? So that there'd be Minnie and herself only knowin'. They'd pass if off as the farmer's child, not a soul in the world the wiser.

But suddenly the bad egg in the pot rose up. How long since the babe'd been begun? Too large too soon and there wasn't a one—includin' the farmer and Brian Maughan—but'd hear a bad cock crowin' in the haggard. Ach! Ach! God help the lot o' them.

Feverishly she calculated the weeks needed for the nephew's wedding, with the writings not yet signed. They couldn't risk him knowin', or the girl either. Especially the girl. Her grand fine dowry'd float off to the hills, had the O'Bannons a hint. One breath of a bad character and they'd never give over.

Ah, Lord save, wasn't it secrets kept the world turnin'?

She set out cake plates, smiled this way and that at the guests, stepped out into the music for a few steps of a jig. "It's a grand day for the lot of us," she smiled back at Annie. "Indeed, indeed." Annie, laughing, swept past in an eight-hands-around.

The leavetaking wore the trappings of a wake. Katie Maughan, though fidgety, was all smiles but old Maughan exuded sorrow. He held the reins, cap over his eyes, while Morgan hitched the horse, and everything about him seemed dispirited. When Katie whispered he'd the look of the long road he pulled the cap even lower.

"Isn't it the way of the world?" he muttered, the thud of

despair in his voice. He gazed over at Minnie, who stood somber yet determined by the door.

Katie Maughan, suddenly flustered, asked if Minnie'd all she needed. "Yeer little bag?" Minnie sent Katie a long stare. "Is it my needs yeer inquirin' after?" A cloud, hostile even if muted, hung in the afternoon air. There was a silence. Minnie fastened her shawl on her shoulders, and with a constrained tightness she smoothed down her hair. "My needs is my own," she said.

"Ah, darlin', isn't it every bride has needs?" Katie laughed, but Minnie sensed the uncertainty. The ma was unsettled, and well she might be. For it wasn't every day a daughter went off, sold for a rise in the world.

"Now, ye'll have a grand life," said Katie. The crowd around the stout barrel were plainly listening. Denny O'Donnell, whiskey in hand, had just stumbled out the kitchen door. "Now, don't be lookin' sad," he said, lurching towards Minnie. Whiskey splashed from his glass and she pulled away. "Ah, Minnie, give us a kiss," he wheedled foolishly, trying to grab her. But quickly Morgan stepped forward. "We've to be off," he said, growling, and Denny retreated.

"Ah, now don't be cross," said Denny. He took a long gulp of whiskey. When he appeared about to fall Morgan grabbed him, settling him gently onto the ground. "You've a drop taken," said Morgan, but his anger had evaporated.

"Sure, I meant no harm," said Denny. He sank back in a sprawl. "It's only the whiskey . . . I'd wed Minnie myself, had I the place o' four cows." He launched forth on the barrenness of his life, the agony of being a boy forever. "Years o' waitin' have made me a buffoon, God help me," he slurred. "Sure, there won't be a bark o' the dog left in me. I'll be too old to wag my tail."

The crowd surrounding the stout barrel laughed. There was nudging, a bit of pushing and shoving. Two of the liveliest, a pair of brothers who were neighbors, pretending to be dogs. One brother barked loudly, while the other cavorted on all fours, calling out, "Watch close now, and if yeer lucky ye'll catch sight of me tail waggin'." The barking dog, as far along in his drinking as Denny, sidled over to Morgan. He'd steal the bride himself, he said, given half the chance.

Morgan laughed good-naturedly but John Maughan glared.

He pushed his cap from his eyes. "It'd take a strong man," he snapped. "My Minnie's not for stealin'."

Katie Maughan stepped forward but her husband shook her off. "Begone to yeer kitchen, woman," he growled. "Ye've done yeer deed for this day. Be off! I tell ye."

There was a muffled gasp from the revelers. No one spoke.

Katie stood her ground, goaded to rashness. "And what is the deed I've done?" Wasn't it his idea as much as her own, when he'd sight of the fine connection? But she backed off, himself still lookin' so fierce.

When Morgan saw Minnie turn crimson he moved quickly to her side. "Now, you've all to be at ease," he said mildly, taking Minnie's little bag to stow in the cart. "Won't we be hiring the cart in a month for the visit?"

He shook hands all around, first with John and Katie Maughan. "There isn't a grander thing than the joining of families," he said. "Won't you be coming yourselves in no time?"

"Ah, before ye know it," said Katie, forcing a smile. She stood apart from her husband, so no one would have it to say he'd have given her a cuff. Sure, wasn't it the drink itself the half of them came for? And envy for a daughter that's off to Kilmaragh?

Morgan assisted Minnie up into the cart, settling her comfortably on the cushioned seat. Annie sat on the opposite seat, struggling to seem joyous. They *had* done a foolish thing. This odd scene was the proof. People with skirts to the ankle and shawls at a wedding were no crowd to tie in with. The Maughans were backward people, no doubt of it.

She anguished over the enormity of their mistake. The years and years ahead, no one putting a tooth in saying that Morgan and Annie Riley'd gone a long way, indeed, to keep the name from dying out.

She smiled at Katie Maughan, who pranced next to the trap, proclaiming there wasn't a thing in the world but happiness for a bride lived close to Westport. "Isn't it them all'll be wishin' it was themselves had such good fortune?"

"Ah, now," Morgan protested, but he laughed. "Remember we're three miles out."

"No matter," cried Katie gaily, snatching her husband's cap

to perch it on her head. "And this is the new hat I'll wear, for won't I be visitin' ye often?" Rapid thunderclouds gathered on Old Maughan's face, so she hastily returned it.

"Now, aren't I only foolin'?" she placated him, but for the second time it looked as if he might hit her. "Now, do ye want me off to Westport with no hat?"

"Ye heard the farmer," growled John Maughan. "She'll be three miles out." He moved toward his wife, arm upraised. Minnie gasped, her face gone white. Morgan moved quickly forward. It seemed for a moment Minnie would topple from the seat.

Old Maughan retreated, shaking his head and muttering. He spat. Wasn't losing Minnie bad enough, without herself carrying on like a fool?

Minnie's color returned, and the crowd by the stout barrel laughed. There was much uneasy shuffling, some moving in the direction of the house. "An ugly scene," whispered the fellow who'd barked. His brother hit him in the ribs. "Be quiet."

"Don't worry about the three miles," said Morgan, his voice carefully cheerful. He wished to God they'd not made the girl uncomfortable—wasn't a wedding difficult enough? He patted Minnie reassuringly. "Shall we be off?"

Minnie responded with a nod, setting her shoulders resolutely. She wished they would get moving, wished it with all her heart. There was nothing to be gained by delaying. "Be off," she said, but when the da rushed to solemnly shake her hand her tears welled up.

"It's a heavy heart goes with ye," said John Maughan, knowing the part he played in her going. Wasn't Minnie the light of his days? He grasped her small fingers in his seasoned farmer's hand.

"Ah, don't be grievin', da," Minnie said softly. "Isn't marriage the way of the world?"

"A father's heart has its own ways. Mine is full near breakin'." He began snuffling. First one large tear and then another dropped on Minnie's fingers. For one wretched moment she feared he'd break into sobs, but he rallied, swallowing his grief. He grasped her fingers and she sat mesmerized. Not for the world would she pull away. Her own grieving heart spoke to his. Don't cry, da, she begged wordlessly. It's the end of me—if ye weep I'll never stand it.

The last she saw of her da was with his head bowed, and there wasn't another sight nor a sound, it seemed, she'd ever want again after the pain of it.

CHAPTER
10

Once beyond the flat plain and the village Morgan's attention was absorbed guiding the cart over the rough two miles down to the more gentle slope of grass and rocky pasture. Past that, the road, though rough, had less of rocks and ruts. So eventually, whenever he could, he cast a backwards glance at Minnie.

The two women, occupying seats on opposite sides, rode in silence. There was something almost regal, Morgan thought, about Minnie's posture. She was pale, calm, and there was a look of new life. Annie, on the other hand, gave not a thing to be fathomed of her mind. Her face was a mask. Not since Old Maughan had nearly taken a swing at the wife had it been possible to know what Annie was thinking. Quick as it happened, Annie's face took a pose, where you wouldn't think butter'd melt in her mouth. And she'd stayed that way.

Annie remained a puzzle throughout the last farewells. While the ma and Chrissie O'Bannon ran waving after the cart, calling out, the crowd gave a great loud cheer. Denny O'Donnell's drunken tenor rendered The Valley Lay Smiling Before Me, the last sweet sound echoing and re-echoing across the green and sun-drenched hills. Annie'd been an enigma. There wasn't a fault you could find with the set of her lips, her cool and pleasant eye.

But Morgan was worried nevertheless.

Was there something hidden in Annie's heart? Was it doubtful she was? Unsure of this marriage? Not knowing they'd already a nice talk of the cows, with Minnie reassured?

On the side seat Annie struggled mightily. At times her heart beat fast, at times her breath came shallow. Mother of God, whatever would they do? Her only hope was to hide her shock. She clung to hope the girl was young enough. That she'd married before there was time for her to become one of them. Annie's other hope seemed even less likely, that the ma and da'd only wished they'd a knock at one another. For if it was long years of that, there wasn't a thing in the world but Minnie'd be doing the same. Wasn't it the way with them backward people? Bouncing a boot off one another if they'd a mind to? Glory be, wasn't it a long way into the hills Morgan'd gone to find a wife?

They were nearly past the uplands now, and after a scattering of coarse grass and green moss they arrived at the bogland. Here on the outskirts the bog was thin, and still mountainy, but there were clusters of villagers already working, two or three in a group here and there. Some were deep in the waterlogged cuts, creel baskets perched above them. Others stood on the bank itself, stacking the dripping turfs. Below, the diggers stood in the muck. There were whole families, many with young children, piling the scraw, where they'd cut through the tough, matted roots.

The nearest group, two men and a woman, worked close to the road. They paused at the approach of the cart. The older man, facing the turf bank, had been in the act of cutting, his spade ready to thrust. Up on the bank the woman's hands were raised to catch the turf. Just at that moment Annie cried out and the old woman let her hands to her sides. "Isn't it the weddin' crowd?" she called out excitedly to the husband.

Morgan drew in the reins and Annie leapt down, a hand pressed to her lips. "Is it ill ye are," said Minnie, scrambling from the opposite seat. "It's the jouncing," said Morgan. "Sure, I'm sick myself," agreed Minnie, full of sympathy. She thrust a clean white handkerchief at Annie, who grasped the side of the cart, pale and with her face clammy.

"Oh, ye've to grab her. She'll faint," cried Minnie, but Annie insisted it was nothing at all, and her color did seem to be returning. "Didn't I make a pig of myself, with all the goose and the cake?"

"Well, sit on a rock," said Morgan, leading her. It was only then he noticed the three by the side of the road. They'd moved up out of the cut, the old man with his cap in his hand, while the wife tried frantically to clean her hands on her smock.

" 'Tis the O'Neils," said Minnie, smiling shyly at young Mick, who hung back, blushing fiercely. The young man managed a smile, and then broke into a grin that showed the gap where his tooth was missing. He beamed at Morgan.

"For the love of God." Morgan shook hands all around.

Annie struggled to her feet, saying there wasn't a thing but that a bit of air and steady ground wouldn't cure it. (Who in the name of God were *this* crowd?) She stared at the mud-caked strangers. The wife wore her dress to the ankles, and over it a blue smock. The smock was spattered, and the black dress had mud to the hemline. Oversized boots peeped out from under the skirt.

Glory be to God, puzzled Annie, was there no sense in these backward people, not knowing to cut from the bank? Kilmaragh never cut in the muck.

She forced a tight smile. "And isn't it a grand day for the turf?" she said.

"Ah, yes." John O'Neil's bony face lit up. "And will ye see the pile we're after diggin'?"

Black, oozy, heaped-up turfs stretched from the deep cut to the road. Mud dripped from a filled basket, and Bridey O'Neil had already begun filling the wheelbarrow next to it. Another creel basket stood empty. "What do ye say to that? Are we the great workers or are we not?" O'Neil said, breaking off a handful of black wet sod to crush it. He rolled it between his fingers, spitting a mouthful of brown tobacco juice onto the ground. "How's that?"

Annie's stomach retched. But she breathed deeply, managing to say how grand it was they'd a son to help them.

"Oh, he's a grand worker." John O'Neil beamed at young Mick.

Annie fought to hide her disgust, taking a careful check of her new shoes. She climbed up into the cart, saying how nice it was to sit down, especially when you were a bit taken. She pulled her face into an appearance of friendliness.

"Ah, ye've to travel more to get the hang of it," said John O'Neil. He ran an admiring hand over the shiny black paint of the cart. "Take a look," he said to young Mick. The son felt the smoothness too. His ma stood silent next to the wheelbarrow.

Her grey, withered face had grown animated, her eager eyes devouring the scene. She gazed at Annie's store frock, hungrily tracing the chainstitched embroidery, the graceful, box-pleated skirt. "Did I ever think I'd see the like?" she whispered.

"Don't be buttin' in," said the husband, but she ignored him. Her eyes fell on Annie's shoes, and a groan of pleasure came from her lips at Annie's length of tan cotton stockings. "Yeer legs, no less," she said in awe.

"Didn't I be tellin' ye?" roared the husband. For a terrible moment Annie feared he'd hit her. She leaned forward from the seat, but the old woman moved off, almost to the cut. There, at a safe distance, she studied Annie's shoes. "And is it yeer own feet is in them?" she whispered, breathless with admiration.

"And whose feet do ye think, idiot? Is one of the fairies doin' her walkin'?" O'Neil's voice had grown even harsher, and he dismissed his wife with a wave of his hand. But she was not to be stopped. The old woman slowly sidled around him, eyes fixed on the shoes, to where Minnie waited by Morgan. "And won't I be honored?" she purred, grabbing Minnie's hand to shake it.

Minnie blushed. "Aren't I country people like yeerselves?"

"Ah, no more ye are. Ye've status now. Yeer a woman that's wed, God save ye." The old woman's face shone. Again O'Neil seemed about to intervene, but the son stepped between them. Mick's warm gaze rested on Minnie, and every time she lifted her eyes or smiled he blushed beet red. "Sure, isn't she Mrs. Morgan Riley now?" he said, pride and envy in his voice. "We've not many like her," he told Morgan. "Yeer luck is Kilmaragh's gain."

Morgan slipped an arm around Minnie, struck anew at the prize he'd won. "That's good of you to say."

During all the smiling and blushing, a change had come over Bridey O'Neil; the grey eyes turned piercing. She stood close to the girl, examining her in an odd way, as if struck by a new thought. After a few additional cordialities, Morgan saying they'd a long journey ahead, she spoke. "Ye'd best be on yeer way, out o' the dark time."

She looked at all of them. Her face was altered, no longer excited. "Nothin' good's abroad in the nighttime," she sang in a monotone, turning directly to Morgan as if moved by a spell.

Morgan grew flustered. What in the name of God?

"Keep yeer bride from the blackness o' the night."

"Sure, what are ye sayin'? There's no danger can touch when a woman's been wed." John O'Neil bristled.

"Take the word of an old woman." Bridey O'Neil looked directly at Minnie. "It's never abroad in the nighttime ye'll be." She'd seen that girl, O'Malley himself with her, slippin' across the fields. Him not comin' home 'til the sun was barely rising.

Suddenly Morgan erupted into nervous laughter. "Well, for the love of God," he said, pushing Minnie up into the cart.

The woman was daft. This was crazy talk. Whisht!

He tipped his hat to all of the O'Neils, flicked the reins and away they swept. The cart swayed off down the road, wheels banging. Rocks and stones flew either side.

Annie's gaze was to the north, where the bog stretched off toward the mountains. Stiff, straight, she rode like a stone.

To the south Minnie faced low mists over the brown reedy lakes and there were birds on the patches of mossy, coarse vegetation. Occasionally a great cloud of them soared up into the greying late afternoon sunshine.

Minnie was silent, her heart frozen by the memory of the old woman's words.

Bogland passed, and she was amazed at the breadth of it, the long wet miles. A new world stretched from one low rise to another, to miles of low hills in the distance.

Morgan, hard at the horse, saw only the road to the west. Not a rock or a rough spot but didn't make him push all the more for Kilmaragh.

Among the three there wasn't a word.

In Minnie the turmoil was greatest. Sickened by the old crone's spying, she seethed at the injustice. Spying was a sin against a poor girl's only bit of happiness. Bridey O'Neil'd stolen the one happy memory she'd to take with her. Herself and darlin' Mattie were now to be bandied about the countryside, every tongue waggin' over their happiness, dirtyin' it, callin' it what it wasn't.

Her indignation soared. For surely she knew, that old woman? Surely she'd seen her boltin' the bog to O'Malley's. The two o' them, herself and Mattie, racing for home in the dark. She knew, that old woman, because she was there. Waiting. Lingering at her own cabin door. Seein' her come and seein' him go, not leavin' her bed 'til the morning. Waitin' to pick and poke at their happiness, relishing it as if it was hers.

Minnie clung to the swaying cart.

Why did they do it, the old women who spied on the young? For wasn't that the way with them? Secrets? Hidden bits and scraps. No happiness of their own, so they scavenged the bliss of the young. Greedy. A fragment here, a fragment there. 'Til when they'd grabbed enough they spit it forth in the sunshine, blackening the light of the day.

The Westport road was drawing near. As if reflecting the changed scenery there was a perceptible easing of tension. Curiosity stirred Minnie. She scrutinized the passing flatlands, the scattered patches of yellow furze. And the late afternoon shadows gave the here-and-there tall mounds of peat an ancient, brooding look.

There was the perfume of bog myrtle.

Annie, too, felt better, with the Westport road drawing near, a real road, more than this barren cart track. Her body relaxed. Soon she was deliberating about a conversation. (Even backward people liked friendliness.)

The vows after all were now said—no one could alter that. Not even the old woman. A marriage vowed was a marriage made; the thing now was to make the best of it. Sure, wasn't that all life was anyway, making the best of things?

"Are you able to knit?" she said, above the noise of the cart. (Household duties were as good a start as any.)

"Oh, yes," said Minnie. "The ma taught me to spin and knit."

"I only knit, myself," said Annie. "Isn't it too bad we've no wheel?"

"Well, we've no sheep either," Morgan joined in. "We'll need a herd of sheep. Then the two of yez can trot off to the pounding mill."

"Oh, we carded the wool ourselves," said Minnie. "The ma'd be at the wheel and I'd be helpin' her card."

"It's grand skills you learned," said Annie. (But why in the name of God did they make those bunchy dresses? Why not something pretty, with a bit of color?)

"Turnin' the wheel by the hour ma'd be, with me cardin' a handful of rolls. Before I learned how to spin."

"Why haven't we ever had sheep?" Annie demanded of Morgan. "We've everything else?"

As far as Morgan could remember there'd never been a sheep or a lamb. He'd really no notion, he said. "Maybe the old fellow feared they'd tumble down the cliffs." He laughed, full of good humor now. It was a grand thing to see the women getting on, after the bad scene on the bog. Wouldn't you think the crone'd have better things to do, not putting a hex on a young one?

"I'm sure it wasn't that," said Annie. "He'd have a fence . . . Who knows why he did what he did, or didn't do?"

Morgan turned to Minnie. "We'd an old fellow set in his ways. Stern. Damned stubborn."

"But a good man," said Annie quickly. Bad luck that kind of talk. Speaking against the da on a wedding day. "Do you think you'll miss the spinning?"

"Ah, no. There'll be plenty else I'm sure." But she would miss the sheep, the bleating, their gentle ways.

"And did you have a loom?"

"We took the yarn to the weaver—it was only to one of the cottages. Wasn't it my job? And then I'd be runnin' to see if the flannel was done. Sure, I loved doing it." Minnie's voice had grown trembly. She blinked back tears.

Morgan caught a sideways glance back at Minnie. He saw the strain. What in the name of God was at Annie? Couldn't she tell she'd unsettled the young one? He cleared his throat. If nothing else, he'd drown out the weaver talk. "There's grand shops in Kilmaragh," he announced in a loud voice.

"But we order from Westport, don't you know? You'll not mind, I hope?"

"And why in the name of God should she mind?" cried Morgan heatedly. Annie showed no sense at all. Planting the wrong ideas. Setting the young one to grieving. "She'll have whatever she needs," he said fiercely.

Annie stiffened. "Sure, aren't I only making conversation?"

"Life's different, that's all, in Kilmaragh," Morgan said. "We'll have to get her accustomed."

Annie shifted in her seat, miffed. When had Morgan ever spoken so loud?

Morgan glared stubbornly ahead.

* * *

At the Westport road the weather turned raw and heavy. After they'd gone a mile or so, the Atlantic fog rolled in, obscuring the sand and the rocks. The shore disappeared. "There'll be other times," said Morgan. He turned the cart for Kilmaragh.

Minnie's first view, brief as it was, revealed an amazing scene. Endless water, as far she could see. An eerie sky and lowering clouds, cliffs in the distance. A strange, piercing light illuminating the strip of rough sand by the road.

"The world!" she exclaimed. She feasted her eyes until the fog lowered. After that there was the continual roar of the breakers to remind her.

And quickly, when they reached the boreen, a heavy greyness gobbled up the fields. The world became invisible. Nothing but low scraggly bushes marked the edge of the cart track. Passing O'Donnell's, a glimmer of light was the only sign, muted, raggedly yellow, a thin ray barely cutting the grey. Halfdarkness gave way to black shadows. Night closed in, with only the sounds of cartwheels and the soft plop plop of the horse's hooves. An unseen world passed silently.

Minnie's mind reeled with curiosity. Were there cottages? Families? A wet softness fell now, little pinpricks of cold on her face. She pulled her shawl over her head.

What was to be the look of the house, the ma sayin' it was grand? A slate roof, the da said. A wondrous thing, to be sure.

But where was the town with the shops? Were they passing it, somewhere in the blackness? Could she be runnin' for sugar, like skippin' down to McNulty's? Or was it Morgan'd be makin' the journey, them having no cart?

If Annie'd a bike, was there chance of a wheel for herself?

Occasionally a hawthorn scraped, so that she pulled her feet close. Thorns scratched and snagged. Ah, for the love o' God, it was a lonely place. Not a thing at all like home.

Remembrances flooded in, blotting out the fog-world. She rode now on a grey cloud, a floating, woolly void. Morgan disappeared. Annie faded into the mists. There was nothing now but pain and grieving. Somewhere, between the new life and the old, she hung suspended.

Loneliness overcame her, weakening her, leaving only a great forlorn aching, so that she feared tumbling from the seat.

She grabbed at the side of the cart. With both hands she held fast.

Silently she prayed to a Power adrift in the mist. A Floating Power. A Being known only to the void. This Floating Power would assist, ensure she'd not falter.

Faltering'd be the end of me, she thought. I'd be destroyed. And there isn't a thing in the world worth bein' destroyed for. Not the memories, nor even the strangeness ahead. There's only life and ye've to live it. Little else. Ye've every day the Good Lord gives and ye put yeer mark on it somehow. Nor let it be said that ye stumbled.

She waited for the strength that would fall with the mist, giving sustenance.

The Power answered. *You know,* was all that it said. The words spun down through the woolly void, parting the mist and the clouds. *You know.*

"We're here," cried Morgan. "You're home, darling wife."

CHAPTER
11

Morgan lit the lamp and hung it on the wall. Yellow light played softly over the blackened roof beams. The morning's fire, white ashes heaped, still smoldered, and a thin stream of smoke trailed lazily upwards. Minnie watched the grey wisps disappear into the blackened chimney.

Outside, quite without warning, a wind picked up. The door, left open, slammed shut. "At least we'll get rid of the fog," said Annie. She righted a partly burned candle, fallen over in the gust.

From out in the haggard there were animal sounds, hens clucking, geese, pigs grunting. "The animals don't like it when it's sudden," Morgan explained. Minnie said shyly that there was often a wind off the mountain, even when you least expected it. "We may get a storm," Morgan said. "This close to the sea."

"Isn't it the way, even in April?" Annie rustled the ashes and threw on fresh sods. Morgan snatched a scrap of paper, stuck it into the red coals underneath. He lit the candle. "We've to buy more candles," said Annie.

The fresh turf ignited quickly. Soon there was a fire burning. Minnie pulled her chair close, enjoying the warmth on her cold hands.

Four slabs of bacon hung from the ceiling, making her think of her da. How he'd climb on a chair, knife in hand, cutting down thick slices. "I'm killin' a pig for dinner," he'd joke, and she'd laugh along with him. Usually they ate the fried bacon with cabbage. Or there'd be turnips.

She studied the sturdy planking. The beams were solidly
butted, the cross-beams well-made. The ceiling was black with
soot, but solid, and the joints were caulked with pitch. She'd
see the roof slate for herself when daylight came, but from the
look of things here there was hardly need. It'd be a compliment,
though, for them to show it, and for herself she could say how
nice it was. She'd tell them it was strong against the wind.
That'd give them great comfort.

"I'll see to the cows," said Annie. "They're milked already
but they've no feed yet." She disappeared out to the haggard,
Morgan following, saying he'd see to the Westport horse. "They
won't want him with a game leg," he joked, adding quickly
wasn't it a fine job, considering the rocks and the rough spots?
"My own half-dead nag would've dropped."

"Ye'd a long trip to get me," said Minnie, but Morgan said
he'd have gone farther than that. "There aren't many your like."
He blushed.

Alone in the kitchen Minnie listened to the rain spattering
the windows, and outside, from the haggard, odd clatterings
and bangings. The doors, front and back, rattled from the
sudden sharp wind but, surprisingly, the kitchen was cozily
warm.

She carefully examined her surroundings. The dishes. The
table and chairs. There were china plates and a cut glass dish
on the dresser, which was painted a bright blue, as were three
small stools near the fireplace. The four chairs, stained and as
nicely made as the table, were smooth and fine-grained, and
the set was of good finish. How often did she see tables and
chairs matching? So what need for six chairs, with no one sitting
on the half of them? Besides, the cottage was clean, the milk
buckets next to the dresser well-scrubbed, and both sides of the
hob nearly as scrubbed as the buckets. There wasn't a thing in
the world couldn't be helped by cleanliness. Six chairs, indeed.

The wind blew harder now, and from the distance came a
new sound that could only be the ocean. A fearsome force, it
seemed, so that she tried to imagine the waves against rocks.
Wild breakers hurtling towards shore.

But the solid lay of the house gave ease and she dozed in
front of the fire.

Later, after the animals were fed, Minnie surprised herself
by eating a plate of potatoes, and a second cup of tea, with

three thick slices of soda bread. Annie fetched extra butter from the barn.

Minnie was beginning to feel comfortable. The kitchen was hospitable, and if the rest was as fine—she felt sure that it was—the arrangement might work after all, though there'd never be an end to the heartbreak. Sure, wasn't it the whole world she'd lost? That she wouldn't ever forget a man such as Mattie.

She touched her belly carefully. The brief contact gave comfort. Little Mattie's heart, beating beneath her own, made up for the privations. Mattie's child would see her through, she could depend on that.

"Eat up," said Morgan. Annie fetched three small glasses and a bottle of wine. "We'll have a toast," she said, thinking that the girl would work out after all. Only there with that backward crowd did the whole thing seem a mistake. The ma and the da so surly together. And the crazy old woman. For wasn't that all it was? A daft old woman too long on the bogs, raving about girls in the nighttime?

But seeing the girl here, the firelight on her lovely hair, her eyes so bright with wonderment, a sweet smile whenever you said a thing to her, musha, there wasn't a doubt they'd done the right thing. She filled the wine glasses a second time. "Sure, it's good for you," she said when Minnie protested. "And besides, it's only wee."

"The glasses were ma's. She wasn't much for drinking," said Morgan.

"They're very pretty." Minnie sipped the wine. "But today's the first I ever had. And I was dizzy."

"Sure, isn't it dizzy everyone is on their wedding day?" Annie laughed good-naturedly, and Morgan joined in. "And some is more dizzy than others," he joked, remembering Denny O'Donnell earlier. But why wouldn't poor Denny take a drop, long years with no sign of the land? They'd a way of hanging on, the old fellows, keeping you a boy forever.

"But we won't give you enough to make your head spin," he reassured Minnie. Energized by the wine, he looked directly at her. The soon-to-be-realized finale overwhelmed him. Only feeding the animals, swinging the buckets of turnips and oats, had he relaxed. And shoveling the dung helped. But now, thanks to the wine, he was at least able to look up, to consider the approaching miracle.

The girl was his. He'd a wife in the full sense. Or soon would before the night was out. Minnie'd be a real wife. One in the flesh. Part of him. Joined in that other way, the way he'd barely dreamt of, so foreign did it seem.

A new essence was come to pass—he'd be the old Morgan, but at the same time, new. A man whose flesh had a counterpart. Fitting him, the way his shoes fit. Or his cap when he went to the fields. It was that kind of thing would be born this night.

"Did you know Denny O'Donnell is distant cousin to the woman our brother Martin wed?"

Morgan pulled free from his thoughts. Annie was making conversation. "Martin married Eileen O'Dowd." She rattled on, and suddenly Morgan was irritated. Wasn't it time to close the evening and here was Annie launching forth? He threw a meaningful glare. But Annie settled back in her chair, pouring herself a third glass! What in the name of God? It wasn't at all like her, readying for a chat at this hour, not a sign at all of tiring.

"Martin and Eileen is in America. There's letters I could be showing you. And there's two darling children. Both girls."

"Minnie doesn't want to be hearing," said Morgan, but immediately he regretted. Wasn't it hard for Annie, seeing his own grand happiness? He tried to look amiable.

But Annie was hurt. She set her wine glass on the table. "I've moved my things to the loft," she said, with a doubtful glance at the steep, narrow stairs. "I hope the room's satisfactory."

"We don't want ye inconvenienced," said Minnie. Twas a poor place, the loft. At home it was only the storeroom, not anyone sleeping.

"Now, doesn't the man and his bride get the best room?" Annie mouthed the words cheerfully enough but her face was woeful.

"Had we only a 'west room,' " said Morgan, "there'd be no need for the loft." Indignation swept him. His da'd been an odd one. So that no matter the pleas there was no adding on. No fine west room for a sort of parlour. Sure, wouldn't the Maughans themselves be settled in as soon as the nephew came?

Annie, too, longed for the fine west rooms of some. She had moved to the foot of the stairs, one hand on the railing, but her feet refused to budge. Life in the loft loomed intolerable. Three narrow beds. One straight chair, a chest. Only a candle against the blackness. The low rafters, oppressive. Wasn't it queer ways gave a west room to a backward place like the Maughans, and here they'd none for themselves? The bride, indeed, must be wondering.

Outside a gust of wind slammed against the house. Rain pelted the windows. A stack of buckets in the shed rattled. "Sure, you needn't be off yet," said Morgan. "It'll be wild up next to the roof."

"No matter," said Annie shortly.

There was a squeal out back from the pigs. Another gust. The cows mooed noisily. "Shouldn't you be out to them?" Annie blessed herself, moving away from the stairs.

"Sure, don't they be knowing the wind?" said Morgan.

"You'd leave them troubled?"

"Isn't it one or another kind of trouble everyone has?" But Morgan shrugged and rose from his chair.

There was another blast, even more violent. A bucket crashed in the cow house, followed by a loud, smashing clatter. "I'll be gone but a minute," said Morgan. A swoosh of wind swept the kitchen when he opened the door to the haggard. On the table the candle swayed.

"Oh, catch it," cried Annie, too late. Hot wax spread across the smooth, fine surface. Annie righted the candle.

"Aren't we forever scraping the wax at home?" said Minnie.

Annie looked irritably at the hardening wax. "Don't we have the life?" she said. Minnie ventured that it was nothing at all, but when Annie continued glum she fell silent.

"It's a hard life we women have," said Annie, gathering up the dishes. She set them into a pan of water on the dresser. "I'll clean up in the morning," she said, refusing Minnie's offer to help. "There'll be time for work tomorrow. This is your wedding."

"Sure, the cows are fine," Morgan announced on his return. His trousers were soaked, his hair plastered to his head, but he made no move to change into dry clothing. In his eyes there was desire. He'd waited long enough. "Isn't a few buckets tipped hardly a thing at all?"

"I'll be off," said Annie quickly. She mounted the stairs to the loft.

Minnie blushed. Apprehension gripped her. The time had come.

But, surprisingly, with Annie gone, Morgan showed no sign of rushing to the bedroom. Instead he resumed his seat by the fire. "We've the house now," he said, lighting his pipe. Before long the kitchen was blue with smoke, and Morgan appeared to be thinking deeply. There was a half-dreamy quality to him, as if he'd all the time in the world. What ailed him?

Ah, it was a strange wedding night. Not the fierce romp it'd've been with Mattie. No shame at all they'd have had, those two. It'd've been bang, slam, wham. Him between her legs, her arms around his heart. Ah, it'd've been a wonder!

The rain poured, and the wind had risen. Close by, the sea pounded. Fury everywhere and yet, despite her misgivings, she'd something near peace in her heart. Not fulfillment, surely. For there could be none. Fulfillment came with Mattie and, in parting, the end of that forever. But there was a kind of contentment, nevertheless, knowing she'd done as expected. Kept her part in life's bargain, hard though it was. For wasn't that, after all, the way? Life givin' ye breath, and in return ye walked by its pathways? Whatever was laid out, ye did it?

Up in the loft sleep eluded Annie. She stared into the emptiness, and the blackness leered back. "Old woman," it mocked.

I'm not old, she protested, straining for sounds from the lovers below.

"Don't be listening," chided the blackness. "Lovers' words for the likes of you?"

The jeers ricocheted from the rafters, driven by the thud of the rain. The slates clattered. The words pressed her into the sagging mattress. She covered her ears, body rigid. With an especially violent gust she felt the house move. The window rattled. Annie wept.

Musha, to be banished here, she sobbed. All alone. No man of my own. Not a chick or a child to leave after me. Not a soul that'll know that I've been. Ah, musha, it's a hard life, hanging on in a house with a bride.

"Then travel," rasped the voice from the darkness. "The match for the one means the miles for the rest. All must travel. To the far or the near but it's journey you must. Off. Off. Off."

But I've no cause, pleaded Annie. I'm to help them. Like I've always done. Morgan's not told me to go. He wants me here.

"You can go to America like brother Martin," droned the rafters voice. "Or the shops in Kilmaragh? Aren't they after always seeking? Be a shop girl."

Annie was desperate now. All I've known is the farm, she wailed. I've no shop skills.

She pulled the blankets tight to her chin, shivering from the window draft. Still cold she rose, crept to the low chest for the ma's thick afghan, listening above the wind and rain for any possible sounds from below. Sounds that might blot out the merciless accusations.

But except for the storm there was silence. What had she expected? Screams from the bridal bed?

The terrible thought, once fullblown, had no stopping. Was there great pain with the duty? Was life's really bad bargain only now taking shape down below? Given her choice, would she stay with the rafters?

There wasn't one she'd met in the village—or outside of it either—but wasn't forever complaining. "Ah, we've the duty," they'd moan. "Life wouldn't be bad had we not the duty." Only Sunday last it was Colman Ronan's wife put it that way.

Was it Minnie Maughan'd be saying the same? Annie struggled to imagine the scene. The new Mrs. Riley telling it out after Mass of a Sunday. Not putting a tooth in it. How it was a hard life with a man in your bed. Saying Morgan was nothing but trouble.

She battled to banish the thought. The others, maybe. The town boys. But Morgan, surely never.

Yet wasn't it the way? So it'd probably come to that.

Oh, musha, God help the lot of us, thought Annie. Was there one life of suffering but didn't meet another even worse? She grabbed her rosary beads from under the pillow. The nuggets were smooth and round in her fingers. She savored the cold hard metal of the crucifix. Was this what life had spared her, the old fellow holding onto the land, not giving over? Was it a fortunate tune she should sing?

Downstairs the silence was heavy. At first there'd been fitful conversation but now only the fire crackled, along with the shriek of the wind. The rain had lessened, and there were occasional sounds from the animals. But once, when a wind gust wrenched the door to the tool shed, there was a great clattering and banging. Morgan leaped to his feet, as if escaping. He rushed to the haggard.

The minutes dragged. Minnie waited.

Returning, Morgan said the weather was easing. That it sounded bad yet would clear. "That's the way by the sea," he said. He took the lantern from the wall. "Will you be coming?" He waited by the door to the bedroom. His energy seemed to have left him, and he had a pallor. He was afraid. With the moment arrived he'd only paralysis and doubts. He was flooded by apprehension. Where was the benefit in never having done it? Wasn't it the boys behind the hedges had gathered all the skill?

God help him, what skill had he? The girl would find him clumsy. He'd strive for delight but might give only pain.

Or was there always pain? Even at the back of the hedges?

A girl was a gentle thing, soft, fragile. No knowledge at all of the thrust of the bull, the lunge. It was only waiting they knew. Peacefulness. Acceptance.

He waited, uncertain. Confusion and worry swept him. He set the lantern to the floor, gazing like a mute puppy at the woman who was his bride.

A new thought struck him. Was she fearful too?

Minnie rose from her chair, stared pensively into the dying fire. Resigned, she moved from the hearth, advancing slowly toward her husband, who stood by the little bedroom. She stared at the open door, into the blackness beyond. Abruptly her resignation faded. Where was the fire and the glory? The grand magnificence? Her heart screamed for the wedding night with Mattie. Mattie riding her into the magic valley, where only pleasure dwelt.

She studied the stranger by the door, saw his strained, hopeful, eager face. Unexpectedly she felt his tension, his indecision. He was a gawky youth, fearful, uncertain. Her sympathy stirred. The man was afraid. Forty-three years and fearing a woman.

Compassion swept her. Her own confusion and anger evaporated, her misgivings. She was filled with an urge to calm him. Teach him there was nothing to fear. "It's time," she said softly, moving past him into the blackness. Morgan followed with the lantern.

The room afforded scarcely space for the bed, with a small, makeshift table to one side. Three or four nails had been driven into the wall for clothing, and there was one tiny window. Morgan set the lantern on the table. "We'll go in to Westport," he said, following Minnie's glance. "You can pick out a chest."

"Then it'll be my first. I never had more than a shelf."

"There's little things for the house we can buy," said Morgan. "There never was need before."

"It'll be grand, I'm sure."

Morgan sat on the edge of the bed.

At first Minnie lingered by the door. But then, moving gracefully, she came to sit beside him. They faced one another, Minnie with her hands in her lap.

Morgan folded his arms on his chest, content for the moment merely to sit, nourishing himself with his new bride's presence. The miracle of her. Her eyes were gently comforting.

His fears eased. Doubts had begun to fade, and he felt consoled. No longer was his bride distant, or sullen as at the wedding. And the haunted look of the day of the match, that was gone too. This bride was a soft woman, patiently solacing. He moved closer. Minnie allowed him to take her hand. They sat quietly, neither one speaking. "Shall we begin?" Minnie said at last, and Morgan turned down the lamp. "Put it out," said Minnie firmly.

"It's darkness you want?"

"This time at least," said Minnie. There was still a faint hearth light from the kitchen. Morgan moved to shut the door but Minnie stopped him. "Leave it. We've still to find our way."

Silently they removed their clothing, Minnie taking a night-dress from her little bag. Morgan reached out to touch the gown. "Is it silk?" he asked.

"It was ordered from Westport. It's rayon. The ma didn't want me ashamed."

"Oh, there could never be shame for a girl like yourself."

Minnie slipped the embroidered gown over her head, her arms through the lace-edged sleeves. She buttoned the gown to the neck, slithering her underwear to the floor. "I'm done," she said briskly, shivering slightly. Away from the fire the room was cold, and there was a draft from the rain-lashed window.

Morgan had removed all but his underwear. The drawers were long to the ankles, and in the dimness Minnie saw his full breadth. He was stocky as well as tall. A strong man.

She moved toward the bed, slipped beneath the covers. When Morgan lay beside her he lifted the silky nightdress, and quickly began fondling her. Her breasts grew taut beneath his hands. Quickly he became tense. He panted, pulled open his underwear. With a loud cry he moved swiftly to thrust himself between her legs. "Ah, darlin'," he cried, and there was a great push and swell. He came in a rush, then lay back, exhausted.

Minnie crept from the bed to wipe herself clean. She returned to his arms and shortly they slept.

In her dreams she ran in the sunshine, laughing and singing. From high in the white clouds came the strains of a penny whistle. Mattie chased her. Light and fast, she led him through the hay rows, pausing for kisses. Blinded by sunlight, they fell in the hay, where the great, splendid body came to her. She wept in ecstasy. Half awake, half asleep, she cried aloud. "Ye'll never leave me?"

Roused from sleep, Morgan spoke soothingly. "And why would I?"

Minnie felt tears on her face. She sat up in the darkness, listening to the howl and rush. She felt the force of the wind on the house. "Ah, musha," she said.

CHAPTER
12

Turf work was hard. Morgan cut the sods, Annie lifted. And when she pitched them, dripping, Minnie stood waiting to set them in the barrow. It was wet, long work. The turf had to be spread, and when it was dry they'd to move it again, piling in tall hand-stacks in the haggard.

The worst problem was wetness. Barrett had had his way. The entire village was out, with Morgan still convinced they shouldn't have started 'til May. April meant waterlogging—wet feet, trousers muddy. Every dripping sod flung spray and Minnie was doing the catching. A hard job for a bride.

Now, after a week's cutting, there was little in the evenings but to sit by the fire. Naturally, no one visited. The quiet hung heavy. So that a letter from Maughans was a treat.

"The nephew's comin' in," said Minnie, when she'd read it.

"Your ma's prompt. You've the news like you lived there."

"She knows I'm keen to hear. Wasn't Brian like a brother? He's worked da's fields for years. The whole of my life, doesn't it seem? And wasn't he doin' it long before?"

"That's the way, when you've no son. Sure, wouldn't it be the case with myself but for Annie? Almost as good as a man she's been."

"It's a terrible curse, no sons. But I don't know why my da says it, with all that Brian does. Cleanin' the ditches, repairin' the walls. And if not, he's layin' in seed. The two of them plant the root crops. Better than a son he is."

"Then it's only fitting he should have the land," said Morgan.

"Shall I read the letter?" said Minnie, a wistful smile on her face. "Or do ye want to wait for Annie?"

"Ah, no, she'll be a while." Morgan noted the fatigue around Minnie's eyes. Sure, mightn't she be nodding off? "Let's hear," he said.

"We'll have tea with Annie," said Minnie, hanging the kettle from the crane. She sat next to Morgan, spreading the letter in her lap. "Ye were hardly wed," she began, "when the plans got under w⁓ Yeer own ink was barely dry.

"The writings are signed and the fortune's handed over. In another week we'll make over the farm. Brian's to get seven of the cows, the horse, the pigs, and the chickens. We'll keep one cow and just enough grass—Brian'll have the land. And, of course, we'll be moving into the west room.

"I'll hardly know myself, in with all the finery. Though sharing the hearth will be strange, getting used to another woman.

"I know it's too soon for yeer visit, so we'll be travelin' to the weddin' alone. They'll all be there, the O'Bannons. A full house, God bless them.

"Keep a good heart, Minnie. With the future bringin' ye blessings. Regards from yeer da to the farmer. With a fond heart, yeer ma."

Annie came in from the haggard as the letter ended. "You've let the fire low," she said, cranky with exhaustion.

Annie's boots were caked with mud and her dress was spattered. Her hair showed specks of dried bog water. But when she saw the letter she brightened. "News?"

Minnie got up to stir the coals. She threw several sods on the fire. Immediately a cloud of smoke billowed out into the kitchen.

"Glory be!" said Annie, coughing.

Minnie flushed a deep red. She rushed at the fire with a poker, but the grey-white smoke continued to billow. "It's my doin'," she wailed, shamefaced.

"Ah, no," said Morgan, "it's not your fault at all."

"And is it mine?" said Annie. "Isn't it her job, bringing in the turf?" She clutched at a stitch in her side.

"Twas only the wrong pile," said Morgan, "and it's yourself that complained of the cold."

Minnie raked furiously, separating out the damp, smoking turf.

"You've not to be blamed," said Morgan, opening the door to the haggard. "Isn't it mixed up we all get?"

Annie recoiled as if struck. Her eyes, already red and watery, filled with tears. She fled to the haggard.

"Oh, ye've to be kinder," cried Minnie. "It *is* my fault. What was I thinkin', not knowin' the damp from the dry?"

"Now aren't we gone all day, struggling in the muck?" insisted Morgan. "So how could you be learning?" He snatched the poker from Minnie, jabbing at the sods.

Out in the haggard Annie mopped at her eyes. Was this the beginning? The first step, 'til they'd turned her out on the road? Oh, it was a sad day, Morgan going so far for a bride.

By the hearth Minnie was miserable, too. Poor Annie, hard enough she'd to sleep in the loft. And it was high time she knew the right pile. "Oh, come in, Annie," she pleaded from the door to the haggard. A breeze had picked up, sweeping clean air through the kitchen. The smell of the sea filled the room. "Sure, the smoke's gone now," said Morgan, ashamed of his own outburst. "Will you come in?"

When they were settled again, the fire burning with a red glow, Annie felt ashamed. She poured the tea, realizing there wasn't a thing Minnie'd not know, given a bit of time. "And will you read your letter now?" she said, hoping to avoid hard feelings.

Minnie unfolded the letter.

"So you see, we've new relatives comin' in," she concluded.

"This Brian's da'd no farm of his own?" asked Annie.

"Oh, yes. But there's brothers. And Brian's always been close with my da. Like a son, ye know . . . But they couldn't marry 'til I did." Minnie stopped in embarrassment.

"But they're quick doing it now," joked Morgan. "We must've been just off in the cart when they was doing the writings." He threw more sods on the fire, which burned properly this time. The kitchen became warm and comfortable. "Do we need the lamp?" he said, but Annie shook her head.

Sitting was more cozy in the firelight. "Will you be to the wedding?" she asked of Minnie.

"Ah, no. It's too soon. The month's not . . ."

Before Minnie could finish Morgan interrupted. "It's only the custom. If you really want to go?"

"The month will be soon enough." Minnie was thrown into turmoil, but she kept her voice calm. The last thing, right now, was a visit to Ballyrea. Dead tired, with rings around her eyes? Exposin' herself? Chrissie O'Bannon'd be starin' and wondrin', askin' why she ate so little. And the rest'd be actin' friendly, but all the while they'd be countin', makin' jokes on her pale face. Sayin' wasn't it soon she'd the sickness?

Ah, no. She'd stay where she was.

Later she'd go, after the months were forgotten. When there was no chance of disgrace. Sure, wasn't the farmer good to her? Tellin' her to rest while he fetched the cows, urging Annie to fix the feed? So why risk shamin' him?

But then a new thought struck her. Was it only for the chief duty he saved her? The begettin' and birthin' an heir?

"We can't have you worked half to death," said Morgan. The week long, since the morning after the wedding, she'd looked tired.

He and Annie were used to the work in the springtime— they'd done it all their lives. Not so, Minnie. The ma and da'd kept her sheltered. Except for the cows and the sheep she'd only to help with the spinning. He squeezed her hand. Wasn't it other tasks went to a bride, not field work? Her chief duty lay with a child.

His heart beat fast and he felt his face redden. Oh, it'd be a wonder, a babe in their arms. He daydreamed up into the smoke, envisioning the future, his wife with a child.

Images swept over him of the nights between the sheets. The wrassling and thrashing. Minnie the bride of a week with near the heat of a man! How had he done it? What was his secret? Musha, weren't they the wild dogs the two of them, after only a quick look the day of the match? Who'd have thought it?

So there wasn't a chance in the world he'd let her wear herself out with the work.

But what then? Keep her chained by the fire? Only himself and Annie doing the cutting? Tell her, Stay rested, darlin', for the feast that we'll have in the nighttime. Would that be out of place, him mentioning an embarrassing subject?

"Do you want to go out on the morrow?" he began tentatively, avoiding Annie's questioning glance that seemed to be saying, "And are we to work ourselves to death?"

Annie felt resentment rise. Wasn't it every spring they'd worked together, a delight it was in the old days? The whole village out, themselves in a happy, small cluster. Paring their own scraw. The old man cutting and tossing. Judging the depth of the face. Morgan catching. Herself piling the turfs on the barrow. And it was smiling Morgan'd been, giving encouragement. Jollying her along. Now his big smiles went to Minnie. His heartening words. The pats of reassurance. For herself there was nothing but silence and drudgery. Where was the good of it, the new life? Yet wasn't it the way? The husband's eyes for the wife—musha, he belonged to her.

But didn't it give the feel of a cast-off? An old shoe, thrown up in the loft? So that the days on the bog were an effort, she'd to struggle to make herself go on.

Was it for this she'd rejoiced in the marriage?

Musha, if there was only a stray buck, or an old fellow, searching a woman for his hearth, wouldn't she give more than two winks? Perhaps be a bride herself?

"Isn't it a shame Barrett's such a foolah, having us out so early?" Morgan's dry comment catapulted Annie back to the hearth.

"Weren't we always fine in May?" Annie said crossly. "Without Barrett pestering, so that we'd all be getting our feet wet?"

"Oh, it's not he wants us soaked," said Morgan. "He gets ideas, progress, he calls it. Aren't we all that way sometimes?"

"You're defending the man, with ourselves half killed?"

"Oh, now, Annie." Morgan was sorry for speaking at all. Wasn't it past time, and the three of them still by the fire? He looked over at Minnie, whose eyes were closed. She seemed to be dozing. "No matter," he said.

"Wasn't Barrett even pushing for breasting?" snapped Annie, not to be pacified, so strangely unsettled she was. "A sad lot, full down in the muck. That he'd do better to leave us alone."

"They do be breastin' at home," said Minnie shyly, rousing

herself. She stretched her arms and yawned. "It's the deepness, don't ye know? Had they these thin bogs . . ." She yawned again, too tired to debate the matter. Besides, who cared? As long as they'd turf for the fire? She stood up, looked expectantly at Morgan.

But Annie persisted. She felt almost as if the old serpent had gotten his hooks into her. She glared at Morgan, as if it was his fault the village was out so early. Indeed, it seemed he *was* to blame. Morgan, not Barrett, had tampered with the cutting. Given them all wet feet.

She threw reason aside. "Haven't I seen the Ballyrea breasting?" Recent memories of those backward people down in the muck, their flat spades having to make two separate cuts, flooded her. She saw the O'Neils clear and plain. Father. Son. Crazy old woman. Mud-spattered, the lot of them. The old man jabbing his slane horizontal into the turf bank, the turfs like severed heads dripping with bog-muck. And above them, on the bank, the black, oozing piles.

Then another thought struck. Morgan's performance in the old days. Unforgettable! A splendid sight. Cutting precisely, one swift jab of the foot slane. Strong thrusts, then little jabs that cleared the peat from the spade. Beautiful to watch. "Ah, you were a wonder," she whispered, too low for Morgan to hear.

On Sunday following, the men came in. All the regulars were there, Pat O'Gavagan in his place by the fire, old Mulrenin, Pat's crony, seated also in a chair. Pompous Colman Ronan rocked back and forth on one of the low painted stools, while O'Dowd, following Ronan's lead, took a second stool. Pat O'Donnell stood by the hearth. Barrett, seemingly no shame in him over the turf cutting, occupied a third stool. He sat calmly blowing smoke rings, completely missing the anger.

The evening was mild, very mild, but Morgan had nevertheless made a good crackling fire. It'd give them something to look at.

Duffy the bachelor could decide neither to lean on the hearth nor to sit on the hob, a chair being out of the question, given his poor land and no cow. Instead he hung by the door, cap on his head. Only a nervous twitching, a sporadic shift of his shoulders, proved he was breathing at all. As usual, he said nothing. But then, as Ronan insisted, the little weasel'd hardly a thing to say wasn't already said twice over, unless he was braggin' of the Yank brother. And what braggin' was there, since the year the brother'd lost the wife?

Finally, after Morgan was officially seated, Duffy made himself comfortable on one side of the hob. Ronan glared. When Duffy's head lifted slightly there was a brief, awkward moment as his pensive eyes met Ronan's.

The evening was in full progress when Minnie suddenly appeared from the haggard. Just finished the milking she stopped short at sight of the visitors. She blushed furiously, considered slipping back to the cow house. But when Morgan noticed her there was nothing to do but be seated.

The men gaped. Never had they beheld such a sight.

Her eyes showed strain, her face tired and white, but nevertheless she was heaven. The girl was an angel in earth clothes.

"Are you going to introduce us?" Colman Ronan, the first to speak, stepped boldly forward. But with the angel's hand in his, the brashness gave way. Confusion swept him. He stammered and stuttered. And when the celestial vision smiled his heart came near to stopping. He collapsed back on his stool.

The rest fared no better. One by one they stepped forward, eager, but when faced with the girl they faltered. Even the two old men, O'Gavagan and Mulrenin. Only Duffy maintained dignity. "I'm happy for yez," he said bashfully but with deliberateness, and Minnie's green eyes were grateful.

Later, when Annie came in, there was tea and cake, and sweets. And bread with bright yellow butter from the shed. Morgan served whiskey all around. The evening grew special.

But the whiskey was barely finished, Annie pouring the second cup of tea, when Ronan, itching for trouble, blurted out what burned in his mind. They'd no business in the bog so early. "We've other to do," he ranted, "even if the corn is in. That we needn't be out so soon."

"We always wait until May," added O'Dowd. "Sure, is there anyone but Barrett doesn't know?"

"This *is* May," Barrett retorted.

"But we're not really *into* May," insisted Ronan. The words hung oily, supercilious, provocative.

We're in for it now, worried Morgan, looking over at Minnie. What would she think of the hooligans?

But Minnie's face was serene. She sat quietly, paying no attention, daintily drinking her tea.

Ronan stood up, pompous as a rooster, his regular abrasive self. "You had us out in *April*. You sent us into the muck. Like the backward crowd does be."

"We should've waited," said O'Dowd piously, crossing himself.

April's the driest month," snapped Barrett. "Not near the rain." His face reddened. "April's grand for turf. If you'd taken my lead we'd've been cutting earlier."

The outrageous statement hung like a noose in the air. There was only the crackling of the fire. A wave of disagreement began at one side of the room, near the door to the haggard. It swelled, moved ominously across the hearth, past the yellow licking flames, swept over the visitors. The silence deepened. There was only the pulsating motion of energy.

A full-scale battle threatened. Morgan's hackles rose. Not so much over Barrett's foolishness as the group's taking him seriously. Their disgraceful belligerence. Couldn't they ignore him? Had they no sense?

"Many's a day I spent in the bogs," Ronan said, "that I'd let a streeleen tell me how. But there's no quieting you. So that didn't I fall in, with water to me neck, and didn't I near to drown?"

"Indeed. Ronan nearly drowned, God help us." O'Dowd's hushed voice fell on the solemn gathering.

Barrett knew they had a point. Bog holes were dangerous. Ronan was stupid, not spotting the edge of the bank. Too busy, as usual, expounding. It served the damn fool right. "You've no mind blaming me," he shouted, his nose in Ronan's face.

Instantly the rest were on their feet.

Ronan's fist was at Barrett's nose, barely missing. The two men glared. As yet, no blows. It seemed for a moment they'd settle it.

Then Ronan struck. Swiftly. A blow on Barrett's chest. They grappled. Blows rained. Barrett shouted, reeled.

"Drown me?" yelled Ronan. "It's nothing at all that ye'd *drown* me?"

The unready Barrett floundered, regained his balance. "Blame me?" he shouted. "Yourself a bag of wind! Why weren't you dead in the bogs these ten years, so little mind you pay?"

The fight raged. The two men clung. Around them, in a knot, the spectators tried to pull them apart. A cut appeared on Ronan's eye.

"Give him air! Give him air!" O'Dowd yelled, but no one stopped to listen. Not even the old men. They were hoarse along with the rest. "There's a lad!" crowed Mulrenin. "Give 'im one!"

"*Omathon! He's hurt.*" O'Dowd struggled in vain, tried to separate the brawlers. The knot refused to give. "There's an injury, you fools!"

A thin red stream trickled from Ronan's eye, and his face had a deadly whiteness. "Fookin' clod!" he screamed. "That ye'd bang me eye, I'll kill you!"

Abruptly the fight was over. Morgan had just cried, "Great Jesus, will you stop?" when Ronan slumped, exhausted. Barrett collapsed. "No more," cried Ronan, and Barrett agreed.

Annie fetched clean water. A rag was put to Ronan's cut and when his face was clean a new calm entered the kitchen. Everyone shook hands with the pugilists. Even Duffy stepped forward, saying it'd been a grand showing. "I've never seen the like," he said.

But Morgan was mortified. They were hooligans.

He looked around for Minnie, aware suddenly she was missing. The fight had frightened her. But to leave so quiet, and not a word said?

Immediately came a call for whiskey, and more tea. Poor Annie was run off her feet, with everyone putting away at least two cups of tea. Ronan and Barrett drank three, after their whiskey gone in a gulp. So that not until the pipes were lit, smoke fogging the air, was Morgan able to reflect.

He sat tense on the edge of his chair, eyes on the closed bedroom door. Was it there she was? Crying alone from these ruffians? For wasn't it taxed she was, these past days? The bog work, surely.

He'd put a stop to it. She'd only bring the cows out, do the milking. Or whatever easy work suited. No more catching the sods and then piling them. Bog work was too much. He'd talk to the sister, lay down the law. Before real harm was done.

He slipped quietly across to the bedroom and opened the door. She was not there.

CHAPTER
13

Minnie had fled to the cow house, so that by the time the battle entered full swing she was long since settled, perched on the edge of the feed trough. She sat quietly, inhaling the fragrance of cow breath, the moist softness.

What ailed these Kilmaragh men? Couldn't they borrow good sense from the cows?

"Yeer the darlins," breathed Minnie, running her hands over first one then another. Letting one cow nibble her, another lick her face. Later she pulled the milking stool to the door, out into the half light.

Evening had deepened. The twilight was ripe with fragrances, strange perfumes mingling exotically with the rich smells of the cows. Across the sharp-sloping field the salt smell of the sea.

Beyond the bare oaks, far down, waves beat against the sand, swept the shingle. Threw it against the rocks. And when the shingle slid back it clinked down onto the flatness below. From out in the rapid darkness came the cry of an odd, remote bird.

Minnie slipped out of the cow house. Past the bent oaks, down the long sweep of grass. The sea spread itself before her, cliff edge beckoning. Below, grey-silver water beat against the granite outcroppings.

She crept to the cliff edge, sitting quietly, staring out at the bay. The light had grown faint, only a grey luminescence. Two dark shapes, narrow, side by side nearly, were faint against the horizon. Fishermen? She watched the boats approach. The curved bows cut the water like knives. Three men in each. A single set of arms, moving in unison. The curraghs neared the shore, rowers cheering. Answering cheers from the shore.

Beyond in the bay, the horizon grew still with the dying day. "Glory be," she whispered.

When Morgan found her she had fallen to her knees. He rushed to her, shouting, but she appeared to almost not hear. "Haven't I been calling?" he cried, snatching her back from the cliff edge. "Why did you go off? And we not knowin' what side of the heaven or earth to be lookin'? The men wondering if I'd still a wife at all."

Minnie struggled to rouse herself. "But we'd hardly a puddle or a bit of a lake at all," she cried. "Ballyrea'd only an old cow pond, or a rocky stream. Sure, and just the bogs." She burst into angry tears.

"Well, there's ocean enough here to be drowneding you!"

"Am I the fool, that I'd be throwin' myself in the sea?" Her eyes grew fiery. "Haven't we the world to be lookin' at, that we aren't to be all our days slavin'? Missing the wonders?" Ah, if only dear Mattie were here, not this farmer. Wouldn't Mattie be one for the amazement.

Morgan's anger evaporated. "Ah, no. Ah, no," he said, reaching out to touch her. "I know you've to be seeing. But there's dangers, don't I be knowing? That you might slip and fall down from the cliff."

"Haven't I sense? Ye've no trust? And where's yeer concern for my needs?" Despair overwhelmed Minnie. She felt a great, empty aching. Wasn't it a strange world, allowing a taste of enchantment, then heartlessly snatching it away? Giving a commonplace in exchange?

"There's many's fell from the cliff," said Morgan. "They do be reaching for the flowers. Or a wee child chases a bird. The last one, hunting plovers' eggs he was. And they'd a job getting him up, the poor bones that was left . . . So you see it's no imprisoning I'm wanting. Only for your safety."

"But I've never seen the sea," she said. "Only the few waves, the day from Ballyrea. And there were no fishermen. They're below now, don't ye hear them?"

"It's no mind you've to be taking of the fishermen." His

tone had grown sharp. "We're farmers. That you needn't to be running down here in the nighttime."

"Well, isn't it stern ye are, now that we're wed?" Minnie's tears spilled over again. Her own husband suspecting her. Believin' the old crone. She began weeping freely, and Morgan grabbed her tight in his arms, caressing her, though she struggled. He begged forgiveness, squeezing her to him.

Later, in the bedroom off the kitchen, he again asked forgiveness. He took her in his arms, spoke shyly of his pride, said she was the wonder of his life. "Didn't the men gape, each knowing I've a jewel?"

"Ah, no. It only seemed." But Minnie knew they'd stared. She'd seen their yearnings.

Morgan kissed her feverishly. When his passion was over he dozed. She heard his quick snore, felt the weight of his head on her breast. But even after he slept deeply she was awake, her thoughts riotous. She was drenched with love for Mattie.

Annie was off to Westport—it was the Sunday following the fight—and no sooner was she on her bike than Minnie lay down for a nap. Morgan himself was tired, the week had been long in the bog, but better use, he lamented, should be made of Annie's absence. Yet wouldn't he be the streeleen, asking the duty in the daytime? What wife would put up with it?

Still, he wrestled with himself. A burning had started and soon began to spread. Sure, there wasn't a thing but the closed door stopping him? He leaped from his chair, moved swiftly toward the bedroom, changed his mind, sat down again. Minnie was tired. Wasn't it only this morning for Mass that Annie'd urged her not to go? (Of course, off she went anyway, saying the prayers would do her good.)

He resigned himself to his chair, emptied his pipe in the low-smoldering fire, took another pipe-fill. He tapped the bowl a tender tap. The tobacco began to settle. "That's the girl," he crooned. "Ah, yes," and he exhaled a sigh of contentment. There were the pleasures, thanks be to God. And wasn't it enough she never refused in the nighttime? So that when Denny O'Donnell showed up at the door, Pat O'Donnell quick behind him, wasn't it almost a relief, with the matter settled for him?

"Sit down," he said. He swept Annie's knitting from a chair. What in the name of God had Denny the ten miles? Nothing better for a Sunday afternoon? "When herself's awake there'll be tea," he said.

"Minnie's well?" Denny threw his cap on the table, fitting himself into a chair as if it were the only thing on his mind. But Pat was ill at ease. "Resting is it?" he said, indicating the bedroom. "They do be tired."

Denny nodded, as if he'd a wife himself.

"And Annie?" Pat puffed vigorously. "Isn't it resting all of them does be, when they get the dinner into them?"

"Ah, no. She's off to Westport since dinner."

As by prearranged signal Pat got quickly to his feet. "I'll be leaving yourself and Denny." He looked meaningfully at his cousin. Denny flushed slightly, snapping his suspenders. "Well, be back," he said, "before Morgan has the tea."

Morgan sucked on his pipe. The silence deepened. From the bedroom came sounds of the bed creaking.

"Oh, before she gets up," said Denny in a rush. He pulled his chair close.

Morgan put his head in at Minnie's door. "Have no mind," he said. "It's a private word Denny wants."

"Ah, now," said Denny, when the door closed. "It was Duffy's brother wrote him," he began, pulling the words from his mouth carefully. He put his cap on again, lit his pipe.

Morgan was puzzled. That poor bachelor Duffy had Denny all the way here on a Sunday? "Duffy?" he said.

"The brother wrote Duffy from America." Denny removed his cap, jiggled it on his knee. "Myself read the letter."

"The brother that lost his wife? Isn't it a sad world? All the way to America and then to be left alone."

"That's the one," said Denny, sitting very straight. "There's only the two brothers. Not a sister either."

"I'd hardly know him, the long years he's gone."

"Well, Duffy'd know him. He puts great store by the brother. Sure, Duffy grieved for a year when the wife died, even though he'd never met her."

"How would you know of his grieving, he never opens his mouth, the little weasel?"

"Now, Morgan, Duffy's not a weasel. You're not to be sayin' it."

"Ah, sure, I'm only kidding. Don't they all say it? We've got to be having some little joke."

"Like I said, Duffy's had a letter." Denny's tone grew inflated.

"Isn't it quick the news is?"

Denny ignored the sarcasm. "Here's the proposition. There's a boy, you know. Tommy. Ten years old."

"There is indeed. Isn't it the only time Duffy opens his mouth, when he's a picture for showing round?"

"Are you interested in what I've come for, or is it just to be jabbin'? Duffy's only fault's bein' a quiet man, so poor the father left him."

"Quiet indeed. Now you're talking. And poor. Isn't his best crop only rocks?"

"Now, is that Duffy's fault?"

The door to the bedroom opened and Minnie slipped into the room. She took the blue-painted stool by the door. Denny looked at her nervously. "Now, I'll get to the reason Duffy sent me," he said.

"Duffy sent you?"

Even Minnie looked up in surprise.

"Him bein' a bit shy, all these years a bachelor."

"And what else could he be, nothing but stones growing?"

"That'll change. Duffy's come into something. That's why he's asking."

Suddenly it was Morgan who grew flustered. Minnie leaned forward. "Isn't he a poor man?" she asked. "And likely to stay that way?"

"Duffy was a poor man, until the letter from his brother. Ye'll be glad enough to know him, once the news gets out."

"Glory be to God, Denny," burst out Minnie. "That you'd have us sittin' on our seats dyin'?"

"As I'm after sayin'." Denny grew magnanimous. "Though you may not have picked it up, Duffy's poverty's a thing of the past, once the marriage takes place."

"Marriage?" A shiver ran down Morgan's back. "Who's the bride, will you tell me?"

"Now, I don't take kindly to your sarcasm, Morgan. When he's come into his good fortune, ye'll be glad to claim acquaintance."

"What good fortune? Rocks, poverty and squinty eyes?"

"You'd better be listenin' hard or it's never forgivin' you Annie'll be!"

"Annie?" The name burst from Morgan and Minnie at the same time.

"Don't make me get ahead of myself."

"You're wearing me out." Morgan shook his head in confusion. "Make us the tea, Minnie. Don't wait for Pat."

"Wait." Denny's voice rose to a shriek. "America's been good to the brother. Except for losin' the wife. He's a little business. A butcher shop."

"A shop is it?" There was respect in Morgan's voice, despite himself. "So the boy'll get a shop?"

"No," said Denny firmly. "That's not what the father's in mind. He's to come and live with Duffy, the boy is."

"In that poor shack?"

"It won't be that poor shack, as you've so tactlessly put it," Denny said. "It's not alone the boy'll be comin'." Denny paused dramatically. "Somethin' else's accompanyin' the boy. Money. The brother's made a lot of it, and more every day."

"A boy with a satchel of greenbacks?"

"Will you let me finish? There's a lawyer. Duffy's to get an allowance, more than enough for the boy. Enough to fix the house. Oh, Morgan, you'll be bitin' your tongue."

"And the boy'll be eating rocks?"

"You will bite that tongue." But Denny laughed. "Rentin' land, that's what Duffy's to do. Crop land. And a meadow for the cow."

"Sure, Duffy's no cow?"

"And a new cow in the bargain."

"But what'll the boy do when he's grown? America like the father?"

"That's what the lawyer's for. The boy'll get it all. The house. The land. The cow. All his. He'll be, as it were, son to them both. When Duffy's ready to give over, it's the nephew'll step in. And the brother'll be sick of the beef racket and he'll be back himself. Him and Duffy's both set for their old age."

Morgan shook his head in bewilderment. "But where's the benefit? Motherless with the Yanks or motherless with Duffy? No one still to wipe his nose?"

"That's where Annie comes in. Duffy needs a wife."

"Jesus!"

"Now, don't be carryin' on, Morgan. This is serious business."

"Oh, I'm not carrying on. I'm just watching the crazy birds fly over your head."

"I'll be damned if I'll put up with this." Denny jumped to his feet. Minnie put a hand on his arm. "Sit down now, won't ye? Morgan, give the man his chance. How do you know what might suit Annie? There's some goes late in life and all the happier for it."

"Thank you, Minnie," said Denny. "The thing is, Annie would suit very well. There has to be a wife before the boy sets foot on the boat. And a young wife won't do. There's got to be no question of giving over, when the time comes. And if there's a young wife, well, it could be complicated. But with Annie . . ."

Minnie sat motionless. Mother o' God, what would Annie say?

Morgan's face was expressionless. He plucked his pipe from the dresser. "The little fellow's ten?" His voice was deceptively mild.

"That's right," said Denny, choked with emotion.

Morgan pondered deeply, letting his eyes roam to the ceiling. "Nothing wrong with the boy?" he asked. "That you're forgetting to tell me?"

"It's a hard man, you've become, Morgan. From the quiet fellow you was at your own match."

"All right, the boy's fine. But sending off your only son? The other side of the world?"

"Don't you see? He'll come some day himself, the brother. They'll be reunited."

"But the boy'll have hair on his face, surely, before he'll be getting the farm?"

"Now, I'm only here to put it through. I haven't a thing to say what the brother should do with his life. I'm merely the speaker, sent to draw it down."

For nearly an hour they haggled, Morgan finally asking forthrightly what fortune Duffy'd be requiring. "Two hundred? Rocks instead of turnips? Not even a cow?"

"But what have I been tellin' you? You'll never see the like when he's the brother's money. Yeerself'll look the poor country boy, I'm thinkin'."

"Well, isn't it a fine slate roof Annie's used to? That she'd put up with the bit of raggedy thatch that Duffy's got? Didn't the hens used to roost in the roof? And didn't an egg or two fall in the soup, them sitting anxious below?"

"You're a disgrace, Morgan. The things you do be sayin'." Denny broke out in a sweat. So near. So near. "But isn't many has hens in the roof?" he said. "And glad for the eggs near at hand? That ye needn't be puttin' the hex on poor Duffy, a man that does what he can."

"Maybe so. Maybe so."

Minnie, too, struggled. Life without Annie? Who'd be to do the heavy work? Her own slim hands? Visions of the haggard rose up. The peat bog. Herself hard on the black dripping sods. Pitching the foul spatter, her own skirts muddy.

But not only the bog work, wasn't there the hens? Feedin' the pigs? The fire? Washin' and mendin'. The knittin'. The lamp lit early on the wet days.

Or in the springtime. With Morgan at the plow wasn't it Annie always followin', droppin' the hard bright corn wherever the rows? A sure hand. And the hay, savin' it. Rakin' and stackin'—didn't Morgan brag? Bindin' the sheaves, as good as a man by his side?

Ah, musha, wouldn't it be a sad day if Annie was a bride?

Yet poor Annie, what of her happiness, a chance for a home of her own? A good heart and a strong back, hadn't she with all a womanly nature, could give a man ease by the fire? Duffy'd be lucky. So that it'd be a queer one indeed that'd deny her? Or complain at her leavin'?

Minnie broke the silence. "Have you a snapshot of the boy?"

She gazed at a thin little face, the sweater and knickers, the child holding a wee spotted dog. The camera caught him lowering his head to rest it against the dog's. "Look, Morgan," she said. "The sweet little fellow. But sore in need of lovin'."

Annie cried all night after Morgan told her. The idea was crazy, for a spinster long past marrying. But morning brought the sunlight. There might be something in it after all. A child. And sure Duffy wasn't a bad sort, and it'd give Morgan and Minnie the house to themselves. Besides, there were worse things, with the new roof tin.

And, sure, wasn't Duffy a modest man, for a quiet sort like

herself? Placid. Not one for arguing and fighting. Weasel, indeed! The rest of them would do well.

Yet at the thought of a man in her bed, not so much as a rosary bead between them? She trembled.

Though perhaps Duffy wasn't much for it either? Long years, with not a hope? They say the need does be dyin'.

No, Duffy'd grab for it, the chance presenting. She'd have the duty, too. But it'd be worth it for the sake of the child.

In the end a letter was sent, the brother to begin sending money. And with the new roof, a cow and the crop land, they'd appoint an evening. Duffy and Annie'd walk out. The important thing was the work on the house. That done, the talks could proceed.

Two weeks following, again on a Sunday afternoon, Minnie spoke to Morgan. "We'll walk up the hill." Wasn't the sun bright and the ocean serene? (Annie was off at the neighbors, and all needed doing was done.)

Word of the child could not be delayed. And it must appear his. Lying was a hard thing, and sinful, but the truth was out of the question. And there'd be a second lie with the babe coming early. How could she explain that? Early births ran in her family?

Morgan followed her out to the yard, to the plain where the field rose. "We'll go up and look at the view," she said.

The hill was steep. At the ridge of rock, Minnie suggested they sit down. "That was a short walk," joked Morgan. " 'Til I've me breath," said Minnie. Morgan grew concerned. "Were you up to this?"

"Ah, yes."

"You've looked tired. It's the bog work."

"Perhaps. But we've to talk. There's news. There's to be a child."

"Good God!" Morgan jumped to his feet. "And I'm after letting you walk the hill? Ah, Minnie. Are you sure? Doesn't it take a while to tell? We're hardly the month wed?"

"The weddin's a month and two days. And doesn't a woman be knowin'? I've not come 'round. I've the queasiness."

"God help us, a child. I'm to be a father. Morgan Riley of Westport, the father of a son."

"Ah, we don't know that."

"Of course. Wouldn't I treasure a daughter? Ah, Minnie. Are you truly sure? Did I ever think this day could come?"

"You're to be a da, and there's not a bit of a mistake in it. We're to be a family."

He clasped her in his arms. "We've to go back to the house. There's love's way for me to tell you."

"Not now. We'll sit a bit. Later perhaps. Before Annie's back."

CHAPTER
14

Ballyrea lay bathed in sun, the wild, riotous sheen of midsummer coloring the days. Mattie O'Malley had been long on the hill. Since daybreak he'd lain on the slope in the grass. Eyes closed, cap over his face, he slept. The gun lay by his side.

Only later, in the clear light, the sun full up, did he pick up the gun, examine it. He searched the hill for signs of life. "They're up!" he exulted softly, at the puff of grey smoke from the chimney. The Maughans' cabin had come to life.

He turned in earnest to the gun, and removed the shell.

Gently he stroked the waxed casing. "Smooth, ye are." He dropped the shell into his pocket. With the shotgun between his knees he leaned back, bracing his body against a rock. Slowly, methodically, he worked at the grime, polishing until grey steel emerged from the rust. "A gun is fer wreckin'?" he muttered, cursing the uncles, their bare, half-ruined cabin. "Old geezers." He rubbed and rubbed. There was no sound, only the rag on the barrel.

The morning deepened. Occasionally a bird screamed. A rabbit raced for its warren. Warm July sunlight poured down on the slope. In the distance the bare rock mountain grew vivid. A breeze rustled the long grass.

Only after he had oiled the gun, wiping away the excess, was Mattie satisfied. He held the shell, stared at it reflectively. A final act remained—sentimental, maybe. Foolishness even. But Minnie would understand. He raised the shell to his lips, tasted the brass, slid his tongue over the wax coating, ending with a long full kiss to the tip. "Now yeer ready." He slipped the shell in the breach.

He held the gun to his shoulder, shutting one eye. Sighted. The cabin in view on the hill above, he swung the gun to the right, swept sideways, went rigid as Old Maughan appeared. He grasped the gun, threw himself on the ground, slid forward. Slowly. Uphill through the deep grass, a watchful gliding forward, knee-high grass hiding him. His shirt became sweat-drenched. Anticipation swept him. Sweat broke out on his brow, dripped into his eyes. Shit! Pausing he wiped his face with his shirtsleeve.

He attained the rise, trembled, lay motionless. Voices? Very clear, close. He saw the cabin just above him. His breathing quickened. The thrill of near danger honed his senses. He moved the gun forward, cocked it, sighted again, cursed under his breath—there was only the nephew, the new wife behind him.

He looked again. Now there were four. No, five. Old Maughan and the wife. Christ. Herself decked out like a pig for a fair. Denny O'Donnell holding a camera, the rest smiling and grinning, holding their hands against the sun, parading their Sunday clothes. Denny separating them, moving them closer, telling them, "Smile."

Mattie drew in his breath, felt the weight of the gun on his shoulder. He decided to wait.

Activity intensified at the cabin, one snapshot following rapid on another. "Cows front and center," roared Denny, master of ceremonies. Old Maughan and Brian stepped lively. The haltered cows were moved to the front, kicking their hind legs. John Maughan, two bridles to a hand, coaxed them, so that, finally, the old man and the four cows stood smack in front of the door. "Well, isn't it a grand cow house it'll look like we have?" John Maughan laughed heartily. "But sure, isn't it crazy we are, doin' all this? When did we ever have a picture?"

"Ah, but Minnie wants it. She misses us. And when Annie marries that Duffy won't she be showin' them 'round?"

"I suppose. They'll all be envyin' her fine relations."

"Don't ye be doubtin' it. Annie herself is gettin' grand. It was probably her idea for the snapshots. Thinkin' Minnie might be thought backward. Hasn't this Duffy the great new set-up? Two rocking chairs. A rug by the door, concrete coverin' the dirt. Three shelves on top of the new dresser, with matching cups and dishes. And with all that, a new roof. Have ye ever heard?"

"And now d'ye want the pigs?" Denny asked.

"We'll get the pigs with the rest. Just snap the cows. Quick! I think they're goin' to poop." Sure enough, great oozy mounds covered the ground by the door. "Did ye get it?" said Maughan.

"Come on now," said Denny. "I've only three left, and we've not the lambs or the pigs. Ye need the hens, too. Though I think I've hens in them all."

"Yeer hard put not to, the way Katie's them runnin'," said John Maughan cheerfully.

"They're Chrissie's chickens now," said Katie with a quick laugh, giving the look of a wife well rid. "Pen up yeer birds," she snapped at the bride.

"A bit of a fence might make them mind." Chrissie tossed her red hair, nose held high.

"Ah, what's a bird or two?" put in Maughan, the peacemaker since the wedding. "It shows them how we're livin'."

"How are we livin'?" asked Chrissie.

Katie, miffed, searched for a sharp retort. "We're class," she said.

"Katie." John Maughan put an arm around her waist.

"We *are* class. And we should've gone to Westport. Had real pictures taken, never mind the snapshots."

"Don't mind." John waved his arm. Brian Maughan led up the pigs. "We'll be to Westport before ye know."

Almost at the moment the shutter clicked, a rustling began in the grass. A long grey gun barrel, reflecting sunlight, rose up. Steadied. Immediately there was a roar. An explosion of smoke and fire and smell and sound.

From the cows, a leaping and roaring and bellowing. Great frantic honks from the geese. Squealing pigs. Mewling from lambs and the sheep. The chickens gone crazy. And silent in the midst of it, his only movements a frenzied twitching, John Maughan bloody in the dust.

Minnie, when they told her, fell dead to the floor in a faint. Brian Maughan, spent after the ten-mile race in the trap, watched helpless. Morgan, fetched from the top field by Annie, went nearly daft himself. "Murdered!" he roared. "Minnie's darlin' da's been murdered?"

Near collapse, the nephew told and retold his wild story. How they'd been all of them having a grand time, just finished the animals. Old Maughan moving backwards, giving a quick look down the hill. And didn't the gun let loose and he all but fell dead on the spot? "And if he wasn't yet dead in the instant, wasn't it in no time at all that he was? Blood like ye've never seen. An open wound, the front of him. And ourselves not seein' the O'Malley, so deep hid in the grass he was."

"But what grievance?" Morgan was beside himself, with Minnie so still on the floor. "Who is this O'Malley?" he shouted. "That he'd pull down the wild wrath of heaven? For there'll be no forgivin', mind my words. No forgivin'. Not for a crime such as this."

"They're a backward crowd, the O'Malleys. But what it was came over him, sure I couldn't say myself. And there isn't a word to be had out of Katie. Wasn't she screamin' to high heaven, and still in a fit when I left? . . . Poor Denny. Himself half killed with the grief, so thick he was with Old Maughan."

Minnie stirred, cried out sharply. "What is it ye say of O'Malley?" she gasped, seizing Morgan's arm. Sickness swept her again and she lay back. When she awakened she lay covered by a sheet, a pillow supporting her head. She was in her bed. "Morgan?" she called out, aware of pain in her throat. "Morgan?" Quickly he knelt by the bed, reached for her hand. "Darlin'?"

"Was it killed they said was my da?"

"Ah, Minnie. Have no care." He kissed her fingers, stroked her hair. "Think of the child. Be calm."

"I've to know." She closed her eyes. She waited for his answer, for the reassurance. Her da? Shot by an O'Malley? Mattie? Ahhhhhh!

Minnie's screams bounced from the ceiling, hit the white-washed walls, skittered up into the loft-room, out the rafters.

It was only later, well into late evening, with the doctor fetched out from Westport, that Minnie lay soundless, calmed into a deep, sedated sleep. "And in the morning let her be off to see for herself," said the doctor. "Only the brown shroud will convince her. There isn't another thing will do it. I've seen it before."

"But what of the child?" said Morgan. "'Tis only begun."

"No harm. It's the mother herself you've to be careful. The child will be fine."

He paused at the door. "This is the dangerous time," he said, "before they know it fully. You've to be certain she's kept from the cliffs—don't leave her. She'll be fine later, when it's settled in her head."

Minnie stared at the da's dread face. Colorless. Alien. Already nearly unrecognizable. Slack mouth awkwardly drooping. Chin pillowed, a second pillow buttressing the shattered cheek. The flesh had loosened. "Da?" She stood in the doorway, transfixed. It was this that Mattie'd done?

Katie Maughan turned from the corpse. "Ye've come," she said, bewildered eyes on her daughter's face. Her voice was hoarse. "Come in and see yeer da, daughter."

Minnie moved forward into the packed kitchen.

"Catch Minnie, she's falling!" "Make space!"

But Morgan had her.

There were gasps, wheezes. Little cluckings and keenings, scraping sounds, as even the borrowed chairs were moved forward. The room quivered.

What would he say, the farmer? The husband. Did he know? Or had she denied it? She led him on, that Mattie. It was her that set him to it, as much as if she'd been there. Surely, she'd a hand on the gun?

And as for the O'Malley, he'd earned the noose, God forgive him. Oh, the shame of it. Once they'd caught him. But the sweet wee girl with the look of an angel to her devil's face, oh, she'd go scot-free. No end of the rope for her, musha, God save us. Yet the sign of the whore in her heart. Where was the justice?

Morgan moved swiftly, parting the crowd with his urgency. They fell back. Tenderly he carried Minnie to the hearth chair, placed her upright, supported her slumped head.

"Isn't it hard taken she is?" said Chrissie O'Bannon Maughan. She rolled her eyes, swung her red hair. For wasn't the murder shameful? One and all but wouldn't be ruined? And who knew the half of it? For many was kissed with a pat on the buttocks but few took a gun to the da.

She turned to look at her husband, challenging him.

"Make no mind of it," he ordered.

"Isn't it on all of us?" she snapped. Her bright, hill-country
eyes flashed. There was a gasp and the room fell silent. An old
woman coughed, and spat noisily. Brian Maughan's gaze was
on his wife, fixing her where she stood. He shook his head.
"Make no mind of it," he repeated. "The deed is full done, so
see to the girl." Chrissie obeyed, assisting Morgan. Morgan's
embarrassed glance swept the nephew and his wife and then,
in confusion, turned to his own wife. Christ and the great saints.
What was it?

Chrissie gave a little swipe of her apron to the sweat on
Minnie's brow. "The whole long trip in the cart and this for
yeer reward?" she commiserated. "It's a pity." But she assessed
the watchers, gauged the loyalties. Who'd hang firm? Who
couldn't abide? Were they all disgraced? Was it already decided? Or would it be, "There's a bad one in every lot"? The
grand cows and the six chairs holding them?

Surely, they weren't all to be banished? Herself and Brian
Maughan with a life bare begun? A stain on their unborn
children, and their children's children alike? Which way would
Ballyrea see it? How judge them? She tried to sort the faces, but
they were impassive now, impossible to know.

Only later, she decided, in the deep night, would they do
their heavy settling, their adjudicating. Only after some had
crept off to their cottages, leaving the poor half-dead widow
with her corpse, with her daughter, the two of them to smell its
deterioration together, make their peace as best they could.
That's when the judging would take place. By morning Ballyrea'd have it all decided.

And by morning it was settled. The nephew and his bride,
new owners of the six chairs and seven of the cows, were
absolved of the crime. Innocent along with the widow, not a bit
of a stain on their good name at all. Only Minnie shared the
O'Malley guilt.

During the night the decision had begun to be obvious.
Morgan had taken Minnie into the little bedroom and Annie
had slipped into a quiet back chair in the shadows, only leaving
it while the rosary was being said. It was during the gathering
near the body for the rosary that the change became noticeable.

The room was ablaze with light, candles at the head of the
table, another three burning fiercely by the feet of the corpse. A

bright lamp hung from the roof, several additional lamps on the dresser, brought from the nearest houses. Brian Maughan stood to lead the praying. "Hail Mary, full of grace! the Lord is with thee; blessed art thou among women, and blessed is the fruit of thy womb, Jesus." He waited for the response. There was a long, constrained moment of silence, as if the mourners were deliberating.

Then the room burst into prayer. "Holy Mary, Mother of God, pray for us sinners now and at the hour of our death. Amen."

After the rosary there was a definite quickening, a neighborliness, a settling-in as the night wore on. The barrel was opened and porter sent round. Whiskey and a glass passed from hand to hand. Brian Maughan broke out the clay pipes, and whenever the bowl of tobacco appeared to be emptying he rushed forward. "Don't be shy. There's plenty more."

Chrissie saw to the tea and the jam. Fresh plates of white bread, so there was always a supply on the dresser. After every great rush, a new round of butter. Sweets in a jar, and there were peppermint sticks set out on a plate. "Isn't it good to see them enjoying themselves?" Chrissie whispered to Brian, taking a lick on one of the peppermint sticks herself. "Ah, it was a close call, so be mindful," he cautioned. "We're lucky."

Next morning, towards noon, the body was brought to the church. But first came the box from the cow house, with the body tenderly lowered, the lid nailed sorrowfully shut. Four men hoisted, and it slid sideways onto the trap. Then the procession formed.

"Leave Minnie to me," ordered Morgan, when the nephew put Minnie with Chrissie. "Oh, to be sure." But the widow argued violently. "Let her accompany her family this last day. For we'll not be seein' one another." In the end Morgan gave in. But what did the ma mean, "this last day"? And what was this talk of "not seeing"?

The nephew led the horse, at his side the grieving widow. Chrissie and Minnie behind, with Morgan and Annie following. The crowd fell in line after.

Morgan walked silently, matching his footsteps to Annie's. Didn't his wife belong by his side? And the look of her and her attitude, Minnie's own? Saying nothing. Face chalky. Her shawl like a shroud—wasn't she wrapped from her head to her toes? A ghost. Was it the grief that had her so?

And what of the neighbors? So distant? With the coffin being nailed, the sighing and groaning, wasn't it all of them only crowding the ma? Hard put to breathe she was, the same for the nephew and Chrissie. But Minnie? Not one had a glance for poor Minnie.

A strange place, this backward town.

Abruptly the procession halted. Minnie had shrugged off the sister-in-law, broken free, moved quickly to the coffin. Ignoring the ma's cries she patted the box tenderly. Placed her hands on the lid, touched the entire length, the sides, the underside. "Da?" she whispered. "Yeer goin'?" She had to be pried from her hold, eased off by Brian Maughan.

The procession set off for the second time, Minnie moving woodenly, noticing nothing, not even her sobbing ma. A corpse herself, an apparition. Even after reaching the flat plain, with the straining cart moving easier, she only quickened her steps. Her face remained frozen, her body stone.

Inside she was in chaos. An immense pressure squeezed her chest, so that drawing her breath was an effort. She felt pummeled. Stripped. Mattie's deed had taken away hope. The crime defied justification. There was no understanding it, no excusing.

Life was a black song. There was no happiness. No deliverance. No redemption.

Da! she cried silently. Me darlin da! Wordlessly she screamed out to him, demanded his presence. But there was only silence. Da lay strapped to the cart, cold and dead in his box, his poor dead face disfigured, his body riddled through. Destroyed by the man that she'd loved.

Ahead of her the cart slowed. They were approaching the village. Before them was the chapel, the priest by the door. On either side straggling villagers, stone-faced, black shawls drawn close. The children silent, great round eyes curious. There were the McNultys, dashing from the shop, the shades fresh-drawn. Behind them old Nellie McGavan, who'd birthed her. Shawn Brady, who made shoes. His old mouth was shut tight, and he laid on a fierce glare. Minnie shuddered. But forcing herself to rouse, she fixed her gaze on the churchyard, on the tombstones. She stifled a scream.

CHAPTER
15

Minnie grew hysterical when they arrived at the church. Morgan, ignoring the ma, was quick at her side, telling the nephew, "I'll see to her now." Among the onlookers, the tension escalated.

First, as the coffin was eased from the cart, Katie Maughan fell down in a faint. Grabbing for her, the nephew broke into tears, then stumbled under her weight. Before anyone could assist he'd gone down in a rough heap himself. But scrambling up he brushed aside the offers of help, carried Katie to the doorstep, where the priest stood waiting.

The coffin was set down. Katie, reviving, threw herself on top of it. The mourners went wild. Their pain broke through. Katie wept. They wept. "Jasus!" "Wisha, save us!" "Mercy!" They flung themselves against the coffin. "Saints save us!" They poured out their love, called down blessings, curses. Why did he have to die? Finally, grief spent, they turned to rage.

"Hang the O'Malley!" "Vengeance!" "A curse on the womb of his ma!" Old Shawn Brady, spittle on his chin, shouted curses on the Civic Guard. Wasn't he dead since yesterday forenoon? The murderer still with his freedom. "Where are they? What's takin' them?"

Faster and louder the cries came. Turn the crime over to headquarters, to Castlebar. Forget the barracks. Get Castlebar. As the coffin was moved inside all control vanished. Where were the O'Malleys? They'd tear them to bits. They'd slaughter and hang every one of them.

Fortunately the priest kept his wits, fixed his eyes on the frenzied crowd, held them. He was a presence, God's emissary. A large man, Father Delaney nearly filled the doorway. He stood silent, the stole around his neck. The anger went out of the mob, wafted mysteriously through the air, became tangible again in the person of the priest.

"Would ye be profanin' the Lord's house?" The great booming voice brought a chill, threw a cloud across the noonday sun. Sent children to their ma's and the ma's to their husbands. Even the old women grew quiet. "For shame. That ye'd be callin' for a hangin' in these holy precincts. Hangin' can wait. We've to bury the dead." Moving quickly he splashed holy water over the coffin. The long box dripped with blessings. "This is a Christian funeral," he shouted. "We'll seat no pagans. We've a soul to send to paradise. And let ye not be forgettin' it."

Meekly the crowd filed in, Morgan ushering Minnie to the front pew, taking his place beside her. Annie struggled after. She grabbed a quick seat before the nephew could stop her, moving close to Morgan's side. The widow glared. There was a look from Chrissie Maughan. But Annie opened her missal, searched hurriedly for the burial prayers. The Maughans filed in beside her.

"Oh, Heavenly Queen," prayed Annie, closing the prayer book again. She turned instead to her heart. "Save dear brother. Don't let this unruly bunch swallow him up in their madness. Their wicked, blasphemous wildness."

The priest made the Sign of the Cross. "Introíbo ad altáre Dei." I will go in to the altar of God. Annie opened her book, prayed silently. "Confíteor Deo omnipoténti." I confess to Almighty God. Her attention wandered. She leaned forward, saw Minnie pale and drawn in the pew, the coffin not three feet before her. Half dead herself. Yet would you be thinking she was the same Minnie, all smiles and bright laughter at home? The joys and the good things of life, not a bit of a worry but getting her work done? Then the dread news. Oh, misery. She was a sweet girl. She did make brother happy. Wasn't it near killed with joy he was, poor man, since learning the news of the babe? His own son.

But there had to've been trickery. Minnie's own turned

against her? The ma herself saying, "Ye've to go." Her very own child for the road? Oh, God save us, where was truth?

Fast on this, Annie had another thought, a terrible realization. Her own life rose up, played against the candle light. What of her own situation, her future? The *match*. Her blood froze. Musha, God give her strength, her own chance was done. Her match lost. Duffy'd want quit of her—the brother'd see to that. Sure, what Yank in his senses would send a boy to them that murders? Or them that has even a connection to a murderer?

Musha, God save us. It was herself had hit the hard times. Herself that needed the solacing.

For, worst loss of all, there was Duffy. That was the misfortune. Duffy. For wasn't he sweetness itself? Not at all what they said of him. Not a sign at all of a weasel. Not a bit of a brag on him, with all the good fortune.

Quiet by the fire, any night he came over. The two of them talking over the life they'd have. Him smoking his pipe. The aroma so sweet, knowing it was your own man was puffing it. His two steady feet on the hearth. Oh, it was grand. Grand.

And now it was lost forever.

"Dóminus vobíscum."

Annie jerked to attention. Glory be to God, but she'd wandered.

The priest moved to the Gospel side. "And let ye not be sleepin'," he said, giving a cuff to one of the servers, a pinch to the ear of the second. "Sequéntia sancti Evangélii secúndum Joánnem." There was a short pause. Then he hitched up his cassock, shook the folds of the alb, gathered the people into himself, into his bulk, into the long full flow of his vestments.

He repeated the Sign of the Cross. On his forehead. His lips. His breast. "Chapter eleven, verses twenty-one to twenty-seven," he announced. The crowd, on its feet, waited humbly.

The priest hesitated. He held the book.

What stopped him? We're waiting, the respectful faces seemed to be saying. Tell us the good news of salvation. The Word. Give us hope in our misery.

But in the front row the family's heads were bowed. Only Annie and Morgan had their eyes on the priest. The rest stood unseeing. Unhearing. The priest waited. Said a second time, "Chapter eleven, verses twenty-one to twenty-seven." He began to read.

"Lord if Thou hadst been here my brother would not have died." On and on flowed the voice of God's priest, raising the poor ragtag bunch of country folk to the heights and the glories. He wove them into his omnipotence, his ascendancy. Made them part of himself. " 'Thy brother shall rise,' said Jesus."

The packed chapel listened, rapt. Sure, wasn't it only through the priest anyone ever found the way to heaven at all? Him bringin' Jesus right out of the clouds of heaven, deliverin' Him in the Sacred Bread? Unleashin' merciful forgiveness, whatever sins the poor deceased committed in life? Right here, in his nailed-shut box, the priest'd send John Maughan flyin' up to paradise. Musha, thanks be to God for the priest.

The Gospel concluded, Father Delaney tooled up for the sermon. Prepared himself heart and soul to speak.

Now the filthy murderer would get his due, wherever in the wild hills or black bogs he'd run to. Now attention would be paid.

And wasn't it also the wayward machinations of this unkempt village that needed addressin'? Bring the lot o' them face to face with their own sins? Their own unruliness?

Father Delaney moved forward, stood directly in front of the coffin. "And isn't it a miserable lot the whole crowd of yez is, that I've to be comin' here today on such an errand?" He turned his full force on the upturned faces. "Murder!" he shouted. "Murder! Can you believe it? When in the long life of these far hills did anyone take a gun and blow holes in his neighbor before? Never.

" 'Thou shalt not kill!' says the Good Book. It's God word. He forbids it. And to them that condones or encourages, or even provides sustenance to them that engages in it, the Almighty's wrath knows no bounds. Aren't I tellin' ye?

"It's to be givin' up yeer sinfulness ye've to be devotin' yeerselves. Ye've to be takin' on a new light—the light of God's brightness. His holy grace. Let the Almighty flood into yeer hearts. Savin' ye. Showin' ye the good road. And let ye be never more harborin' the likes of them that blows holes in their neighbors."

Who in the name of God was he talking about? Morgan looked worriedly at Minnie, who'd slumped against him. Look what he was doing to the poor girl, with his ranting and raving. Exhausting her. Giving the last bit of a blow to her strength on top of the terrible thing of losin' the da. Get finished, he muttered under his breath. Finish your damn blathering and let me get the girl to her rest.

Annie too glared at the grim judge standing over them. What was wrong with the man? Wasn't it enough for poor Minnie without the babbling fool railing away in front of her? That he couldn't save the fire and brimstone until they caught the one'd done the fearful deed? Lash the guilty not the innocent. But what could you expect, with the backwardness of the place?

Through all this, Minnie leaned brokenly against her husband's shoulder. Eyes closed, shawl before her face, she rested motionless, not a sign even that she was awake. A deathly hush seemed to hover around her.

Morgan placed one of his big hands on Minnie's, gave a squeeze.

Father Delaney paused for breath, searching each frightened, upturned face. Coming to rest finally on the bowed head of Minnie Maughan Riley. The deceased's daughter. The seductress. The cause. "And as to them that bears a special responsibility in this matter," he said quietly.

The congregation leaned forward, keeping their ears front, some of them, so that not a word would be missed. Now that one'd get what she deserved. That Minnie Maughan with her swirly hair had everyone gapin'. Small wonder she'd gotten into such a peck o' trouble, the good Lord havin' give her more than the rest o' them, with not a bit of humility to go with it.

"If there are them that knows," the priest said, tapping softly on the book of Prayers for the Dead in his hand, "them that has reason to feel personally responsible for the dread deed of this Wednesday past. Not that anyone here had a hand on the trigger, mind ye. Not at all am I sayin' that. No. But there are ways of lendin' assistance. Bein' party to the deed. Bein' part of the 'intention,' so to speak.

"And as ye all well know it's the intention makes the sin grievous. What's in the heart is the whole of it. Givin' incentive and motive by whatever means, do ye know what I'm sayin'? Is it the third-grade education that all o' yez thinks passes for schoolin' lets ye have an inklin' at what I've in mind?

"And then there's the matter of bad seed. Bad seed growin' in all of us. And there isn't a thing even the Lord God can do

Himself for any one of us until every scrap is rooted out. Bad seed must go. D'ye hear? Wherever it is there's a bit of the devil's own progeny hidin' it's the duty of one and all o'ye to cleanse yeerselves. Cleanse the community. Purify it. Purify it. Bring the grand love and blessings of the Almighty Saviour pouring down into yeer hearts and homes once again. So that we may all be what we're intended to be, the children of our most precious Lord and Saviour.

"Think on it, Christians. *Think on it.*"

"Credo in unum Deum . . ." Father Delaney launched into the Creed, followed quickly by the Canon. The Communion. The faithful marched eagerly forward, received the Holy Bread. The chapel quivered in silence. A beam of sunlight hit the coffin, leapt upwards. Light fell on the mourners. Lit the brave faces. Rippled the rough surfaces. Sanctified them.

"Inítium sancti Evangélii secúndum Joánnem." The Last Gospel.

The Mass was ended.

"Holy water."

The servers rushed forward. The coffin ran with blessings. "More." Holy droplets oozed to the floor. Splash went sanctifying grace.

"Incense," roared Father Delaney.

The holy fragrance swept upwards. It hung over the mourners. Bound them indelibly into the act of salvation, the priest's holy deliverance. One and all stood ready with the deceased, prepared for redemption, to be flung into paradise.

Finally the absolution ended; John Maughan was freed of sin. ". . . through the mercy of God rest in peace."

Four men hoisted the box, eased it slowly forward. At once the sad crowd surged, wailing. They swept into the aisle, surrounded the coffin. "And will ye be seated." Father Delaney turned crimson. "Ye've to be waitin'." Ballyrea became obedient. Slowly the long brown box passed unimpeded, grand in its majesty. It moved through the narrow aisle, reached the door of the church, sailed smoothly into the churchyard, where it rested finally on the shoveled dirt. Waiting.

The bearers gazed on the open grave, at John Maughan on the dirt pile, strapped into his long brown box. Their old comrade. Ready for the long road.

Ah, musha, cried one. The Lord save us.

Was there a thing in the world that could give reason or sense to killin' their hope for the future?

For wouldn't the lot o' them'd been off to Westport, too, with John goin' regular? Visitin' all the new kith and the kin? And with the lay o' the land, the dangers pointed out by John, what'd stop anyone who'd a mind? A regular procession there'd've been. Hardly a one feared o' the trip or the trottin'. Old Maughan havin' the goin' nicely under his belt.

Westport.

And now what was there?

Oh, the grief of it. Himself shortly six feet down, the lovely daughter banished. Who'd be goin' to Westport now? No one. Only these rocks and the hills for the lot o' them.

Inside the church was in uproar. First Father Delaney had rushed back of the altar to remove his outer vestments. The family would be after the coffin, he'd cautioned. "Ye just sit tight. It's the family's to lead off."

But hardly were the words spoken when Shawn Brady, the shoemaker, was up on his feet. "She's the cause!" he shouted. He pointed at Minnie cowering in the front. "Let the Civic Guard take her." Bolting the length of the aisle, and before Morgan or the nephew could prevent it, he was blazing away directly into Minnie's face. "Didn't ye lead the young buck on? Ye stirred him."

"What in the name of God?" cried Morgan, jumping up, giving a shove to the older man's chest. "*Move off now.*" Shawn Brady stumbled backwards.

"This is a sacrilege," shouted Father Delaney behind the altar. "Yeer in the Lord's house, do I have to remind ye?"

"It's the girl that's caused it," cried Shawn, old age and anger getting the better of him. "She was the one in the hay."

"Ah, isn't this the disgrace?" cried Nellie McGavan, two rows behind all the Maughans. "It's the girl's character yeer destroyin'," she screeched. "Destroyin'."

Musha, wasn't it herself had birthed that young one? That she'd be lettin' Shawn Brady be murderin' her name? For murder it was, destroying a girl's character. "And there isn't a thing on God's earth gives it back!"

Exhausted, she crossed herself. Musha, wasn't it only after buryin' three Maughan sons that she was able to birth the poor girl at all? That she'd be lettin' a streeleen the likes o' old Brady put a hex on her? Regaining her energy she took to thumping her stick on the floor. "It's murder! Murder!"

"Now, will ye stop that," shouted Father Delaney.

"For shame, Shawn Brady," piped up Mary McNulty, from the far end of the row ahead of Nellie. "Ye've every right," she encouraged the old midwife.

"For shame yeerself," whispered her husband. "Isn't it old Brady's great for givin' the orders, that ye'd want him buyin' for the shoes elsewhere?"

"Ah, no, Michael. What's a customer here and there next to the poor darlin' girl?"

"Here and there, is it? Well, I'll tell ye now. Be quiet 'til ye see what the rest o'them sez."

"Michael. Michael."

"Now I'm orderin' ye," hissed the publican. "They'll be takin' themselves off the books, not a thing left o' the shop, ye go against them. So, be still, darlin' Mary, God forgive me. See which way the most o' them's goin'. Then ye can speak yeer mind. The right mind."

There was an ominous, low-rumbling buzz. It grew louder and spread from one end of the chapel to the other. Shouts broke out, the first wild cry down near the back by the door. Then louder, from the other side, where the road outside led off to Maughan's. Last of all from the far side. Cries everywhere, calling for Minnie's ruin.

"Do ye hear them?" shouted old Brady, wagging a finger at Morgan. "Do ye know the fool ye are?"

"Oh, Mother of God and the saints," said Annie, grabbing for her dear brother's arm. "What is it?" A riot was breaking out! In the church, God save us! "It's even yourself they're accusing, not just Minnie. Will you look at them? The place is going mad."

Minnie shrank against Morgan. She was terrified. He planted his feet firmly, and when the first of the rioters drew near pushed her quickly behind him. Fists clenched, a deep rage overspreading his countenance, he faced the crowd. "Let ye be putting a hand on my wife to your peril." He took a step towards Shawn Brady, who led the pack.

"Isn't it a fine sort o' woman yeer defendin'," he hurled at Morgan, "mister grand farmer from Westport. And yeer after comin' into a poor hill town destroyin' the happiness o' the community. A backward out-o-the-way village never did yeerself a day's worth o' harm."

"Tell 'im, Shawn."

"This is God's house," came Father Delaney's roar from the back of the altar. "Yeer blasphemin'."

Petrified, Minnie huddled behind Morgan. Annie, at her side, sent prayer after prayer up to heaven.

"This is the man's daughter, for the love of God," shouted Morgan at the mob confronting him. "Have you no sense?"

"Daughter, is it? Daughter? She's his betrayer. It's her caused it. Her that's responsible. Ask her why the wild man shot him."

"Scoundrels," shouted Morgan. "Givin' the bad name and the lie to the darlingest girl in the world. You're scum. Fit for the dung heap."

"Do ye hear him?"

"Is it a wonder a crime had to happen?" yelled Morgan, gone wild with fear and rage. "It's not. Not a wonder. The marvel's the rest's here at all. That ye all haven't murdered the lot of yez. How anyone's alive's what I'm asking. In such a wild place. And the way you're carrying on?" Morgan cradled Minnie with one arm, kept the other fist at the ready. His thoughts were in chaos, one frenzied notion tumbling after another. Something had to be setting them off, crazy as the accusations were. What was it? What poor innocent deed had darling Minnie thoughtlessly done? Giving them the wrong idea, leading them to say 'twas her fault? Was there an indiscretion? A bit of walking out, setting the tongues to wagging? A look or a smile? A laugh with the lad? The false idea he'd a claim?

Or was it nothing of the sort? All of them mad with the grief? Could there be more?

A cold, sickening chill began at the base of his spine, sped upwards until it stiffened the back of his neck and made his mouth go dry.

"Tell 'im, Shawn. Give him news o' the romps in the hay."

Morgan blanched.

"Dear God," said Annie.

Morgan tried to speak. His tongue stuck. With an effort he held Minnie to his side.

Minnie gave a choked cry. Tears streamed over her death-pale cheeks.

"Dear Christ," Morgan whispered.

"*Hold it,* all o' yez!" Father Delaney pushed through the crowd. "We've a body needs buryin'." One by one the congregation yielded.

"Start the procession," said the priest. "Heaven's waitin'. Would ye be temptin' the satyrs o' Hell? Poor John left in Limbo, floatin'? Kept from joinin' the Faithful? It's sacrilegious, that's what it is. Not speedin' him fast on his way. Be quick, now. The family first. Then the lot o' yez. And no more accusin' or blame."

Brian Maughan stepped forward. Then the widow. Chrissie assisted. Morgan led Minnie, still weeping. Annie filled in at the rear.

"And now the rest o' yez," said Father Delaney. "The deceased's waitin'. It's absolution ye'll be needin', the lot of ye, if ye does be delayin' me any more in my holy task."

Outside, when they were all assembled, a profound silence settled over the grave site. The might of the heavens stared down.

Father Delaney ordered everyone present to kneel. A heart-rending wailing broke out.

"O God, by Whose mercy the souls of the faithful find rest, vouchsafe to bless this grave." Father Delaney sprinkled holy water, incensed both coffin and grave. Holy angels were called upon—they were to guard the body. And the deceased was to rejoice forever, from all bonds of sin released.

"Through Christ our Lord."

"Amen."

The body was lowered, accompanied by the silence of the crowd.

Abruptly wailing burst out again. An old woman begged God's mercy. Minnie shrieked. Brian Maughan wept soundlessly.

At length it was over—a final sprinkling, the empty holy water bottle thrown in on the coffin. The time had come to close the grave. The priest tossed the first shovelful.

"May he rest in peace."

"Amen."

The coffin bearers took over. Earth covered the coffin. Hid it. Until at last there was only a soft, loose, heaped-up mound.

Afterwards the villagers fled to the pub, McNulty and his

wife in the lead. A few stragglers waited. But there was little left to be seen. Katie Maughan said nothing, merely covered her face with her shawl. "Sure, aren't ye fine now?" said Chrissie.

Minnie hung back, but Morgan came forward to shake hands with the family. "God speed you," said the nephew. He helped the widow to the cart. Chrissie sprang up after her. "Be off," she said sharply, so Brian gave a flick to the reins. He turned the horse toward the hills. The cart moved.

For a long, pained moment Morgan watched them. Then he took Minnie's arm and, with Annie following, set out on the long walk for home.

Later, at McNulty's, there were some who said he'd cried. But others denied it. The farmer had more sense, they argued, than to weep for a man he scarce knew.

CHAPTER
16

They reached the cottage after ten, with the late evening sun just gone down. Duffy stood at the door, his face alive with concern.

Minnie let him kiss her cheek, and Morgan shook his hand. "Didn't I think you'd stayed the night," Duffy said.

Annie refused to meet his eye, so he grabbed her two hands in his own. "I've a letter," he cried eagerly. "You'll be delighted." But Annie pulled away. She hung her shawl on a hook, dropped heavily into a chair. "I'm tired," she said. Her grey knot of hair had come loose, and she pushed it over her shoulder, letting it fall carelessly.

"That you'd have no one bringing you home?" said Duffy, after a pause, and with a glance of apology at Minnie. Then gathering courage, "And that you'd be out on the road at this hour?"

No one replied. There were only the animal sounds outside, and in the distance waves hit the rocks.

Morgan sat down.

Duffy rushed to add the turfs. He stirred the embers 'til they glowed. "Pull over here to the fire," he urged Morgan, who turned his chair toward it. "The tea'll be done in a jiffy." Duffy swung the crane toward the fire. "Isn't it your own hearth that gives the best welcome?" he said.

"It's a grand spread you've fixed," said Morgan, eyeing the fresh-baked bread on the table. "See, Annie, what your man's done?"

There was jam and butter, hard-cooked eggs to the side. There was boiled chicken; someone had sliced the pink, juicy meat. "Pat O'Donnell's wife came in," said Duffy by way of explanation. "Wasn't it grand of her?" He drained the boiled potatoes.

"It's kind yourself's been," said Morgan morosely.

"I'm sure the day was a hard one," said Duffy, to break the silence.

"There's days that's worse than others." Morgan reached for bread and jam. "You'd think it was fall, so cool the evening's turned."

"Was it clear and fine in the hills? I suppose it was, Annie?"

Annie remained silent. She filled her plate with potatoes and an egg.

"Annie?"

"We've heard more than enough talk this day," she snapped, and Duffy, smarting, said gently, "Time and enough in the morn." He stood. "I'll be over early to hear." He took his cap.

"You'd hear, would you?" said Annie, the look of a trapped fox in her eyes. "There'll be plenty eager to tell."

"Ah, now, Annie," Morgan began, but Annie burst into tears. Minnie pushed her stool backwards, near to the wall, eating silently.

Annie paused by the stairs. "Don't think ye need come in the morn."

Duffy looked to Morgan, who said nothing. He sat down, pondering. What ailed Annie? Was it the Maughans, sending them off the ten miles the same day? A strange crowd.

"Now have a good meal," he said, getting to his feet. "And don't be thinking over the day. There's sadness comes to us all." He put on his cap by the door. "The letter I mentioned," he said awkwardly, "it came from the States two days past. Perhaps you could tell Annie, Morgan. The boy's coming."

"Coming?" Morgan's face grew ashen.

"They've the passage booked. The father's coming too. August third they sail. So we've to act fast on the plans."

"The plans, is it?" said Morgan.

"We'll talk with the priest on Sunday." Duffy blushed. "So when herself's calm," he said. He fled through the door.

There was a long silence before Morgan turned to Minnie.

"You hear?" His voice was strained and rough. "The boy's coming. The Yank with him. *Now* what have you to say?"

"God help me!" Minnie burst into tears.

"It's Annie's chance that's lost, don't you hear?"

"I hear. I hear." Minnie lifted her head, tried to speak. But tears choked her. She shook uncontrollably.

"I've to *know*."

Minnie said nothing. She backed against the wall, her tormented eyes on the fire.

What could she tell Morgan? How justify the day's madness? The shootin'? Them riotin', sayin' she was the cause. Should she start at the beginning? Speak of the wonders, of Mattie? The magnificent days?

Yet what of his own part? Morgan's guilt? Didn't he take her far from the one that she loved? It was his doin', the match. Why not ask him for an explanation?

Then there was Mattie. What words could she find for his deed? Killin' her da in the full light of day, standin' in the summer sun, shot down?

Ah, Mattie, it was evil ye done. *Evil.*

A frightening thought struck. Father Delaney sayin' the bad seed grew in all of us, had to be rooted out. Bad seed must go.

Was that what the child was, bad seed? Murderer's blood mixed with her own?

"I'm waiting, Minnie."

A stranger stood before her. A persecutor.

"Do ye think I've the ease in my mind?" she cried out desperately. "Bring Annie down here. Let her see the judgment yeer heapin'. No, more than the match is lost, isn't it my own heart's near breakin' too?"

"Now, I'm not accusing," said Morgan, voice rising. Sweat poured from his face. "There's a story led up to this day. I've to be hearing it. Without Annie. To a husband and wife it's to be told. No other ears. Sure, maybe there'll be no accusations. Not a thing but a bit of innocent walking out. It's a character's easily destroyed, with some of them backward crowd. Maybe ye did nothing? Who's to say? But I've to hear it."

Minnie's restless hands roamed over her face, tore at her skirt. Why not run out into the black night? Throw herself into the sea before he'd even the wits or thought to run after? Wildly she conjured up an image—her body hurtling from the cliffs, crushed on the rocks below. The tainted child's evil blood swept out by the waves. That'd keep Mattie's child from seein' the light of day.

But, ah, musha, she wept, was there nothing but a second evil deed? God help her.

"Yeer cruel, Morgan," she said. "With all yeer goodness yeer cruel . . . Can't ye see I'm tormented?"

Morgan grew pale in the firelight. "And what of yourself, Minnie?" he hurled in desperation. "What is this thing that you've done? Tell me, for God's sake?" He grabbed Minnie's shoulders. "What did they mean, those hooligans? That you led the young buck on? I'm tormented, too. That you'd have to be blind not seeing it. Mine isn't the only cruelty. *Tell me.*"

Minnie pulled free, white-hot with anger. "Put hands on me, will ye? I left a backward place for this? Yeer cruel. Ye are."

"No, I'll not let you." Morgan forced her to face him. "For the last time, so help me," he said. "The truth."

"The child's not yours," screamed Minnie. Her eyes had lost all focus. "I'd a love o' my own in the hay."

Morgan gasped, a look of dread sweeping over his face. "God Almighty."

There was silence, only the sound of the embers sputtering. Minnie was deathly pale. "Ye made me say," she whispered.

Overhead in the loft a bed creaked. Then a rustling across the floor. "I heard," Annie called down from the head of the stairs. Her voice trembled. In a moment she stood before them, a blanket clutched over her nightgown. Her feet were bare. "Minnie?" She rushed to Morgan's side.

Morgan sat down in a chair.

"And are you for the long road?" asked Annie. "Have you pain, brother?" She touched Morgan's chest, felt the heartbeat, the hammering.

"A different kind." Morgan groaned. He sat motionless. He appeared to be struggling with unseen forces, huge powers. Some gargantuan tyranny that left him no course but to submit. He stared at Minnie in wordless agony. "Because of the child he shot your da?" he said finally.

"He'd no word. Only ye know. Yourself and Annie."

"Why, then?" The words seemed to be coming from some distant cold place.

"Don't ye know what a grief is lost love? That people go

mad?" Minnie rocked back and forth. "Tis an evil deed for a cause."

"That's cause?" Annie bristled. "Don't hearts break every day? That there's no need for taking a gun?"

"Wait, Annie," said Morgan. "Let's hear her out."

"There'd been no murder if ye'd left me back in the hills. I never asked to come. Ye took me."

"Mother of God," said Annie.

Morgan forced his gaze upward, hurled his thoughts heavenward until he reached the Most High. Stood in His presence.

Ah, Ye had a special plan, he raged silently. Even Yourself, the Lord God. Special little tortures Ye hold, for the poor believing farmers thinks there could be something more. Deceiving us, even though anyone with a brain knows better. Ah, musha, wasn't it a deadly fool I've been? Thinking life was more than pigs and hay.

"And you've been tricking me?" he said at length to Minnie.

"I knew there was tricks up," said Annie. "Didn't I feel it there at the church?"

"That's not true! I came honestly."

"Well, now. That's news." Some of the color had come back into Morgan's face. He filled his pipe, lit it. "Tell me about this honesty. How you came as a sweet, blushing bride. And the little business of the child was only what anyone knowing all sides of the case would call a mistake. Something you just forgot to mention. Bein' so busy counting the cows, and gauging the size of the land. Was that it? You were just too occupied?"

"That's cruel," exclaimed Minnie. "Cruel, ye are!"

"But isn't that the pot calling the kettle?" Annie was frightened herself. Morgan seemed altered. Not at all like the brother she knew.

"But ye gave no hint," she accused Minnie. "Bad enough with your da in a murdered man's grave—an ordinary disgrace. But a quick-born child besides? There isn't a one we'd want thinkin' it's Morgan's."

Minnie put a hand to her lips. She brushed away tears with the end of her skirt, waited for whatever was coming.

"And if it's a boy where's the name for the land?" Annie looked for reassurance from Morgan. The Rileys' land for a murderer's child?

Morgan turned toward the fire. His broad shoulders fell

slack, and he seemed to lose vigor. He watched the flames, not speaking. But when he turned again he'd recovered. "Do you see what you've done?" he asked. "After us breaking our backs the long years?"

"And my own match?" burst out Annie. "Ah, musha, didn't Duffy turn out a surprise? Him talkin' love and sweet joys with myself, not the brother's money at all had him cheered? Duffy wants me. And you're after ruining it. It's lost." She began crying. "Not a one in the world that'll have me. Ah, musha."

"Oh, Annie," said Minnie. "I never meant . . ."

"Indeed, I'm sure," growled Morgan. "What didn't you mean?"

"I told ye you took me."

"So that I'd the ten long miles in winter, without yourself in the matter at all? Not even consulted?" Morgan's tone bristled with bitterness. "They surprised you?"

"I had no say," whispered Minnie, ashamed. "Me da was keen for Westport."

"O'Donnell was here with the grand talk and yourself not knowing a thing?"

"I'd naught to do with it. The da and the ma did it all."

"Or was it you'd already the child? Was that the story? So they sent Denny to do what he could? Get you ten miles out of view? And myself thinking you was fresh as the rain?"

"A great beauty, they told us," said Annie.

"A lie. They knew nothing. I saw to the babe. I planned it. Do ye think I'd take nothin' I loved? I'm not that easily man-aged." Minnie leaped to her feet.

"You planned it?" This from Annie. The color had drained from Morgan's face. "Deliberate?" he stammered. "To your wedding, another man's child? On purpose? God help me." He hurled his pipe to the floor. "You're mad."

"Say it was a mistake," begged Annie. "Say it."

"No mistake. I've me own heart's broke. Don't think at all yeer alone." Tears ran down her face. "I'm a woman, and ye've the arm and the fist and the boot. Beat me, ye can. But hear me out ye will. No mistake. I swear. So help me God."

"She's cursing, saints help us." Annie made the Sign of the Cross.

"A curse on the lot o' ye, I'll still have my say." Minnie ran to the far side of the kitchen.

"But he's your husband. Ye mustn't."

Morgan strode across the room.

"Don't touch me," Minnie cried, grabbing a chair. She held it between them. "A woman's life's a cruel joke. We're bartered."

"Minnie."

Minnie heard the pain in Morgan's voice, but she plunged on. "It's true. We're naught but a swap for the land. Life's trade goods, we are. We've to go and bed down where we're told."

"Terrible words, Minnie. For shame."

"Ye'll never admit, but it's true!" The injustices were becoming clearer. "Who ever gave thought to my happiness? My wishes? Asked if I wanted a connection to Westport? If I needed the farmer's four cows? Hadn't I cows enough of my own? A woman's told. No one asks her."

"You're near blasphemin'," warned Annie. "So, think, Minnie. What ye say you may never recall."

"I am thinkin'. And sad for the thoughts that I have." A flood of grievances swept over Minnie, choked her. "But I've the babe," she cried. "A *love child*."

Annie gasped. Morgan said nothing.

"And didn't I deserve happiness? Without myself and Mattie havin' to grab it wherever we could? Snatch it here, grab it there? The hills, the hay, the cow house? Was that any way?"

"Minnie. You've to stop." Annie tried to cover her ears. "Don't say this."

"And the ma sayin' I'd to go off and marry the farmer, no more than a cow or a pig. Not a chance in the world to say, 'No.' "

Morgan groaned.

"Where was my happiness?"

"You're daft!" Annie had grown paler even than Morgan. "For shame on your bad deed," she whispered. "For shame. Dear brother's been treated the fool."

"Ye only think it's for shame, so little of love have ye known. Had ye knowledge, ye'd think on yeer own life so poor."

"Glory be. The devil's handmaid. Morgan, the girl's evil. We've no call to be hearin' this."

"But hear it ye will," said Minnie.

"Stop her, brother."

"Have ye known happiness?" cried Minnie. "The bliss o' the flesh?"

"Say no more," Morgan croaked.

"Na more? When I'd the whole o' creation throb in me? Fillin' me. The force of the world in my arms? That's heaven, I'm tellin' it. The hay is the thing truly real. The rest is foolishness."

"Blasphemy." Annie crossed herself. "The end of the world."

"There's all o' the world in the hay," declared Minnie.

Horror flitted across Morgan's face. Pain. Disbelief. Hopelessness.

"And I'll never be sad that I done it," said Minnie, sinking exhausted into a chair. "Whether I'm kept or I'm thrown in the sea. I've known paradise. Paradise."

CHAPTER
17

When morning came fog had rolled in, hiding the fields and walls. Entire patches of daffodils had vanished—even the rocks were gone. The morning was nothing but grey soft mist. And when about nine the wind picked up, chasing the mist, there was the sound of the waves hard against the cliffs.

Morgan threw off his blanket, stretched, tested his aches and his stiffness. What a fool he'd been. He stood up, moved his neck carefully, eased a cramp. Bad cess to the dunce that sleeps in a chair. He ran a thick tongue over his teeth, spat noisily into the hearth. "It's a bad lot, whiskey." He grabbed the empty bottle, hurled it into the fireplace.

"We'll have to get the cows," he said, as Annie descended the stairs.

"But can't it wait? I'll do the milking after." Annie eyed the broken glass, her brother's pasty face, the look of the whiskey still on him. There were black circles under his eyes. She winced, rushed to stir the embers, lay fresh peat. She swung the crane with the kettle. The fire caught, and there was a sudden rush of flames. Smoke raced up the chimney. "Minnie's asleep?" she asked, before noticing the blanket, the closed bedroom door. God help us.

"I'll fetch the cows," said Morgan, grabbing for his jacket. His movements were stiff. "Wait and have your tea," said Annie. She set out clean dishes.

"I've no heart to eat." Morgan hesitated by the bedroom door. He pushed it inward. "Get up, Minnie," he called out, not looking into the room. "You've to go."

"Brother." Annie rushed to grab Morgan's arm. "Can't ye be waiting?"

But Morgan banged on the door again. "Are you up?"

"Wait, Morgan," Annie pleaded. "Can't we talk after tea?"

But Morgan's face had shut tight. "We said it all last night. There's nothing more. Besides, yourself and Duffy might be able to patch it up, if he sees we've sense enough to be quit of them. I'll have her gone before he gets here." He listened at Minnie's door. "She's up," he said.

"Well, I know she acted badly," said Annie, verging on tears. "But sending her back? And how do you know you'll be let?"

"I'll make it up with the priest tomorrow. Would he force a murderer's name on the land?"

"But who's to say it's a boy? And besides, the ma had three sons dying."

"Stillborn? I won't chance it. There's still the match for yourself. The Yank'll kill it."

"Ah, Morgan, there's a chance we yet might save it. I've slept on it. I've been thinking. You could add a hundred pounds."

"God Almighty. For that little weasel?"

"Morgan. For shame."

"Ah, I know, I know. God forgive me, Annie. I'm not my-self . . . But that's three hundred pounds it'd come to. And me givin' the money back?" Morgan grabbed up a pipe, tried to light it. But his hands shook. "God help me. Isn't it enough that I've lost her?" In a frenzy he rushed out the door.

Minnie emerged from the bedroom. Her face was white and strained. "There's tea, Annie?" she asked faintly.

Annie heated the pot, poured water over the tea leaves. "There's only the bread from last night," she said. "We're just up."

"I know," said Minnie. And when Annie poured out the tea, in a whisper, "They'll not take me."

"Whisht." Annie sliced the hard bread. "Time enough when he's back with the cows."

"But there's matters."

"It's all settled. You're to go back. And the money along with ye . . . Now, drink up your tea."

"Ballyrea's quit o' me, too."

"Whisht. When himself's back. Here. Have a little of this."
Annie pushed the jam pot toward Minnie. "It's some of the
blackberries."

"Jam? When he's turnin' me out on the road?" But she
scraped a tiny bit across her bread. "Doesn't a man always
cleave to his wife?" she asked softly.

"Merciful God, Minnie. And the terrible things you've been
doing?"

"Is lovin' forbidden?"

"What talk. You've to be traveling. Isn't the poor man near
broken?"

"But I've been loyal. Since the vows. And isn't he full o' the
sweets in the nighttime?"

"Minnie."

Minnie felt silent. She heaped a spoonful of jam on her
bread, bit into it. She motioned to Annie for a fresh cup of tea.

"Here's Morgan back. I'll be out," Annie called as Morgan
led two cows around to the cow house. "Oh, but they're heavy,
I've to go." She flew out the back door.

Morgan, when he came in, sat at first with his back to the
fire. In shadow the little tufts of hair over his ears, along with
the bushed brows, seemed to emphasize the strangeness. There
were deep lines by his eyes. "Have you the tea?" he said. His
voice was heavy, and there was almost the look of the long
road. "There's tea?"

"In the pot," said Minnie. She emptied her cup, felt a knot
begin. "Shall I pour it?"

"Do."

When Morgan was settled with his tea he told Minnie to
prepare for the road. "If we'd a cart," he said half apologeti-
cally. "And aren't my trousers near soaked through? I think the
rain's blowing to sea. July's funny."

"I'll take a blanket."

"Ah, do."

Minnie slipped off to the bedroom, began gathering together
her clothes. "There isn't a little bag, or a case?" she said,
coming to the doorway.

"Not a bit of trouble." Morgan rushed off to the seed shed.
When he returned there was a smell of whiskey. "Will this do?"
Minnie accepted the sack.

"For the little ye have." Morgan's voice was gruff, and she

was sure she saw his eyes fill. Again she thought of trying to reason, but then he turned to the tea, hacked off a chunk of bread. "Be quick," he said.

"It's a fine little bag," was all Minnie could answer. There was small use. His mind was set.

The fog had lifted by the time they were ready. Only a thin mist hung on the fields, and there were signs the clouds might part, though the day was chill yet.

Annie, back from the cow house, made a wan attempt at cheer. "Wasn't it quick they were?" she said. She set the pail on the floor. There was a strained moment of silence. A faint flush moved across Minnie's cheeks. "It's time," she said. She clutched at the sack with her clothes.

Morgan jerked towards her. "I'll carry it." But Minnie pulled away. "The weight's nothing."

"Give it here." Morgan grew agitated. "Isn't it enough you've to walk with the babe?"

With a slight shrug Minnie gave up the bag. She settled her shawl, but her hair, which she'd left unbound, tumbled free, spilled across her shoulders, curled unchecked over her breasts.

"Take a blanket," ordered Morgan, rushing to the bedroom. He wrapped her in coarse wool, covering her head, shoulders, pinning the ends across her breast. "The wind'll be off you," he said.

"Will it?" She shivered. For a moment she thought of hurling the blanket to the floor.

"And will you be home?" Annie asked Morgan, red-faced with embarrassment.

"I'll be late back."

"I'll have the tea." Annie seized the milk pail, poured milk into a basin, set it on the dresser. The remainder went into the pail for the pigs. "Isn't it well fed they are?" she said. "And the pigs not doing a thing for their keep?"

Annie's words hung in the silence. Morgan, mute, seemed locked in an inner struggle. He paced before the hearth, fury escalating even as he kicked at the peat by the fire, tipping the basket. "Jesus," he shouted.

Annie added meal to the pig pail. "They'll be looking for it," she said.

"Is it only with the *pigs* you're concerned?" He advanced

toward Annie, and for a moment Minnie thought he'd strike her. Annie recoiled, backed against the dresser. Morgan caught himself.

"I won't be keeping you," said Annie. She sidled toward the back door.

Morgan, in agony, pushed Minnie toward the door. "You've to be off," he said, his voice hardly recognizable.

"God help us." Annie fled to the haggard.

The wind had grown warm by the time they set out. A quick, bright sun swept the sky, clouds only here and there, and the sun had warmed the roses, so that by the doorway there was a thick fragrance.

Minnie breathed deeply. Her eyes roamed the slope, memorizing the steepness. There was Annie's clothesline, empty. Beyond the clothesline, the bay. And then further out, still hazy, the bay stretched at length to the sea.

Amazing, all of it.

She shifted the blanket, felt the fresh heat of the sun. "It'll be a long walk," she said.

Annie came around from the cow house in tears. "Isn't it a sad day?" she called out after them. "God forgive ye." She burst into loud wailing. "Maybe He'll *not* forgive." Minnie stumbled, so touched was she by the cry.

Minnie grew tired when they'd barely begun. "I've the miles in two days," she said, when she caught Morgan's eye on her. "Don't they all be doing it?" he retorted. But Minnie could see he was shaken. By the end of the boreen they'd to stop at O'Donnell's, so that Morgan could ask for the trap.

"Pat?" said Anna, when she poked her head from the door. "Most likely he's shoveling the dung. Run around to the back. I'm sure he'll give it," she said pleasantly. She smoothed her apron, reset the hairpins at the back of her neck.

Two small faces, a boy and a girl, poked out from under her skirts, staring at the visitors. Anna shooed them away. "Isn't it the curiosity they do be having?" she said, though not crossly. She studied Morgan's urgency, the jittery set of his head.

And Minnie's own face, with the look of something gone terribly wrong.

"Isn't it half killed you are from the funeral?" She insisted

Minnie come up to the hearth. "Now, that's a comfortable chair." She pulled up a stool for her feet. "Stay for tea." She swung the crane to the fire. "It won't be a minute. The kettle's just off the boil."

"We've to be moving," said Morgan quickly, but Minnie worked up a wan smile.

Anna reached for the teapot but Morgan shook his head. "We've to be off . . . Isn't it queer for a day in July?" he added hurriedly, as if by way of explanation. "That we don't know if it's rain or the sun we'll be gettin'. When us, the poor fools, are only half the way."

"Whisht to the rain or the sun. You've time for a wee cup of tea." It wasn't the day that was queer. She snatched up the jam pot, plunked it on the table, grabbed the bread board. The table was set in a flash. "The bread's just done," she said. She moved a small metal oven from the fire, eased it off the coals, knocking red coals from the top. She slid the oven to the hearthstone. "Himself's outside," she said. "So, be off and see to the trap."

Alone with Minnie, Anna's anger evaporated. "I'm sitting here for ye to tell me," she said. "There isn't another word from me." She stared at her neighbor.

The silence deepened. Minnie grew more desolate, sitting with her head bowed.

"Now, Minnie," Anna coaxed, her voice gentle. "Look up and show me your eyes." Minnie moaned softly, refusing, it seemed, to be comforted. Finally, she raised her head.

"God Almighty. You're a sight, Minnie. You've death and despair in your eyes. The look of the long road. What ails ye?"

Out back, hearing they needed the trap, Pat set his shovel against the back wall. "The wheel's off," he said regretfully. His sharp eyes sought Morgan's. "The donkey'll do for herself." He pulled a tobacco pouch from his pocket. "Have a smoke?"

"We're in a bit of a sweat, don't you know? There's clouds still."

Pat cradled the pipe in his hand and turned a quick, knowing look at the sky. "Isn't that sun we have?" He began to suck, pulling the smoke fast, blowing it out the side of his mouth. "Have a pipefill," he said, offering the pouch.

Morgan frowned, said they'd be off. "If it isn't too much trouble." He struggled mightily to keep his voice even. "It may rain," he said desperately.

"Rain?" Pat puffed a great cloud. He let his eyes wander over the back field, where the sheep were grazing. "Isn't it quick you're goin' back there?" He watched Morgan carefully. What in the name o' God possessed him, that he'd bundle her off the next day? Was she an old plow horse, that he wouldn't mind her dying still hitched to the blade?

Morgan's jaws tightened. He felt tension spread into his shoulders. Another minute or two of this and he was done. "You say you've the donkey?"

"But he's a bit of a streeleen, you know. Cross. So you've to see herself doesn't fall off. In her condition, you know. Twouldn't do, now Morgan."

"I'll see to't." Morgan's heart pounded.

"If you'd a mind for the first of the week, I might have the wheel on?"

"Today." Omathon.

"Ah, well. Whatever suits." And then after a pause, "Is it the murderer they've caught, that you've been called back? The Civic Guard's no consideration. Not that I've had any business with them. But I've heard."

"News travels." Morgan's voice hit a menacing note, but Pat appeared not to notice. "A bad business. They say 'twas a friend of the girl's."

Morgan's fists went hard at his sides. "You're speaking of Minnie? My Minnie?"

"Who else? Haven't we all an unwise friend in our day? And as for our women, there isn't a thing we do be knowing about the heart o' them, even the fairest." He knocked the ash from his pipe, banged it on the stone wall. "Here," he said, extending the pipe to Morgan. "Have a pipefill now. Enjoy yourself."

"Who brought you the news?" croaked Morgan, shoving the pipe aside. "He was only Wednesday shot. Wasn't it prompt they were?"

"Christ, Morgan. Isn't a bird could fly the ten miles but the news'd be cold before it? Is there one that misses a trick?"

"Who told you?"

"Ah, Morgan. Don't crap on it. Isn't it the duty he had, Denny? Bein' of my own flesh and blood? Himself after arranging with Duffy, wasn't he obliged?"

"Yez told Duffy?"

"Christ, Morgan, Denny's his own reputation . . ."

"Jesus Christ," shouted Morgan. "Will ye give me the ass and be done."

"Ah, Morgan. Cool down."

"Cool down? Fookin' liars, all of them. Fookin', fookin' liars. Liars." He banged his fist on the wall, drew blood.

"Now, don't be taking things badly. Not a bit of a blame to yourself." Pat's voice had a silky quality. He spotted the donkey upland in the fields. "I'll fetch the animal." With a leap he was over the wall, bolting through the golden furze, racing up the low, green hill.

In a frenzy Morgan tore around to the kitchen, dragged Minnie out of her chair, where she had settled, drinking her tea. "Get up," he said. Anna leaped to her feet. "Keep out of this," Morgan roared. He grasped Minnie's arm, "He's the donkey. You'll manage."

"Mother o' God! Isn't it half killing her he is?" said Anna.

CHAPTER
18

The upland air seemed thin. There was a dryness, and effort seemed to bring on the sweats. Morgan paused. He stroked the donkey's nose. "The animal's tired," he said to Minnie, asking her next, was she warm? He reached out to touch her blanket.

"Leave it." She yanked at the blanket so that the coarse wool shielded her face. "There's no one needs to see," she said.

How would she bear it, she thought, the Saturday crowd o' them? Gawkin' and loafin'. McNulty's full out to the door. Half the lot nothing better to do than laff 'til a poor girl's destroyed.

And would Morgan give a word for her? Hardly—him throwin' her out on the road. It'd be, "Here, Ballyrea. Take back yeer pride and yeer joy."

And wouldn't that set them mockin' between the lot o' them, destroyin' her good name before her life'd had a chance to begin? So that she'd be dumped back at the nephew's, with him and his Chrissie bootin' her back. What then? Would Morgan's hardened heart open a crack?

Before them, here in the high ground, scraggly meadows stretched. Boulders dotted the flat plain, with great spreads of rock clogging the road. Just before the snaked curve, black bog cut a wide swath through the fields, with mounds on either side, where the turfs lay piled to dry.

Clouds gathered, yet before the snaked curve was barely passed, the sun was warm again on their backs. A breeze blew off the mountainside. Climbing still higher, they were able to see Ballyrea.

The crossroads approached. There was chimney smoke from the pub, and at either side of McNulty's, old folks sat, a man and a woman, outside their cottage doors. On the other street the church lay deserted.

Shawn Brady sat humped on a three-legged stool. Cuttings of leather littered the ground by his door, and on his lap he held the beginnings of a boot. Deftly he chiseled the leather, smoothing the edges.

To the right of McNulty's, bent and withered next to her own door, Nellie McGavan pounded her blackthorn, alert for anything at all she might see. She pounded the stick rhythmically, surveying the square.

In the square itself there were only a few old women gossiping. Chickens and geese wandered free.

Two cows, with a scraggly calf between them, stood fastened to a post; when they mooed a flock of crows flew off the church roof. The black cloud swept over the square to land shrilly on the grassy plain just past the pub.

Ahead, the public house was busy. There was activity everywhere. In the front, women bargained for Saturday groceries, at every skirt a child or two.

Back of the groceries, past the partition, the pub had every table filled. There was a man on each of the bar stools, with five or six others standing behind. And further back, at the curtained area known as the "snug," there was a constant back-up waiting.

There was a commotion from the front of the shop. Loud cries. An excited Bridey O'Neil appeared in the doorway.

"Quick now. The farmer's the donkey, with young Minnie Maughan." She dragged her husband off the stool, propelled him towards the door.

The crowd was on its feet instantly, surging ahead of O'Neil, who fell in a heap on the floor. "Bastards," he mumbled thickly.

Bridey O'Neil was senseless with glee. "Let the fool get up!" she cried, pushing. "Didn't I tell ye the young girl'd a curse?

"Bringin' her back, that's what he's done. He's turnin' her out. Oh, I've to be seein'." In a frenzy she shoved towards the door.

Denny O'Donnell poked his head out of the snug. "I'm just in the back door," he said. "What's happenin'?"

From outside there was a great burst of shouting. Cries of,

"Murder," followed by "That's what ye done, Minnie Maughan. Killed yeer da."

Denny bolted for the front of the shop.

All of Ballyrea, Morgan thought, had poured in a great shouting mass out of the open half-door. Some were dragging sacks of flour, a few dropped their parcels next to the windows at the front of the shop. A lean, grey-faced farmer, a keg of nails in his arms, staggered over the door stoop and sprawled head-long. Nails scattered in all directions on the gravelly path.

Some of the men still clutched their glasses, half filled with stout. There was the smell of beer and whiskey.

When the cry of "Murder!" went up Morgan felt his heart give a terrible leap. The hand holding the bridle went nearly numb, and up and down his spine raced a chill of fear. What in the name o' God had they stumbled into?

"Give them no mind," he whispered. He gripped the donkey's harness, giving the animal a sharp tug. "There isn't a thing in the world they've right to do to you."

"Isn't it late ye are to think of it?" snapped Minnie. But quick as it came the rebellion left her.

The warm, thick smell of the donkey comforted her, and she stroked the animal. Bridey O'Neil stood wild-faced in front of her and, next to Bridey, pushing and shoving, old Nellie McGavan pounded the ground with her blackthorn. "Isn't the young one better than the lot o' ye?" she screamed. "Birthed her, that I'm to be knowin'?"

"And what do ye know of her doin's?" countered Bridey O'Neil. "There's a curse," she shouted. "I saw ye. And the O'Malley there with ye in the darkness. That murderer."

A gasp went up from the crowd. Men and women penned Minnie in. She let out a frightened cry.

Sweat poured down Morgan's face. Was he going to have to fight for it? The mob lookin' for all the world like they'd tear the girl from the donkey's back?

"Back off, now," he shouted. "Make a path. Let my wife through." What in the name o' God kind of place was this? That they'd have the whole town half drunk on a Saturday afternoon, with nothing better to do than persecute a young one? Oh, Ballyrea was bad, wasn't Annie right?

Mick O'Neil emerged from the grocery to see his ma

squarely in front of the donkey. "What are ye up to?" He pushed through the crowd to her side. "Ye've to back off, ma," he said. "This is the grandest girl in the lot o' them." Didn't poor Minnie look for all the world ready to die? He grabbed his mother's arm, where she'd taken hold of the bridle. "Let go. Ye've to let go."

"Puttin' an angry hand on yeer ma?" yelled Bridey. "Is it for *this* I nursed ye?"

"Ah, ma," said Mick, backing off. "Won't they be callin' the Civic Guard?"

"For the O'Malley, that's who. Isn't it the Guard's chasin' these hills?"

"Ma. I know they're hot for O'Malley. And hang 'im they should . . . But Minnie? God save us . . . Now, let go." He grabbed her arm but she held on.

Losing patience completely, Morgan put his hip to the woman and shoved. "Let go," he shouted. Her fingers slipped and she stumbled. A yell went up from the crowd. "Assault. God help us." "Run quick for the Civic Guard."

"You're all crazy," shouted Morgan, struggling with the frightened animal. Hind legs flying wildly, the donkey struck out at the crowd. When a young fellow, drunk, fell down, the animal stomped him. Minnie held on for her life.

"A mad animal," shouted Shawn Brady, who stood at the edge of the crowd. "Isn't it cowardly yez all is, standin' there? While this criminal and his beast knocks us down?" The old shoemaker called out for the Guard. "Get them."

The crowd parted. Brady planted himself in front of Morgan.

"Get out of my way," Morgan shouted. "Be off, now. Give way."

The donkey snorted and bolted, throwing Minnie, blanket and all, onto the ground. She screamed.

But in a flash Morgan had her up on the donkey. He dragged the struggling animal forward, using himself as a wedge, and pushed on into a narrow opening left by the crowd.

"Let him."

"Give the man leeway."

Slowly Morgan got the donkey moving, until, with steady plodding, Ballyrea was no more than a pair of streets behind them. Once or twice Morgan heard curses behind him, but for the most part there was stillness.

Minnie clung to the donkey's back. Dry-eyed now, she'd flung the blanket over the bridle. The reproach of the crowd still rang in her ears. "Ye've cause now, I suppose?" she said icily. "Now ye hear I've done murder."

"Ah, Minnie," Morgan began.

"Take a gun and shoot me own da? Me darlin' da?" She spat out the words. Dizziness swept her, and she clutched the bridle. There'd be even more accusations, surely, on the hill just ahead. Yet, battered as she was, her resolve stiffened. She'd not beg mercy, for there was certainly none to be found here. She'd not degrade herself.

But what would become of her? Would the Maughans and the ma leave her to starve on the road? So that she'd be forced to run off and eat grass with the cows?

"Isn't it proud ye are?" she said to Morgan. Her voice was low and bitter. "Now that I'm to be crucified."

"Ah, no. No."

"Ye think they'll welcome me? The lot o' them hugging to the farm from the da? Take in the likes of me and risk losin' it? Not on yeer life."

"But they're your family. They have to take you."

"And have the town shun them too? Ah, no. Ballyrea's said I've to go. The ma and the Maughans're sittin' pretty."

"Minnie, you've to stop this. You're killing me." Morgan stopped on the path, held the donkey. "I've not the heart for this," he said hopelessly. "I'm losing *everything*."

He reached to grab her, so that she nearly fell. He was panting now. The donkey dragged sideways, began a frightened whinnying. Minnie struggled to hold her seat.

"Have you no heart?" Morgan gasped. Minnie's hair had tumbled over her shoulders, mantling her. The brown waves shone in the sunlight.

Morgan clung desperately to his resolve. "I told you to keep the blanket," he said. "You were to wrap yourself."

He flung the blanket at her. Hands shaking, he hid the brown curls, stuffing them under the wool. "And let ye keep it out o' my sight."

There was an even greater urgency now. He was near to throwing himself down in the grass.

Feverishly he crushed the wool across Minnie's breasts. "And keep yourself covered," he shouted, giving a desperate thump to the donkey's hide. The animal stumbled forward. Morgan grabbed up a switch. "Move, you stupid beast. Move."

"God save us, it's Minnie," said Chrissie Maughan, on seeing the donkey outside the door. "Brian. Ye've to come quick."

"Christ."

Brian gawked at the visitors, stupefied. "Ma," he yelled. "Minnie's here."

Katie Maughan rushed up to the door. "Dear Jesus. Isn't it Minnie?" Her face rapidly flushed and then paled. "Ye've not to be *seen* here."

"Minnie's home," announced Morgan stoutly, nudging her from the animal's back. "And I'll be bringin' the fortune, too, God help me, the soon as I get to the bank." He steadied Minnie, who leaned weakly on the donkey, breathing hard. Her face had gone white.

"Are ye daft?" shouted the nephew. He glared at Morgan.

"Daft? Not on your life," Morgan shot back. "Minnie's home."

The words hit like a blow to the three at the door.

Katie breathed in loud, uneasy gasps. "Ye'd have us *ruined*?"

"There isn't a thing I've to say on it," Minnie began, but Morgan silenced her. "I'll handle this."

The wife, Chrissie, flounced her red hair. The nephew pulled her beside him. "We've the land now," Brian began.

"And let ye be listenin', now," Chrissie O'Bannon said. "My husband's the wisdom, don't ye be doubtin'."

"And I've the wisdom and I'm giving her back." Morgan pushed Minnie toward them, leveling his gaze like a weapon at the Maughans. "I'm divorcing her."

"Ye are daft. There's no divorce."

"A 'country divorce,' that's what I'll get. I've only to see the priest." Morgan pulled himself up confidently. "There's cause."

"Christ, this isn't the old days." But Brian was shaken. "A 'country divorce' is it? The priest'll laugh ye out of the church. That's only for barrenness. And ye haven't that problem."

"I'm sure all of you know the troubles I have," said Morgan soberly. "There isn't a thing can change my mind."

Minnie could see Morgan was avoiding her. Why not? How

else could he do what he'd done? She eased herself into a chair standing empty by the door. No one told her to get up again, so she rested. Thirst parched her, and she felt numbed.

The tormented little group paid her no mind.

"It's sinful," said Brian Maughan, aware now he'd a serious problem on his hands. The whole town would shun them. They'd be as good as dead for all the buyin' and barterin'. "Who in the name o' God ever heard of divorce?"

"I'd be ashamed," hissed Katie. "Such a thing's not for the likes o' our Minnie. Minnie's a country girl. Not knowin'."

"But it's girls from the country it's for," Morgan insisted. "It's only these backward places."

"Backward? D'ye hear him?"

"Minnie's the wife that God wed ye," said Chrissie O'Bannon.

The Maughans were more than Morgan had expected. But last night's revelations flooded him. God help him. Wasn't it a terrible knowledge, that your wife'd been a whore? The thought of Minnie on her back with another man made his heart nearly stop. "I'm not backing off," he said. "I'll have no more to do with the lot of you. And the money'll be yours as soon as I can."

"We've money ourselves. Plenty of it," said the nephew. "Is that all ye think we've concern for?"

Suddenly Morgan grabbed the donkey's bridle and threw a leg over, seating himself like an avenging warrior atop the animal's back. "I'm done with ye," he shouted, giving a kick. Before one or the other could stop him he was off with a cry down the hill.

"Faster, ye dumb beast." He beat the animal with blows of his fist. "Faster. Faster."

CHAPTER
19

"Ye come back here," shouted the nephew. "Deserter," screamed Chrissie. "We'll get the law on ye."

The ma, speechless, tore back and forth in a daze. At one moment she'd stop to look with anguish down the hill, the very next she'd rush over to stare hopelessly at Minnie. "D'ye see what ye've done?"

Minnie, herself, sat still. The figure on the hill was fast disappearing. "Glory to God, what'll I do?" she whispered. She tried not to look at the Maughans. Chrissie O'Bannon had taken to jumping up and down, screaming; the nephew strode this way and that in a rage, and for a terrible moment it seemed he'd run off down the hill. Finally, grabbing a stick, he pounded violently on the wall near the door.

"Has he come loose of his senses?" asked Minnie.

"Isn't it a fine thing ye brought on us?" screamed Chrissie O'Bannon. "The long days he's waited? That ye've to destroy his new life when it's barely begun?"

"I never asked to come back here," said Minnie. She stood up, struggling to maintain dignity. "So I'll thank ye to say none of that. I've a heart in me breast like yeer own."

"Ye brought this on us," shouted Chrissie. "It's yeer doin'." She took Brian's arm. "We've to be settlin' this." But after peering down the hill, where Morgan and the donkey were only a faint blur, Brian froze. "I'm sorry, Minnie," he said. "There's no place for ye."

"But we can't turn her out," gasped Katie. "She's with child. A 'love child.' Where can she go? This is her home."

"It was her home." Brian's voice faltered. "They'll be after shunnin' us," Chrissie hissed. "Isn't it for less that many's an outcast? They'll be claimin' we've no heart at all for the honor of Ballyrea. We'll be as good as dead. They'll disown us. Much good the land'll do us."

"Ah, musha, Katie, there's not a thing we can do," said Brian. "The disgrace would kill us." His eyes were full of pleading. "Can't ye be knowin'? Minnie's nothin' but a world of trouble."

"So she's to starve on the road?" Katie folded her arms. "Minnie's my child."

Brian shrank back. "Oh, isn't it a terrible thing when a man's tormented? Terrible. Terrible." It almost seemed he'd burst into tears. "Ye've made me a monster. A betrayer."

"Will ye lookit?" screeched Chrissie, running to her husband. "Come to yeer senses, will ye? We've paid for the land fair and square. No betrayal. Isn't it only the old couple's name's writ in the writings? Not a young girl with a babe?"

"Oh, it's true. It's true," Brian agreed.

"It's not ye've destroyed her character. It's that murderer."

"True."

"And whatever she done with him."

"Ye've the fortune," Brian told Katie, in what he hoped was a reasonable tone. "And ye'd a firm hand when ye signed the writings. Yeerself and John."

At the mention of John Maughan's name Katie began to weep. "John, me darlin' man." Her wailing filled the barnyard. She flung herself on the ground. "John. Will ye be comin' for me?" she wailed. "Take me out o' this cauldron of woe."

"Ma. Ma," cried Minnie.

"Ah, Minnie, yeer lost to me now," sobbed the mother. "As if it wasn't enough with my John. My only child besides."

"Now, Mrs. Maughan, yeer forgettin'," said Chrissie, "yeerself was agreed. Remember?"

"I know. I know. I'm denyin' none o' that. Didn't himself always say ye'd the land? But what is my daughter to do? He's divorcing her."

"Oh, ye'll see. Minnie's kind always manages," snapped Chrissie. "Ye'll be in touch."

"Can I visit her out on the road?" Katie drew herself up. "I thought I'd be goin' regular to Westport. What was to stop me?"

"Brian," snapped Chrissie, "let ye be gettin' inside." She pulled Katie Maughan with her. Katie, dazed, allowed herself to be led, while the full implications came through. This was the end. The end of her Minnie. The end of her own hopes. Fresh tears fell, and she began to sob.

"The law's on our side," said Chrissie. "The whole town knows it."

"If only my John'd never died."

"Well, we'd all like that," snapped Chrissie. "Most of all John . . .But what of poor Brian? Hasn't he the work by himself now? Not a bit of a hand by his side?"

"Oh, yeer hard. Hard. My poor John not yet cold in his grave . . . And will ye be able to manage, daughter?"

"I'll manage," said Minnie quietly, blinking back tears. "Though where I'm to go I don't know."

"Wait," said Chrissie. She rushed into the kitchen to return almost instantly, thrusting a pan of biscuits at Minnie. "We've just had the tea. Ye can eat them on yeer way."

Minnie clutched the biscuits. "I've nothing since morn," she said by way of thanks.

Chrissie rushed out again with water. She pressed the cup into Minnie's hand. "Keep the cup. It's an old one."

Minnie tried to swallow but she choked. She spat the water out on the ground. "Don't trouble yeerself."

"Ah, sure, the Lord save us," screamed Katie. She struggled towards Minnie, arms outstretched. "Daughter."

The Maughans leaped forward. Pulling and tugging they dragged her inside. The door slammed.

Minnie could hear the struggle. There were the ma's screams and the nephew's pleas. And over all the racket, Chrissie in command.

"There's not a family around'd take a murderer's child."

Minnie set off down the hill. Tears nearly blinded her. Halfway down she grew weary. Above her the sun was brilliant, the hills green and fine. She breathed the air, full of the smells of grass. A hot breeze bathed her face. She lay down in the tall grass and felt comforted. Hay piles beckoned. A breeze carried her, soft, through the windrows. She lay covered in hay. Memories flooded.

Together with Mattie she romped in the fields. Tasted gentle lickings, kisses, deep probings, fillings and emptyings. Naked across the green meadows they danced in the hay.

She knew what to do. Rising, she smoothed her clothes, picked bits of grass and weeds from her hair. She threw the blanket over her shoulder and, clutching the cup and biscuits, made off down the hill.

Skirting the farms, she walked steadily to where the valley turned off at a sharp angle, the mountain and hills behind her. She pushed along to the lowland and struck out across the swath of bog. Cautiously she circled the O'Neils' cottage and made for the O'Malleys'. The farm stood at the outermost reach of the plain.

At first she saw no one. Not even smoke from the chimney. Had they all fled? But coming closer, she saw the littlest girl, alone by the door, holding the infant. "Mama. It's Minnie. It's Minnie. Come quick."

"Mother o' God," came a shout. A crowd of O'Malleys, wild with apprehension, rushed noisily through the door.

"Isn't it our Minnie?" Mother O'Malley, pale, stumbling, yanked her trailing dress from under her feet. "Yeer da. Yeer da," she sobbed. "Our Mattie's after shootin' him." She swept Minnie into her arms.

The two women clung. "They've thrown me out on the road," Minnie said. "I've nowhere."

"Ah, musha. Sure, how do they think yeer to blame? Wasn't it only the devil made it happen?"

"Twas the devil made brother kill yeer da," said Nora . . . "Oh, Minnie, will they hang him?" She burst into tears. Her sister Clare, too, broke into loud wailing. "Maybe they'll hang all of us."

They led her inside. Minnie realized for the first time how desperately frightened they were. She sank to the hob at the side of the hearth.

The cottage was even more decrepit than usual. No fire at all. Only gray ashes. A battered pot containing a few scrapings of congealed oatmeal. Even on their worst days there was some semblance of cooking.

Shaun, Michael, and Owen, squatting, appeared caught in a cloud of despair. "Shaun's hard taken," said the ma. "He thinks if only he'd a gun he could rescue Mattie."

"Christ. If I can only find him before the fookin' police,"
burst out young Shaun. "A *gun's* what I need."

"A gun?" Minnie felt the blood rushing to her head. Hadn't
there been enough guns?

Mrs. O'Malley rushed outside to pluck the forgotten infant
from the yard. She held him to her breast. "Himself's not here,"
she offered forlornly, as if Minnie had asked.

Minnie's heart jumped. "But isn't he always?" Worriedly she
recollected the scene earlier. No Con O'Malley at McNulty's
either. And on a *Saturday*?

"And what of Mattie," she asked softly.

"Con'll hide him," said Mrs. O'Malley. "He might have a
chance in the hills."

"But the Civic Guard's over the land," said Minnie. "So
what's the use?"

"The use? They're after 'im dead or alive." Her voice had
fallen to a whisper.

"They've even a guard on this house," Shaun said. "I'm
surprised they didn't plug ye."

"But what for?" gasped Minnie. This was craziness . . .

"Ye came here. Ye showed yeerself one o' us." He strode
angrily toward the door.

"Don't go, Shaun," cried the ma. "They'll plug ye. Ye'll not
get a mile from the door."

"I'm goin' after me da. Two can search better than one."

"No, gossoon. No."

"But, ma. They'll hang 'im." Shaun appeared close now to
tears. The tough, angry set of his face crumpled. "Mattie's me
brother."

"Oh, Mother o' God," cried the ma. She dragged him over
to the battered chair, pushed him into it. "Don't let me lose *two*
sons."

Young Shaun, gaining control again, pushed aside her
hands. Cold determination surrounded him.

"I'm goin', ma. There's a place not even the Guard can
find." With that he was out the door.

"It's where dada makes the poteen," said Peggy, laying her
head against her ma, who'd collapsed into the chair.

"How've ye to be knowin'?" asked the ma. "Ye've not been
to the hills."

"We all know da's the still," said Nora.

"Ah, God help us. Isn't it the whiskey has us licked?" Minnie followed the distraught woman's gaze. Dirt for a floor? Scattered with straw? Half-painted walls. Festering with mold. An old battered shoe left on a sill. Soiled clothing heaped. And thrown near the hearth, a wheel off a cart.

"It's the still's undone us," said Mrs. O'Malley. "Ah, Mother o' God, we're hopeless. Hopeless."

"Drink's bad," said Nora. "Don't ye be goin' near the poteen now," she said, in a perfect imitation of her ma. "It's the whiskey that's undone our da."

"Ah, don't ye be even sayin' the word," said the ma. "Poteen's ruined us."

Minnie sat dumbfounded. She'd never seen the like. "And Mattie?" she whispered. "Did he go to the still?"

"Ah, Minnie, it was drink planted the thought fer yeer da. I'm sure of it."

"Ye knew?"

"Never a word. I'd've stopped him."

"He was drunk? That was it?"

"Not at the time but for three days before. Con took him up there."

"But why? Why? Mattie was never a drinker. He swore to me."

"He brooded and brooded since the day ye was wed. Not one o' us knowin' what to do fer 'im. Two months it went on."

"God help me!"

" 'Til an even worse misery took hold o' him. And he'd be shoutin' sometimes. Almost not right in the head. So that Con got the idea. The two o' them went up there. But when he come back there was no reachin' him. I know twas the poteen . . . And the very next day didn't he shoot him."

Grief consumed Minnie in a great wave. And whenever she tried to lift her head to keep from drowning, the wave grew larger. Until at last it threw her limp on an imaginary shore.

She lay on the dirt floor, exhausted. She felt crushed. Unwittingly she'd contributed to the death of her da. God help me, she thought. The guilt'll kill me. And all for the love I gave to a man.

"Nora. Clare. Get out the fiddle. Fetch the penny whistle. Be quick now." The girls ran to obey. Before Minnie half knew what was happening they'd put her on the stool by the hearth.

Almost at once the music soared, heartfelt, melancholy tunes. Despite her grief, Minnie listened. Softly at first, then with a stronger voice, Nora began to sing. First the songs of the ancient poets, then songs of Thomas Moore. The sad, beautiful words flowed over Minnie. "Has sorrow thy young days shaded?" Ah, yes, she thought. Isn't it long, sad tears I'll be weepin'?

Nora's sweet, high voice moved smoothly into "The harp that once through Tara's halls . . ." Minnie thought her heart would break.

God help me, my heartbreak will be my survival, she resolved. My broken heart, all the world seein' it, will show my da's alive. I'll stay on with the O'Malleys, with the music and song to keep me in mind of it.

Mother O'Malley's voice broke into her reflections. "Go dig the potatoes, Michael. Owen, run beg for some tea. Be off with ye now."

After, when the potatoes were done, Minnie passed around the biscuits. "Wasn't it nice of her to give them?" said Mrs. O'Malley, when she heard of the nephew's wife. "And the little cup. Nora, fill it with tea."

Later, with only the light from the candle and fire, Minnie went off to bed. "Now don't be givin' it a thought," sang out the ma.

Minnie slowly climbed the ladder to the loft.

"And ye just take Mattie's cot. We'll think o' something. Not a thing stoppin' us, when we've the help o' the morning's clear light. Good night now, darlin'.

"And if nothing else ye've a home here with us."

CHAPTER
20

———————

On reaching McNulty's, Morgan stumbled in for a quick pint.

Ordinarily he'd hardly have given a thought to drink, but his chest was tight, his limbs near useless.

What in the name of God had he done? What could he have been thinking of? So what she'd another man's child. So what she'd deceived him. Who cared for the land?

God help me, he moaned. Give me my Minnie.

He pushed through the open half-door. The grocery was crowded.

All activity ceased abruptly.

"There he is." (He heard the whisperings.) "What can you expect from a man out o' Westport?"

He pushed his way through.

"Well, isn't it brave ye are?" said Mary McNulty, the publican's wife.

"I've need of a drop," Morgan apologized, and she softened. "Go in to himself," she said.

His knees were wobbly in the short hallway, and he slipped quickly through to the bar. The room was crowded, not a single table free. Despite the warm day a fire blazed in the hearth.

"A pint," he called out to McNulty over the heads and backs crowding the counter. No one but McNulty moved. Morgan felt his own back stiffen.

"Comin' right up," said McNulty. He thrust forward the foaming glass. Again no one moved. Morgan was forced to reach.

What business was it of theirs, he fumed.

Draining the glass he called for another.

"That was a hard thing ye did to the girl," came a voice. Morgan went rigid. Angrily he studied the heads. Fookin' backward scum.

The room had grown suddenly quiet, but there was movement. The tables seemed to creep forward. The curtained-off snug had emptied, with five or six women having slipped into the room. Morgan threw a quick look over his shoulder. "Another," he called again.

McNulty pulled the handle. There was the sound of beer filling the glass. "This is a peaceful place," he said. "Peaceful. Let none be forgettin' it." He rolled up his sleeves for emphasis. "That goes for all o' yez."

"There'll not be a fight out of me," said Morgan. He spoke more forcefully than he'd intended. But hadn't he enough for one day?

"I'm not fightin' neither," spoke up young Mick O'Neil. (His was one of the backs at the bar.) He turned. "Just that ye've to be knowin' it was a hard and a sad thing ye done."

"Twas hard."

"And sad."

"True."

There was a flurry of movement. The crowd pressed closer. Mick O'Neil rose to his feet.

Morgan emptied his glass, getting the feel of the sawdust under his boots. He noted the doors, in case he'd to make a run for it.

Yet maybe their grief was a show? Didn't themselves call Minnie "murderer" not more than two hours before? "Let me have one for the road," he ordered, letting his voice boom out, but hoping he'd not have to fight. He'd no heart for it. Minnie'd seen to that.

It was her expression'd done it. The look of horror. And the disbelief. When he'd leaped on the damn donkey's back . . . Oh, if he could take back that leap!

But what had she been hoping for? Forgiveness?

What choice had he, knowing full well what she'd done?

And she wasn't really sent out on the road, not in the true sense. The Maughans'd take her. Katie'd make them, Minnie being the one child she had. She'd have to.

Or would she?

"Let that be yeer last." McNulty's own voice boomed out, and he pulled the handle reluctantly. "The pump's dry after this one."

Mick O'Neil, a few glasses ahead of the rest, stood in front of Morgan. He tried unsuccessfully to square his great, gangling shoulders. "There's not many's sent out on the road," he said, "and fewer yet survives."

"Indeed."

"The road."

"Ballyrea's not often seen the like."

The chorus spread across the room.

Cold white anger sent strength surging into Morgan's back. Didn't he know the thing he'd done, that he didn't need this gang to tell him? The shits.

Hadn't he sent his young wife to her doom? God help him.

"Be silent," he cried. "Enough." His vision blurred and the words came in a roar. The glass flew from his hand. Shards of glass showered the group at the bar. Everyone scattered.

"Ye'll stop now," said McNulty. He rushed towards Morgan.

"Fight!" "Fight!" The crowd jockeyed for vantage points.

"Are yez crazy?" cried McNulty. "Ye've all enough in ye, I'm thinkin'." He grabbed Morgan, propelled him toward the door. "Yeer a good fellow," he said. "Ye've a cool head, given the chance."

Morgan stumbled into the grocery, deaf to the exclamations of the shoppers. McNulty led him skillfully through the women and out the half-door. "There now," he said. "Let ye be takin' care on the road." He gave a whisk to Morgan's pants leg, where bits of sawdust clung. "Yeer all set now."

Morgan swayed drunkenly, and the publican steadied him. "There isn't a thing stoppin' ye from a fine walk home. The brisk air'll cheer ye." The women had broken into cackles of amusement. The plight of a Westport man. "And the stuck-up manner o' them."

Morgan's face was flushed and his eyes were bleary. "That little drop ye've taken'll see ye the whole way home," McNulty said. "We wish ye well and God speed."

"I'll be off," Morgan said, wondering how in the name of God he'd make it the ten miles. But McNulty put him up onto the donkey and he set off. "And let ye be thinkin' well o' this

village, if ever yeer rememberin'," McNulty called out after
him.

When Morgan reached the boreen the late evening sun was
mellow. It was nearing ten, and everywhere a golden glow
hovered. In the fields the small haycocks, tied and left to season,
sat plump and yellow, and where the stone walls crisscrossed
there were bursts of yellow furze. The hawthorn was alive with
singing birds wherever the hedgerows bordered.

But Morgan was heartsick, so that it could have been bog
muck, for all that he knew.

What have I done, what have I done, what have I done, he
repeated, with only the donkey's warmth giving a tie to the real
world at all.

Earlier, leaving Ballyrea, when the drink was still on him,
he'd gone daft. Crazy. So that he thought himself dropped to
the reaches of Hell. There were demons dancing, monstrous
creatures, floating soundless over the bog grass. Fluttering the
peaty stretches, the black waters. They sprang from the cuttings,
soaring and plunging, choked him with sulfur—he felt hellish.
And wasn't he swooped up, sticky in demon webs? To be
dropped senseless into the vacantness?

But this was the real Hell, this place of aloneness.

The cottage, as Morgan approached, appeared busy—
smoke from the chimney, with every sign of a visitor or two.
God help him. He slowed the donkey along the boreen, neared
the house with a heavy and desperate heart.

Duffy and Denny sat next to the fire, with Annie opposite.
There was an air of conspiracy. Denny's homely freckled face
had a look of good cheer; Duffy's expression was less certain.

"Isn't it quick you were?" said Morgan to Denny, seeing the
tea cups, the dishes and crumbs. Each of the men held a glass
of strong drink in his hand. Annie sipped wine. "Quick indeed,"
Morgan repeated. "Wasn't it only this noon you were there at
the pub? Fast traveling." A pain started up near his heart.

There were jam tarts on the dresser. Duffy, it appeared, had
brought them.

"Ah, Morgan," said Denny. "Don't be tyin' me in with that
gang. Didn't I leave the moment you left for the hills?" Denny
tried a long-toothed smile, but it didn't come off well. He
coughed nervously, sat back in his chair by the fire.

"But what brings you at all?" asked Morgan, feeling his heart thump. The quicker their business was done the sooner they'd leave him alone with his grief. God help him. He was liable to be dead of the thing long before this terrible night was done. "Let's hear."

Annie blushed furiously, saying she'd have to see the cows.

"But they're long milked?"

Annie fled, almost ran, through the door.

Denny broke the silence. "Fearin' the bargainin'," he said, "Annie's embarrassed."

"Bargaining?" What in the name of the saints gave them to think he'd heart or the stomach this night most of all? I've killed my wife, was the cry near bursting him. "Tell me quick and let me be done for the day."

"This is the plan." Denny looked to Duffy, who flushed deeply, with the face of a man in a snare. "It's hard for me to say," Duffy apologized. "The brother's coming soon. The boat is August third. He's bringin' the boy."

"What's there to come for?"

"Now, wait 'til ye've heard," said Denny. "A letter'd be close, so we thought we'd give it a try." Denny tossed off another of his toothy smiles. "The thing we're proposin' is this."

"Leave it."

"But that's just the point. We can't." Denny was almost prim now. "And who knows what the brother would do? We might salvage it."

"Christ." Morgan pounded the table so that the dishes rattled. "Aren't I near mad with grief?"

"The brother'll be sick, don't ye know," began Denny. "Who wouldn't be? We know he'll never leave the boy, given the circumstance."

"God, yes," muttered Duffy. "Related to a murderer?"

"It wasn't a Riley killed him," said Morgan. "Not a drop of bad blood in our veins. It was that hoodlum did it."

"Ah, we know," said Denny. "But with the connection . . ." He leaned forward. "Now, if the Maughans don't take the dowry back."

"It's promised," Morgan interrupted. An image of Minnie, alone and starving, thin and collapsed on the road, swept him. He heard his heart stop. Then the beating resumed. "The money's the Maughans'."

"But ye've not brought it?"

"How could I? She's only back this day."

"Good. Good. There's a chance."

"There's no chance. I told the nephew. And I'll be bringin' it."

"Now, just for the sake of argument, Morgan—keep cool now. If ye wuz to keep the money, hold it here, it'd be available, so to speak."

"For what? It's blood money. It paid for a murder."

"Not really, Morgan. It's not for the money he's dead."

"Don't mention that," screamed Morgan, his hands on Denny's throat. "That's never to be talked of."

"Morgan. Morgan." Annie had come back and now, with Duffy assisting, pulled Denny into a chair.

"God Almighty," gasped Denny, rubbing his throat. "Yeer daft. Gone daft."

Morgan slumped by the fire. He clenched and unclenched his hands. "You've never to say it."

"Could we go on now?" Only with effort could Denny speak. "When the brother comes we'll give him the lay o' the land."

Morgan groaned.

"Oh, nicely. We'll do it nicely."

"There isn't a thing I want riding on me that'll put me to obligation," Duffy said. "Bernard's got to know, Denny."

"But carefully," said Denny. "We've to save every bit that we can."

"For sure, he'll sell the cow," said Duffy. "And the land's off."

"No matter," Denny snapped. These things took skill. "D'ye think he'll pull off the roof? Or the concrete off the floor?"

"The tin roof," groaned Annie.

"Well, he'll take the chairs and the rug," said Duffy gloomily. "Yes, surely, he will. We've lost that luxury . . . and wasn't Annie in love with the shelves and the cups? . . . Oh, it's a sad day."

"Christ. D'ye think he's a crook, man? What kind of a brother? Draggin' the shelves off the wall."

"Bernard's in business," Duffy said. "Do you think the beef's free?"

"Never mind all that," said Denny, feeling his blood rise.

Morgan was looking increasingly dismal and Annie had a desperate air. This would never do. It was time for a straightforward pitch. "Gettin' back to Annie's dowry," he said.

Morgan glowered. "It's Minnie's you was disputin'," he said. "Trying to talk me from giving it back . . . Save your breath."

"Here's the deal." Denny stood up, hands behind his back. "Ye've a fine home, Morgan. China plates. A cut glass bowl. All the little niceties . . . Ye'd like Annie to have the same?"

"God damn. What're you driving at?"

Denny moved so they'd the table between them. "Money, Morgan. Two hundred and seventy-five. That's what I'm driving at. The fortune Minnie brought. It's yours, fair and square. Not a court in the land would say otherwise."

"Get out."

"Now, wait." But Denny edged for the door.

Duffy jumped to his feet.

"Listen to Denny, Morgan!" Annie cried, a world of longing in her eyes. "Have you no heart?"

"Give Denny a chance," begged Duffy. "Hear him."

"Annie and Duffy'd be well set for life. Annie's two hundred, with Minnie's besides. Four hundred and seventy-five pounds. They'd buy their own cow. The hell with the brother. They could have all the chairs they like. Think."

"Think?" Morgan grabbed a poker. "Think?"

Denny fled through the door, Duffy after him. With a shriek heard halfway to O'Donnell's Annie raced up the stairs to the loft. "Murderer, yourself!" she screamed over and over. "Murderer. Murderer."

CHAPTER 21

Monday morning early, while Annie was off with the cows, Morgan set out, first to the bank in Kilmaragh, then north to the Ballyrea road. Noon found him climbing the hill to the Maughans.

When he set out, there was summer warmth and sunshine, but later came a lowering. Chill rain fell. It seeped through his coat at the back.

The dreary bog road was rocky and rough, the mists lifting only occasionally. Birds darted fitfully, clustering, to hide again, swift, in the thick, silky fog.

"And what is it brings ye?" The nephew spotted Morgan before he was halfway up the hill. He rushed back through the gloom to call the wife.

"Ye've to come in from the rain," ordered the ma, and she led Morgan straight to the fire. "Ye'll need dryin'."

"Hang yeer coat on the hook," Chrissie O'Bannon said, "and set in yeer shoes b'the fire."

There was fresh-baked bread with butter and jam. Katie ran to the cow house, and returned with milk for his tea. "We've scones," she said.

The nephew merely watched, resting his feet on the turf by the fire. "What brings ye?" he asked.

Morgan put off answering. He pulled an egg from his pocket, shelled it. "Ye've salt?" he apologized.

"Sure, wouldn't I have boiled ye an egg?" Chrissie scolded. She heaped his plate with butter for scones. Morgan felt a twitch at the base of his brain, as dread mounted. Where was Minnie?

"I've the fortune," he said finally, wiping bits of jam on the back of his hand. He laid out the notes. "Count it," he said.

The three before him stared. "Glory to God," whispered the nephew. "And I know ye've come a long way."

"Sure, what would we take the money for?" asked the wife.

"Indeed we'll not," said the nephew.

"It's all there," said Morgan. "Two hundred and seventy-five. We're square." He stood up, struggling for a look of steadiness. "I'm not seein' her?" he said.

The nephew thrust the notes at Morgan, ignoring the question. "The money's yours."

"I'll not. You're to take it. And then I'd like a word with my wife." Sweat poured down Morgan's back.

"Ah, would ye now?" Trying to mask his own nervousness the nephew paced the kitchen.

Morgan's mouth went dry. "Ye've Minnie?"

"To tell the truth we don't."

The kitchen went silent.

"Yeer wife's not here," rasped Brian, "so we've no claim to the fortune."

It couldn't be true. "Where is she?" Morgan brought his fist to the table. "Tell me straight out what you've done?"

"Not a thing." Chrissie, face aflame, rushed to her husband's side. "We'd no call. So that's indeed, what we done. Nothing."

"You threw her out on the road?"

"Didn't yeerself?"

"God help me."

"Oh, Minnie. My Minnie," cried Katie Maughan, throwing herself, weeping, into a chair by the fire. "They've killed her, these two. The only child of my womb."

"God help me. God help me," Morgan shouted.

"Ye did it yeerself bringin' her back here," said the nephew.

"Look what ye done," screamed Chrissie, rushing to comfort her man. "There's no end o' trouble with all o' ye."

Brian bathed the ma's cheeks with a rag. "Dear ma," he said. "We'll find her." He counted the fortune, slid it, folded, into a dirty cloth purse. "We're square now," he said to Morgan.

"Are we now?" Chrissie said. "The murderer's moll at our hearth? Indeed."

"No fear," said Morgan. "If we find her I'll not let her go."

"But the disgrace? They'll mock. And whose name will ye have on the land? Meself and Brian may be shrewd and unkind, but we've brains. Yeer daft."

"If it's a boy he'll come into my name. That'll settle it."

"But the blood's wrong. You can't change that. It's the blood that makes the name."

Silence fell on the kitchen.

"Blood's not all," said Morgan quietly, his face pale. He stood resolute. "It's late in life I learned."

"So have it yeer way," said Chrissie. "Give him the money, Brian."

Brian hesitated. He reached in his shirt for the purse.

Chrissie tossed a turf at the fire. She poured hot water from the kettle. "I've not all day. D'ye think we've the leisure o' the rich?"

Morgan pocketed the dowry again. "But have you a thought?"

The nephew reached for his pipe. His hands shook.

Morgan held the match.

Brian puffed a great grey cloud, said nothing. Finally, after a long, embarrassed pause, "We left her outside by the door."

"Ye needn't be tellin' all that," said Chrissie. "Didn't I give her the cup and the buns?"

"Ah, no, it wasn't to starve she went off," said Brian quickly, but he flushed.

The ma rose, blessed herself. "God help ye find my babe."

"I'm going," said Morgan.

"I'll help." Brian grabbed his cap.

"It's the blessing of a ma ye'll take with ye!" said Katie.

"Hush with the racket," snapped Chrissie. But she made the Sign of the Cross.

"God's praise," wept the ma.

Long into the same evening—very late—Con O'Malley showed up at his own cabin door. "Shaun's got 'im," he said. "In the hills, he was."

The ma sprang up. The whiskey smell was clear. "God help him."

Everyone, Minnie included, ran to the door. They hung there, scanning the moonlit low flat plain. It was the clearest of bright nights—not a trace remained of the rain. There was a warm, summer softness.

"It was Shaun found 'im," said Con O'Malley. "Haven't they Guards in the hills and the fields? The shits." With painful, hard effort he eased onto the hob. "But we foxed 'em." He vomited into the hearth, leaned back on the mold-blotchy wall.

"But what're ye bringin' 'im for? To end his young days at our home? The Guard's out there." Mrs. O'Malley rushed to the door, looking at the shadowy shapes on the plain. "They'll plug him. They'll plug him for sure."

"D'ye think they'll strut home in the moonlight? They're fools? Nah! There's quickness in them two." Con's bloodshot eyes came alive. An air of cunning swept over him. "He's crawlin' 'im home through the grass, Shaun is. They've the instinct for huggin' the ground. Besides, Mattie's a gun. And he'll use it!"

"Ah, Con, yeer a wonder. Yeerself and yeer sons besides."

But Nora, the oldest girl, let out a shriek. "I love Mattie. I love Mattie. Don't let him die."

Immediately followed a chorus of wails from the rest. "Don't let Mattie die." "Our Mattie," begged Owen and Michael.

"Quiet," said the ma. She lumbered to her feet, like a general in the midst of a rout. "The Guard's out there. The sons of bitches. And they'll put lead in his pants if they've a hint in the world that he'll try. So, quiet yeerselves!"

Tiny Peggy climbed the old dung heap next to the door. "Brudder," she shouted, waving her arms. Her baby voice was thin, but it carried over the silent waste of white. "Brudder. Brudder."

"Mother o' God and all the saints!" said Mother O'Malley. She yanked the sobbing child into the cabin, slamming the door. "We've to be silent."

Throughout all the uproar Minnie'd gone numb. She sat frozen on the stool by the hearth. Blood cold, mouth dry, she felt a lock click shut on her tongue. Reality seemed to have fled.

Who was this Mattie, this stranger who crept in the grass? Surely not her Mattie? Her ecstasy? The lover'd lain bare at her side?

Nervously she twisted her hair, wound the long silk on her thumb, struggling to envision this foreigner, the outsider they'd whisked from the hills. Even to call up an image proved impossible. Her Mattie'd been part of her. They'd been one. Surely she'd never been two-in-one-flesh with this Mattie, a criminal fleeing the Guard? A murderer.

Or had she?

No. This Mattie was no more than a ghost-visitor. A will-o'-the-wisp fraud.

Agonized, she went to the door. There was only the silent moon. A few wispy clouds hung feathery overhead, while out on the bog the terrible whiteness lit up the scraw. Soundlessly she settled her skirts, leaned her head on the sagging door. Behind her, in the darkened room, the O'Malleys seemed made out of stone.

"What do ye think, Con?" Mrs. O'Malley shifted the child at her breast. "Whatever do ye think we should do?"

"Send him off." The words came badly slurred. "Like the rest does be doin'."

(All feeling rushed from Minnie. America?)

"But the passage?"

"I'll manage."

"Sweet Jesus, d'ye think that ye could?"

"Haven't I always come through in the past? When we'd nothin'?"

"But this is big money."

"Hasn't McNultys the store?"

"Oh, Con. Ye'd rob their little shop? With all they let us owe?"

"Sure, aren't they robbers themselves? Makin' us pay on it?"

"The McNultys been good, Con."

"They're the ones with the dough, so that settles it."

The ma let out a deep sigh. "I suppose ye know."

Minnie sat stunned. Steal? Her mind went into a spin. Were they mad? Giddily her glance swept from the dark of the room to the door. Who were these people? So poor they'd not even a cow, yet they'd give her a home with their own? They'd saved her.

But they were thieves.

Or were they merely daft?

She shook uncontrollably. Had the whole world gone daft? Had Mattie? Where'd been his brains when he picked up a gun? Where was his heart?

Dizziness swept over her. She leaned on the door post,

dazed by all that she'd lost. Life could have been made of such happiness. The joys they'd tasted. But instead life had come to an end, without hope for the future or past.

Abruptly rage flooded her. A surging torrent. A sense of injustice spread crazily, until she came alive. Head, toes, every bit of her body throbbing. They wronged us, her heart shouted. They were wrong when they tore us apart.

Fierce burning swept through her thighs, flowed upward, turned her body into fire. She felt tortured, agonized, enraged. Yet, heavenly sensations swept her, visions of wonder. She was in rapture; now there was pleasure and delight. Ah, Mattie, she whispered. Even yeer memory saves me. Though I die I'm alive in yeer joys.

Gunfire cut through her bliss. Followed rapidly by answering shots. Louder. More terrifying. The O'Malleys stood bunched at the door, the ma screaming. "Kill 'em," bellowed the da.

There were shouts, loud oaths. Flashes of light erupted. A great din blasted the moonlit plain.

There was a pause.

The firing resumed, echoed across the lakes and the scraw. Then came a terrible, quick scream of pain.

There was a momentary lull, almost immediately shattered by pistol shots. The smell of gunpowder fouled the air.

Eerie silence hung on the bog. A brief, grotesque quiet.

Then a voice yelled, fierce, defiant, "Ye shits." A shot rang out, followed by a second. And then wildly, revengefully, a series of deafening roars.

When it was over, silence. Not a sound at all on the scraw.

Shrieking O'Malleys poured from their door, ran crazily through the stunned moonlight. "Mattie!" "Shaun!"

Minnie, eyes glazed, stayed by the door. She stared through the night at the bog.

The cursing O'Malleys ransacked the plain, scrambling for the spot in the scraw. Except for their screams there was a terrible void in the white-drenched air.

Further out, in the cuttings, the scraw ran red.

CHAPTER 22

Three days later Morgan brought Minnie home.

The Maughans had put him up and when he found Minnie, at first she seemed carved out of ice. Her mind could form no thought at all. But after they'd talked there was hint of a thaw. "Why not?" she said dully, when he told her he wanted her back.

The O'Malleys begged and wept. But, "I'll go," she said simply. She stood up from the hob and went off, with Morgan's hand in her own.

The sun was high as they passed through the square. The here-and-there stragglers stared hard.

But as they went by the pub Mary McNulty ran out, a parcel of sweets in her hands, which she thrust at Minnie. "Take heart, darlin'! Ye've a good man to walk by yeer side."

The grocery door was barely shut when it flew open a second time, John McNulty's head at the door. "God speed," he cried at Morgan.

It wasn't long before they'd left the village behind. Occasionally, when Minnie tired, they rested. She'd a look on her face of being done with the thing, so that Morgan sent up his thanks to the stars.

Evening was on when they finally reached home, a golden sun low in the sky. There were purple clouds, and out towards the sea a feathery down drifted softly.

"God bless us, you're home." Annie started up from the seat by the fire. Duffy and Denny set down their glasses. There was an expectant scrape of chairs . . . (And a queer, perplexing air, Morgan thought.)

"Isn't it the great whiskey Duffy's brought?" said Denny, rushing to shake Morgan's hand. (Too prompt and too spry?)

"We've the tea and the biscuits," said Annie. She threw a quick, imploring look at Duffy, who coughed nervously and sat down in his chair.

Morgan eyed the boxed sweets, the tarts, the fruit on the dresser. Apples and oranges, both? The kettle hung and a good fire burned; Annie had laid on a cloth. What in the name of God? On this day?

"You've heard?" he said carefully. Denny turned quickly brash. "Isn't there the bad and the good in us all?" he said.

Three men dead in six days and he's *cheered*?

Grey-faced and exhausted, Minnie sat on the stool by the door. Were they daft?

Annie rushed to the dresser for cups. Duffy blushed self-consciously, but his eyes followed Annie. She giggled.

Morgan pulled a straw from the broom, methodically took a light for his pipe. "What brings ye?"

This time Annie blushed. "Denny thought . . ." she began.

"We settled that," said Morgan. "I gave the fortune back."

"But ye've it again," said Denny. "And a lot's happened."

"I'll thank you not to mention it," said Morgan.

"You've the fortune back," Annie persisted. "Now we've the money to wed, if you'll give it."

"God help me. Have you no thought?" Morgan paced the floor. "Four days like yourself's never known."

A strangled sound came from Minnie by the door. Surely they weren't to speak of the terrible things?

"Ye've to be silent." Morgan, looking ready to fly through the air, positioned himself before Minnie, shielding her. "This is my wife."

Annie shrank back. Duffy tried to render himself invisible.

"Now, Morgan," began Denny, throwing caution away. "Ye've no need for the fortune. While Annie . . ."

"Have you no respect?" Morgan shouted. "Isn't she already near dead with the shame?"

"Ah, we know. We know," Denny said. "A terrible, terrible tragedy. But we've all our sorrows."

"Christ. Will you not speak of it."

Suddenly Duffy was on his feet. "We'll marry. Money or no. I've writ the brother."

Annie's face went pale.

Morgan puffed ferociously. The Yank knew. The world knew.

"God help me, I had to let him know." Duffy's eyes sought Annie's. "We've the roof and the floor. What more do we need?"

"And the boy?" Annie asked. The thin little lad of the photograph danced before her mind, spun her brain into a whirlwind. No child? What kind of life would it be?

"He'll not give him," said Duffy in a whisper. "With the circumstances. So I told him it's off. All of it. There isn't a thing now that'll put me to obligation."

"Oh. Oh," Annie cried.

"I want you, Annie," said Duffy, straight out. He raked a hand through his wisps of gray hair. "And if it isn't myself that suits, we'll call it square. Not a day's trouble I'll give. But I'm hoping you'll come be my bride."

"You want me?" Annie could barely speak, but her words, though faint, were clear. "Though the brother's offer's through?"

"That's right. Only myself I'm offering. Share and share alike. For it's a poor man I am once again. But I'll be rich if I've you . . . There's only my love. Will you take it?"

Annie hesitated.

"Think," burst out Denny. "Think o' the freedom, the two of yez. One and the other by the fire. Quiet evenings. Steady talk. Think, now."

But still Annie held off. She'd not be a mother at all? And there was to be no cow, nor the chairs, nor even the rug by the door? God help us, they'd have nothing. She turned to Duffy, saw the fear and the love in his eyes.

"Great Jesus, give them the money, Morgan," said Minnie. "Give it! Give it!" She rushed to Morgan, shook him. "If ye'll not I'll go back on the road." Her face flamed.

"Mother of God, Minnie." Morgan was stunned.

"I'll not stay. Give over, Morgan. Let Duffy have Annie." Her green eyes flashed. "A man that loves." She gazed on Duffy wonderingly. Glory shone from her eyes. "Yeer a grand man," she said. Then, angry again, to Morgan, "There's true love. No bargainin'. Wasn't it bargainin' meself brought Mattie his death? Wouldn't he still be alive on this day?"

"Good God. Are you goin' to be saying it?" Morgan said. She'd gone crazed. "You've to be silent. Have you no mind for your character? That the babe has it nearly destroyed? Isn't it enough that we've maybe to flee? Go to the States?"

"Flee?" Minnie pulled free. "Will they be drivin' us out, these Kilmara'ns? Yeerself and yeer 'backward place' girl? Is that what they think? That I'm fit neither for hills nor the town? Ah, Morgan, life's hard."

Morgan slumped into the chair by the fire. "I don't know what they'll think."

"Minnie, take hold of yeerself," said Denny. "There's many a destroyed character's fared worse. Yez two might havta run off to the States."

"But the passage. The two hundred and seventy-five. What if I give it? Then how could we flee?"

Morgan's head cleared. He saw Minnie, her glow. She sat quietly in the firelight, bathed with the flush of the late evening sun. Like an angel she was.

"It's not Duffy alone that loves pure," he choked.

"Give over," Minnie said. "Or I swear that ye'll see me no more."

Morgan brought the money from his shirt. He felt a chill, suddenly, where it had rested next to his heart. "Take it," he said after a long moment, holding the packet to Duffy.

Duffy breathed hard. "Annie?"

"Take it," shrieked Denny, but Duffy backed to the dresser. "Take it. Take it." Duffy toppled. Oranges and apples spilled to the floor.

"God help us, the fruit," cried Duffy. He dove for the floor.

"For the love o' the Christ, ye fool." Denny, scrambling and pushing, tore at the oranges. "D'ye think life's food?"

Finally, when Denny'd the money safe in Duffy's hands, he led him to Annie. "Ye have it!"

Suddenly the room fell into stillness. Deep. Summerly warm. Filled with the aroma of apples and oranges. Duffy looked at his beloved, breathed hard. "Annie?"

"God help me. I'm yours," she said in a rush.

Three weeks later Duffy and Annie were wed.

On the first Sunday after the wedding the men came in. It

was a mellow evening. Sunshine bathed the kitchen and there was the scent of flowers. From outside came the sound of bird song.

Minnie was nervous. This was the real test, the visiting. Would they accept her or force her to go?

Morgan strode back and forth by the hearth, gave a stir to the fire with the poker, despite the warm evening. "I think there's a shower on the way," he said. "It'll be cool."

"Yeer worse than an old woman." Minnie laughed. She peered out the door. "Isn't it clear?"

But Morgan knew his weather. The soft evening darkened. A breeze picked up and a grey sheet of rain swept in from the sea. "Crazy," said Morgan.

"We'd nothin' the like at home."

"You'll grow used to it here."

The rain grew heavy. "They'll come?" asked Minnie, and Morgan was sure. "Curiosity'll bring them . . . God help us, here's someone." He rushed to the door.

Colman Ronan, the first in, was followed by Barrett and O'Dowd. The three were drenched but they shrugged it off. "Aren't we the fish?" said Barrett, eyes on Minnie. There were nods and smiles all around.

"Isn't it the missus herself?" said Ronan smartly, throwing off one of his exaggerated smiles. The three took their stools at the rear, and there were hearty laughs.

"Now, won't you by drying yourselves?" said Morgan. He watched the visitors closely. "The night's queer," he said.

"Sure, we'd not've stayed home for the world." Ronan's voice was oily, his eyes roaming the room. Cripes, Morgan'd the knack, all right. Lookit the huge sacks of oats by the hob. There must be two hundred pounds. "Haven't we all need for the talk?"

Morgan flinched. Ronan'd the jealous streak, too.

But Minnie, calm in her chair, regal almost, returned Colman Ronan's look. "Yeer own wife's well?" she asked, knowing a sixth child was due.

Ronan squirmed. (Couldn't you have controlled yourself? the missus had taken to shouting.) He shifted his weight, braving it out.

"Yeer wife and I'll have the tea?" said Minnie. This was the test, this night. But if she'd to lose, she'd lose with a fight.

Morgan caught his breath. Waited. Counted the ticks on the dresser clock.

"We'll see," said Ronan. "I'll ask her. Oh, I'll do that, to be sure."

The rain blew heavier now. Rain hit the front windows. There was a quick knock and the door blew inwards. Old Pat O'Gavagan, his pal Mulrenin in tow, wheezed his way into the room.

"Haven't we the elves?" he said. "Can ye believe it on such a fine night?"

"Ah, now," soothed Morgan, taking his jacket to hang by the door. "You came by the cliffs?"

"Didn't the wind nearly knock us?"

"Scared all the way, we were," said Mulrenin.

"Yez should've stayed in from the rain," said Barrett.

"Stayed in?" O'Gavagan bristled. There was fire in his ancient sharp eyes. "Haven't I right?" His glance swung to Minnie. "We're fit to just rest b'the fire?"

"Ah, no. Wasn't it a joke?" said Barrett, backing off. "Wasn't it a clear, brilliant evening the hour?" He lit his pipe. "Where's Duffy?" he said quickly. "Late, now he's the brother-in-law?"

Ronan and O'Dowd laughed. Even the two old fellows chuckled. They were settled now by the fire. "Duffy's a new man," said Mulrenin. "Hasn't he the dough?"

This brought a second laugh.

Minnie sat silent. Her face burned for poor Duffy. And for herself.

Morgan frowned. They were incorrigible. And with Duffy due soon at the door.

He stirred the fire. "That ought to chase off the elves," he said, pretending playfulness. There was a burst of sparks and flame.

"You've to be careful!" cried O'Gavagan. Along with Mulrenin he moved his chair away.

Sparks sizzled and danced on the floor.

"Indeed." Morgan sat down in his chair, lit his own pipe. There was much shifting and stirring.

Duffy arrived at the door, Pat O'Donnell following. "Twas the rain," Duffy apologized. He hung up his cap.

"Fit for thieves." Pat O'Donnell shook the wet off.

"Thieves and elves," Mulrenin said.

Duffy pulled his stool to the fire, saying Annie sent her love.

Minnie smiled. Wasn't he the wonder, this Duffy? Not a bit of the swank to him, no matter the roof, or the floor.

Duffy held out a parcel. The brown grocery paper was tied up with string. "Something she knitted," he said.

"God love her," said Minnie. Wasn't Annie the darlin' to send it this night.

Instantly a scrape of chairs began, everyone jockeying for a better view.

Minnie held up a sweater and shirt. Along with a tiny pair of stockings. "A wonder," she said, examining the even stitches.

"Hasn't Annie the knack?" said Ronan. "Like yourself?"

"Indeed," said O'Dowd.

Minnie clutched the gifts to her breast. She blushed deeply. They were all staring, and she wantd to flee from the room. A feeling of terror had begun, and immediately it swept from her head to her toes. Could Ronan be going to say something?

"We've the tea," Morgan said.

"The jam's in the dresser," said Minnie, breathless.

There was a tin of biscuits from the store.

After the tea there was whiskey, Morgan filling the cups while Minnie, eased somewhat, took a small glass of wine. There was laughing and joking. Morgan relaxed. Maybe the thing would work out after all?

But thanks to the whiskey, Barrett and Ronan began needling. One threw a jab about field work, the other flung back with the cows. Ronan hadn't the knack with the hayricks, Barrett was slow on the bogs. One piled the turf in wet foots that slipped, the other built no stacks at all.

On it went.

Abandoning his judgment, Morgan poured a second drink all around.

Barrett faced off at Ronan. "Only a fool'd push six kids on his wife," he said.

Ronan went livid. "You're talking of me?"

He gave a shove with his foot to Barrett's stool. Barrett slid to the floor. "The hell," he cried. He jumped up, swaggering.

A shiver of horror tinged with eagerness quickly circled the room. "Aren't we all the young bucks?" said Mulrenin, delighted.

But Duffy grabbed his cap. "I'm off," he said. "Annie's alone, don't you know."

Barrett stopped in his tracks. "Alone?" His eyes were darting and bright. "Isn't it the grief Annie hasn't the boy?"

Morgan gasped. Minnie went white.

"We don't speak of that," Morgan said.

"Sure, there's hardly a thought," Duffy stammered.

"Not a thought?" said Ronan, jumping in. He looked meaningfully at Minnie, who sat speechless. Please, oh, please God, Minnie prayed.

But Ronan had grown pompous, an ominous gleam in his eyes. He turned to Duffy. "I heard the brother took back the cow?"

Duffy shifted from foot to foot, edged toward the door. "Wasn't the cow only on loan?" he stammered. "The money'd yet to be paid." The words seemed to rise from his toes.

"The loan of a cow? Who ever heard?"

"Not a real loan," Duffy quavered.

"I see. The brother would pay when he came with the boy?"

"God help me," muttered Duffy. He threw a pleading glance at Morgan, who stood as if turned into stone.

Ronan, fueled by the whiskey, paced like a magistrate. "And the rug and the furniture, too? Wuz they on the books? . . . You're all hearing?" he said, not noticing the silence, except for his own oily tones. "Lord save us, even the high and the mighty."

Only O'Dowd offered encouragement, though even he seemed half-hearted. The rest simply stared at the fire.

Suddenly Duffy flared. Everyone gawked. Who'd ever seen it before?

"Haven't I the grandest girl in the world for my wife? And you're talkin' of cows?"

But Ronan wasn't to be stopped. "God help us, the brother must've been put out, hearin' the news." He looked directly at Minnie.

With a cry Morgan was at him. "*Ruin Minnie's life,* is that what you'll do?" Hand on Ronan's throat, he shoved him back towards the hearth. Ronan stumbled, fell backwards on a huge sack of oats.

Ronan lay gasping. "I'm the only one saying it."

"Speak the unspeakable?" screamed Morgan. "Fookin' dirty scum."

Finally, panting from exertion, Morgan backed off. "Is there anyone else with a word for my wife?"

"God help us, no."

"Not on your life."

"Aren't we behind yez?"

The two old men stood up. They were stiff on their feet. "She's a jewel," O'Gavagan said. "A jewel worth a dozen and more."

The only sounds were the crackles of the fire. A few flakes of oats skittered across the floor, caught by the breeze from under the door.

"Indeed," said Mulrenin, followed by a chorus of voices. "To be sure." "God save us, you're right."

O'Gavagan steadied himself, one hand gripping the arm of his pal. "And I'll tell it around," he said, "next week when I go in to Kilmaragh."

"Indeed. Tell it around."

"Tell them Morgan Riley's a gem for a wife."

O'Gavagan turned stiffly. He sailed majestically to his place by the fire.

There was silence. Ronan, digging oats from his nose, blew violently into a rag from his pocket. He cleared his throat, said nothing. His breathing was noisy and labored, the sound carrying as far as the door, where Duffy still stood, hand on the latch. "I'll stay for a bit," he said, and he resumed his stool by the fire.

"Aren't ye the grand bunch?" whispered Minnie, eyes alight. Joy filled her heart; she felt the infant move. She looked at Morgan, caught his own gaze of pure happy love. "And yeerself," she said quietly.

Morgan smiled. "You're surely the lass."